I0635986

DOG SOLDIER MOON

The Superstition Gun Trilogy Book 2

MCKENDREE LONG

WOLFPACK
PUBLISHING
— EST 2013 —

Dog Soldier Moon
McKendree Long

Paperback Edition
© Copyright 2019 by McKendree Long

Wolfpack Publishing
6032 Wheat Penny Avenue
Las Vegas, NV 89122

wolfpackpublishing.com

This book is a work of fiction. Any references to historical events, real people or real places are used fictitiously. Other names, characters, places and events are products of the author's imagination, and any resemblance to actual events or places or persons living or dead is entirely coincidental.

All rights reserved. No part of this book may be reproduced by any means without the prior written consent of the publisher, other than brief quotes for reviews.

Paperback ISBN 978-1-64119-500-3
eBook ISBN 978-1-64119-562-1

Library of Congress Control Number: 2019931660

DOG SOLDIER MOON

Foreword

March, 1880

I know many if not most of the people in this work. I mean, I rode with Dobey and Boss Melton in Terry's Texas Rangers during the war, and I've lived with them here for some time now. Those I know were familiar with the rest of the characters, and I've spent years soaking up details from them to put this together. Maybe some of you read my first book, *No Good Like it Is*, to which this a sequel.

The story is as accurate as I can tell it. I've plugged in some assumptions and conversations that are just best guesses, and after so many years, so many viewpoints, and some agendas at odds with others, I can't swear to its accuracy, so I call it fiction. But it's all I've got.

Now, I've seen the work of good writers. One of those fellows is like a guide; he puts you in the front of the canoe, steers you downstream, nothing for you to do but enjoy the float, the gentle rushing of water under the boat, the serene landscapes sliding by. Sure, you have to work with him a little on the tricky turns, and he'll let you wonder about those roaring noises around the bend.

Suddenly he's taken you into the rapids: rushing blasts of water and spray and noise and danger. In these sickening, jigging moves, you must pay attention and work with him to get through, and you do, but the respite is too brief. Before you know it, you're in the crushing rapids again, only worse. Here comes Decapitation Rock, and it's that or Dead Man's Drop – no way out. But then your guide makes one masterful stroke and you're in a quiet eddy and gliding to a sand bar, previously invisible to you.

This is not one of those trips. I'm no writer. I'm a storyteller who writes things down. My language is as childlike as my thought processes, and I only know that because of all the good writing I've enjoyed. But I'm all you've got.

William "Buddy" Skipper Canadian Fort, Texas

1866

Chapter One

Jimmy Ridges was finally able to say goodnight to old Chief Black Kettle, and slip into the tipi he'd been offered as an overnight guest. Black Kettle assured him that the owner was on a hunt, and that his wife and children would share a tipi with cousins whose husbands were off hunting too.

He had hoped to avoid this camp, but a group of Cheyenne hunters stopped him, remembered him from his visit last summer, and insisted that he come see their chief.

And now, he thought, it was really cold, and sleeping under buffalo robes in a tent wouldn't be a bad thing. In the dark, he pulled off his holster, boots, and heavy coat, put the pistol and Spencer where they were handy, and slipped under the robe, to find a naked body.

"Eeeyah!" He shouted, spun from under the robe and pushed the person down with his left hand as he cocked and pointed his Navy with his right.

A soft voice whispered, "Do not hit. No shoot me. Please, Boss."

Ridges exhaled, and flipped the tipi's door flap open to let in the light of the campfires and moon.

There was muted laughter from just outside. The girl lay shivering, afraid to recover herself with that pistol in her face. A very pretty face. She'd been Black Kettle's translator earlier.

"Pretty face," said Ridges, staring at her breasts. He decocked the Colt.

"No. I not Pretty Face. I name Serenity Killer. I put here for you." She recovered herself.

"Good name." His own peace of mind, fragile since meeting Amanda Watson on the trip through here last year, completely disappeared a minute earlier when he'd placed his left hand on this girl's breast in the dark. "Who? Who put you here? This your tent?"

"Tent, Boss?"

"Tipi. House. Is this where you sleep?"

"No, Boss. I sleep at foot of Old Chief. He put me here. Say you big medicine with Cherokee, white men. Must please you."

His breathing was almost back to normal. He closed the flap and eased back under the robe, careful not to touch her. There was more giggling and Cheyenne chatter outside, which he didn't understand. "You ain't Cheyenne. Osage?"

She was. When her father died in her thirteenth summer, a trader named John Shelly bought her. Two years later, he traded her to Black Kettle, saying that she made him crazy. When he tried to buy her back two moons later, Black Kettle refused, and two moons after that, old Shelly shot himself, and the Cheyenne changed her name to Serenity Killer. That was three winters ago. It took her a while and many gestures to tell all that, and the robe kept slipping down to her waist.

"What was your old name?" Sleep was now out of the question. The dim spectacle of her nudity would not go away. And she was more than a year older and more experienced than he. Didn't seem like his combat service as a sixteen-year-old lieutenant with General Stand Watie's Confederate Cherokees come up to a pile of bird droppings in this situation.

"Oh, I was called Moon Dancer. Miz Shelly, Sweet Thang, Honey. Many names." She was running her fingers over a gunshot scar on his arm and occasionally touching his leg, which caused him to flinch and her to giggle.

"Did you make him crazy? The old man?" He pulled the robe up again.

"Oh, yes. Sometimes he hit me, for my talking. He make me take off clothes and hit me on backside. But then he get confused, and we wrestled some more. He say that make him crazy, too."

"Wrestle?"

"Oh yes. You like to wrestle? I hope so, because if I no make you make noise, I get beat some. We start now, Boss?" She started to tug at his pants buttons.

"Hey. Whoa. I have a woman. That's who I'm going to see." "She not here, Boss. Please don't make them beat me. We just wrestle some, make some noise, and you sleep better and I no get beat." She dove under the robes.

"Great moon, sun and stars above!"

He didn't sleep better. Didn't sleep at all. And for the first time in many moons he didn't think about Mandy Watson, or any of the other folks he was heading to see at Canadian Fort.

* * *

"I BELIEVE YOU FOUND YOUR BED warmer satisfactory?" Black Kettle's question was straightforward, sincere, devoid of leering. He probably knew the answer. Probably spent some time outside their tipi with the others. Serenity Killer translated for them, over morning soup.

Jimmy Ridges smiled sheepishly. "Yes, Chief. Very satisfying…uh, satisfactory."

"Please take her, then. She makes me crazy. And my other wife wants to kill her. This one never stops talking and her questions make my head hurt."

Jimmy Ridges hesitated, not knowing what he should offer in return. He'd been planning to ask for her since about three o'clock this morning. In case Mandy hadn't waited for him.

Mistaking the hesitation, Black Kettle pressed him. "She will keep you warm 'til you get to Canadian Fort. I'll give you two ponies and some robes. You can beat her if she keeps talking. And when she makes you crazy, you can give her to someone else. Or knock her on the head."

Serenity Killer frowned as she translated that last part. But she never hesitated, and omitted nothing.

THEY LEFT THE CAMP THREE HOURS before noon, to much good-natured cheering and a few gunshots. They both wore buffalo capes against the biting cold, and Ridges held the Spencer up in a parting wave, as Serenity Killer struggled to pull both his packhorse and her spare pony.

"You may be surprised that I ride. Cheyenne women mostly walk. But old Shelly, he taught me to ride. And other things. But he is dead. I hope you don't go crazy and kill yourself. You haven't beat me. And you had lots of fire and movement last night." She clucked at the horses.

"Listen. About last night …" He lost his train of thought, as he remembered again.

"Oh, that was some good wrestling. Better than with Old Chief or old Shelly. I think your woman much lucky. You can have two wives, no?"

"No. And that's what I wanted to say about last night. You must not talk about that when we get to Canadian Fort. Leastways, not if Mandy is there."

"Mandy is your woman?"

"Yes. And I don't want her to know what we did." "She a good wrestler?"

"I, uh, I dunno."

"She your woman, and you don't know? My old man Shelly say you Cherokee are strange."

"She ain't Cherokee. She's English, uh, white. And she wanted to, uh, wrestle, but I did not want to …"

"Did not want to? You wanted to last night. You very strange."

"Don't interrupt. I was saying, I did not want to make a baby until we can marry. And her father would have shot me."

"Strange. I have made two babies, but they did not live long. Maybe we made one last night. I hope you don't want to make one tonight. Serenity Killer very tired. Do Cherokee women walk or ride?"

Serenity Killer, he thought. *Good name.*

"Listen to me," he said. "When we get there in two days, your new name will be just Shelly."

"Just Shelly? Why, Boss?"

"Never mind," he said. *Because with your real name, I might never be able to sell you, or even give you away.*

"Where we go now? You have friends we go see at this fort, or just your woman?"

"It ain't a real fort. There was some Yankee cavalry there before the war, so they changed the name of the place from Canadian Ford to Canadian Fort, see? But it ain't far and it's right on the Canadian River there in north Texas, and my friend, Captain Walls, brought some people there last summer to help his mother run her trading post. Him and his old sergeant-major, Jimmy Melton."

"They were in the gray army, like you. I saw them when you and them met with Chief Black Kettle six moons ago." She had been there as an undeclared interpreter for Black Kettle, to make sure that the Confederate Cherokee translator was honest.

"Same army, but not with us. We fought the blue-coats just east of here, and they was with the Eighth Texas Cavalry, across the big river. Fought in Tennessee, Georgia, the Carolinas." Ridges watched her eyes to see if she understood.

"I see." Maybe not. She dropped it. "That place we go to, I think the Cheyenne call it Balliett's Post. Old white woman and a crippled man run it, with some Mexicans. Cheyenne trade with them some."

"That's Captain Walls' mother and brother. He had lost track of them for eleven winters before we found them here last summer."

"Will we stay at this place with them, Boss?"

"I hope so. And that's another thing. Sergeant Major Melton is called 'Boss'. I guess you better just call me Ridges."

"I didn't meet all of your little tribe when you were here before. Who will be there, besides the people that run that store?"

Ridges rode in silence for a few moments as he thought about it. "Well, one of them Mexican girls is the woman of that crippled man. He's Tad, she's Carmela, and I think her baby sister is called Manuela. Their father is the old Mexican, Nacio, and he's the black-smith. He ain't got but one good arm. Now stay close. I seen some wolves watching us just now."

"Yes, Ridges, but they were fat. Them wolves won't likely attack us unless they're starving. Plenty of buffalo calves around here. Now, I know these peoples you are telling me about. I have traded with them. Don't you listen to me? I want to know about the new ones, the ones who came with you last summer."

She clucked as she led her pony and the pack horse in a stumbling, sliding descent into a rocky ravine behind Ridges.

"It helps me to say 'em all, for me to remember too." Ridges said. "So, they's also Miz Annette, Dobey's mother. She's Tad's mother too. Then there's the Watsons. Mandy's mother and father, name of Hazel and Henry. And two brothers, Buck and Button. They might not even be there, as they was hot to get on to Santa Fe. Then they's Doc Thomason, who you seen before, and his girlfriend, Junebug. And a large old black man called Big William who used to be a slave. Like you."

Ridges spurred his horse and clattered up the far side of the ravine. "Now he's free and he cooks for them. He shot me once. And I guess the most important is Captain Dobey and Boss Melton's women, Honey and Marie-Louise. They is part black, though it don't show much. They's lighter skinned than you or me. Marie-Louise is the mother. Oh, and she's got another child, Robert. He's 'bout full-growed, big and very powerful, very dark. Called Bear. Good fighter and scout."

Ridges smiled at the memory of his trip with them. "They are good friends. The new ones all kind of latched on to Captain Dobey and Boss Melton as they was trying to get to Dobey's family out here at Canadian Fort, after their part of the Gray Army quit fighting. And they wanted me to stay too, and I surely wanted to, but I was honor bound to go back and stay with my Uncle Stand Watie until he gave up. And now, here I am."

"Goodness, gracious, you talk a lot. Well if you like them, I will too. Even though they shot you. Maybe that one, Bear, maybe he had a different father than the one called Honey. I have seen that happen. Sometimes the mother gets beat because her children don't look the same. Those wolves ran off now. I think they smelled buffalo. Or maybe a deer. Did the big black man shoot you bad? I have fixed many gunshot and arrow wounds..."

Ridges shook his head and rode on in silence. Serenity Killer. Too right.

Chapter Two

"You sure she ain't your Cherokee wife? Shelly don't sound like no Cheyenne name," Mandy asked, her voice wavering with fear and suspicion. She had nearly wet herself with happiness and excitement as she watched her Jimmy Ridges ride in, until she saw the second rider was an Indian girl. A strikingly pretty Indian girl. And older. Now Mandy leaned against him, holding him tight, as the Indian girl put away the horses.

"She ain't Cheyenne, Mandy. She's Osage. And Black Kettle give her to me as a, uh, guide and translator. She speaks English, Osage, Cheyenne, some Comanche and Kiowa. A little Mexican. Now, let me talk to Dobey and Boss Melton a while, then we'll, uh, go for a ride or something."

"Well, I dang sure don't like you owning no pretty girl, I don't care what tribe she's from. What if I had me some handsome-as-all-get-out young Cheyenne boy as a slave? Not too young? How'd you feel? 'Sides, I don't think nobody's supposed to have no slaves now, no how."

She stopped snuffling. Her eyes blazed. Ridges frowned as he tried to digest the unexpected assault. "What's a Cheyenne boy got to do with it, Mandy? I told you she's not Cheyenne. I mean, I didn't buy her or nothing." He suddenly beamed as the solution came to him. "Tell you what. I'll cut her loose. How's that? Set her clean free, just like Big William."

Mandy didn't seem to be all that reassured.

* * *

"SO, Y'ALL FINALLY QUIT?" Dobey asked. He was in the barn with Melton and Jimmy Ridges.

Ridges said, "Yes sir, Captain, back in June. But the Bluecoats said my uncle, Stand Watie, was the last Confederate general to surrender. Three moons after Lee."

"Your people must be proud of that. And I'm just 'Dobey' now."

"Captain, I'll try, but it don't seem right. But anyhows, my people are proud, but now they pay. The Yankees tooken our lands, and gave them to the tribes that fought with them. Given us some worthless flat lands."

"So they moved you again," added Melton. "Dobey, what we gonna do with two Jimmy's? You think we ought to call him James, or just Ridges? I been Jimmy 'round here a long time."

"I hadn't thought on it."

14

"What about Cherokee Jim, Dobey? I already seen a lot of folks out here don't know a Kiowa from a Comanche, let alone a Cherokee. Might save him some trouble. I mean, if he don't mind."

Dobey thought a second. "Probably what he'll wind up being called, whether he likes it or not. You got a problem with that, Ridges?"

"No, Cap'n. That works for me. Thank you, Boss. Well," Ridges looked around. "Y'all been busy here."

Dobey thought about that. They had been busy. In six months, they had built two more adobe buildings and a large wooden house with a two-bedroom loft, two fireplaces, and a third bedroom on the main floor. There were tornado cellars for each of the living quarters as well as the barn. These doubled as storage areas. Though they didn't discuss it, most of the 'captured' cash was split and hidden under two hearthstones at the main house and one in the original store. The cash was a Union payroll taken off the bodies of three deserters who'd been killed by Dobey and Melton as the Yankees tried to rape Honey, back across the Mississippi. They'd been too late to save her father, and afterward, afraid of Yankee retribution, Honey, her brother, and mother had become the first members of the small army that wound up joining Dobey's trip 'home.' And now both Honey and Marie-Louise were pregnant.

"The Watsons would not stay?" Mandy's family had been the next group saved by the Texans, from a renegade town marshal named Fetterman in Mason's Landing, Arkansas.

"They was hell-bent to get to Santa Fe afore winter.

Didn't want to leave Mandy, but her and Marie-Louise put their foots down, and that settled that." Melton laughed. "You remember Buck, their oldest boy? What was he, maybe sixteen? Buck said he had to get the rest of the family there, but he'd be back here in the spring. I 'spect he'll not do that, once he tastes Santa Fe."

"Might avoid some trouble, if he doesn't come back," said Dobey.

Ridges said, "You mean about Junebug?"

"Yeah. He's been moonstruck over her since she rode behind him at Mason's Landing. Kept hoping Doc would tire of her, or start drinking again."

"The good Doc." Ridges smiled. "And how is he?"

Dobey smiled too, as he continued on down that trail of memories. Charles John Thomason was a balding little hard-drinking dentist in the bawdy river town of Mason's Landing when Dobey's group arrived. Pretty much at the end of the line, he was a long way from a successful pre-war practice in Savannah, and the trip had all been downhill. He was still the only medico in town, serving as dentist, doctor, and veterinarian. Dobey had enlisted Doc and his young prostitute girl-friend, Junebug, to help patch up the battered Watson family, after they were rescued from the local 'law.' After they'd all left Mason's Landing, Junebug contrived to sober Doc up, and only then did they learn that he was also a lightning fast killer.

Melton said, "Doc's good. Still ain't drinking. He and Big William is on a scout right now, cross the river. Bear's looking out for them, as ain't neither one perzactly frontiersmen yet."

"Scout? Kiowa trouble? Comanche?"

Dobey answered. "No. Not yet, anyways. Kit Carson hurt them pretty bad just over a year ago, up river a little ways at Adobe Walls. Killed a bunch of their horses and maybe a hundred men, Comanche and Kiowa."

"Adobe Walls? That some place named after you, Cap'n?" Dobey smiled. "No, more the other way 'round. There was an adobe kind of fort and trading post there back in the 1840's. Trader blew it up when he pulled out, left nothing but the walls."

"Who is Carson?"

"A legend out here. Christopher Carson. Old scout and Indian agent, now a Yankee general. He had cavalry and howitzers, but he almost bit off more than he could chew."

"Yeah," Melton chimed in. "They was two villages he bumped into. He ruined the Kiowa one first, but the Comanche had about five hundred lodges. Lotta fighters. They corralled him and the Yankees by this old knocked-down trading post, and if he hadn't of had them cannons, he'd be history. But he's an old trooper, and he slipped away. One of his scouts come by here later and told Dobey's brother about it."

Dobey added, "And since the hostiles was run off, buffalo hunters have been easing back into that valley, camping around the walls. We do business with 'em and it's starting to pick up."

"So, if they ain't no hostiles nearby, what are Doc and Big William and Bear scouting for? Buffalo?" Ridges was fidgeting for some reason.

Melton said, "Naw. You might not have knowed this,

but afore Big William got freed, he cooked for the man as owned him, and once ol' Doc got his tastes back, he learnt Big William's a better cook nor anybody out here has ever seen. They got the idea to open a sporting place. Likker, cards, and Big William's cooking, and maybe women later on. Dobey's momma don't want no likker sold here, so they's looking across the river."

Jimmy Ridges kept looking back nervously at the store where he'd left Mandy. "I sort of want to take Mandy out for a ride, but I don't want to bump into Doc and them."

Melton laughed. "Head up river, most of a mile. Little hill there, by some cottonwoods. Good visibility, all around. River on one side, us behind you, you only got to watch two directions for hostiles."

Ridges thanked them, started away, and then turned back. "The other thing is, where can me and Mandy stay tonight?"

Dobey thought a second. "She's in a room here with my Ma. Room for you in the bunkhouse, with Bear and Big William. Course, once y'all are married, there's another room in Doc's adobe. No bed yet, but plenty of buffalo robes. I'm sure he'd welcome you."

"And Shelly?"

"She can bunk with Manuela and old Gomez in the store. Unless you want her with you." Dobey grinned. "She said she belonged to you."

"Great stars, Captain, no. She near killed me on the way here. Like to have wore me out, and not just talking."

"I believe I would conceal that fact from the women. At least glaze over it."

"Bury it," said Melton.

THREE HOURS LATER, Cherokee Jim Ridges returned from up river to announce that he and Mandy were married. And probably expecting.

1867

Chapter Three

"I BELIEVE you two Cossacks are going just to get away from these noisome brats." Doc held one of the noisome brats, Dobey's eighteen month-old daughter, Millie.

The other, her uncle Mikey Melton, pulled on Doc's pants saying, "Me next, me next." The two, born one week apart, worshiped Doc for the stories he told them, stories the others had never heard, only now coming back to Doc. Stories that the old cook, Flossie, and his mother had told him, forty years ago in Savannah.

"Come on, now, Doc. You wouldn't let the Ridges go by themselves, even if we didn't need to upgrade our hardware. And they got to go. It's been what, over twenty months since Cherokee Jim got here?" Dobey knew that Doc wasn't serious; his comments were more for Honey and Marie-Louise, who were not so understanding. It had been settled last night; the crying was over for now, but they were not a happy pair.

Big William picked up little Mike, tickled him, then set him on his shoulders. "We gonna be fine here, Cap'n. Just y'all hurry back and don't forget them condiments I wrote down."

Melton nudged his horse close to Big William, leaned over, and lifted up his son, holding him straight out and staring into his eyes. "You be good for your Momma, and all these other grownups, too. You do, maybe I'll bring you something from Santa Fe." Melton kissed him on the forehead and put him back on the old black man's shoulders.

Big William squeezed the inside of Mikey's thighs, the baby's favorite tickle points. Mikey squealed, then grabbed Big William's glasses and put them on. "Look'a me. Blind-ass Big William." Mikey had begun walking and talking at nine months. Now a year and a half, he was a pistol.

Marie-Louise slapped Melton's leg and said, "See how you men teach him?" Melton and Big William both shrugged and grinned. Marie-Louise and Honey finally smiled, and Dobey took little Millie for a final hug and kiss. Cherokee Jim Ridges clucked at the two mules, and the wagon pulled away, the spare ponies trailing behind. Mandy and their eleven-month-old, Billy, waved from the back.

Mandy had promised her mother that if Ridges didn't come back and marry her, Mandy would come to Santa Fe, but if he did, as soon as they had a child, they'd come anyhow. Which is probably why Hazel Watson finally agreed to leave Mandy in Canadian Fort back in '65 in the first place.

And, in second place, Mandy missed her family. Her big brother, Buck, despite his promise, had not come back. Her daddy wasn't physically sound, her mother was addle-brained, and baby brother Button was only fourteen. Shoot, she herself was not yet sixteen, with a baby. Of course she was going. It was nice that Captain Dobey and Boss Melton were going with them, even if it was just to buy guns.

ACROSS THE CANADIAN, they angled northwest to intersect the Cimarron Cut-Off of the Santa Fe Trail. They'd take a rest at Camp Nichols on the Trail for a few days, to see if a wagon train came along for company on to Santa Fe. Being as it was just September, there ought to be plenty of traffic.

THEY WERE WELL STOCKED. Two spare ponies trailed the wagon, which carried extra food, water, ammunition, about twenty buffalo hides for trade, a tent, and two shotguns. Dobey had his Henry, and Melton and Ridges both carried Spencers with speed loaders. Each man had three Colts. As an afterthought, Melton put a long Sharps rifle in the wagon with a cartridge pouch of linen .52 caliber cartridges.

"Case we need to do some distance shooting. Like buffalo." "Yeah. Or Kiowa," Dobey mused aloud.

"Hopefully, they're out after buffalo themselves,

Cap'n. You think the others will be all right back at camp?"

"Should be. There's Bear, Tad, Big William, Doc, and Gomez. Plenty of guns. They got Ma, Honey, Marie-Louise, Junebug, Carmela, and Manuela to load for 'em."

"Yes," said Cherokee Jim, "and don't forget Shelly. She can talk any hostiles to death."

"She takes a lot of abuse from everyone," said Melton. "But you got to admit it's good to have someone who can talk to what tribes stop by. And now ol' Ignacio has taught her some Mexican."

"Spanish," corrected Dobey.

"You don't know that, Cap'n. You ain't never talked to no Spaniard. Nor even seen one, far as I know. If you did, you never tole me," Melton said, with a certain confidence.

"I've heard it's the same, Boss. Captain Dobey may be right. Although I did talk with an Englishman, a reporter with the Yankees, and he did not speak at all like you Texans. Or even like the Yankees. It was when we surrendered."

"What the hell did you expect, Lieutenant? He was just a foreigner."

From the back, Mandy added, "I just better not catch you teaching that woman no Cherokee, Jimmy Ridges."

Except for the clopping, squeaking, clattering, and jingling, they rode in silence for a while. Well, the baby talked, but it was a mixture of Spanish, English, Cherokee, Osage, and French, and nobody understood him.

* * *

26

THE TWO BARRELS of water they'd lashed to the wagon were not too much for the eight-day ride to Camp Nichols. The only good thing about that one hundred and fifty miles of scorched earth was that most hostiles were too smart to be out there in the late summer heat.

Dobey and Jimmy Melton had made the trip before, when they escorted the Watsons to the Cut-Off two years earlier. They knew what to expect. They'd learned to travel early and late, sleeping for several hours at midday, in or under the wagon, with a guard.

As they approached Camp Nichols, mid-morning of the eighth day, a rider left the fort and rode slowly toward them. As he neared them they could easily discern at least five canteens and a water bag on his horse and pack mule.

"Heading for Texas?" Dobey hailed him.

At fifty yards they could see he was tanned brown, a lightly mustached young man, lean, maybe eighteen years old. Well armed.

"I sure am." He smiled back at them. "And I guess y'all are bound for Santa Fe."

Mandy screamed, terrifying the baby. "Oh my God, Buck. Oh, Buck. Stand William Ridges, you hush. It's your Uncle Buck."

* * *

THE MEN WERE STANDING behind the wagon, five minutes later, laughing as Buck tried to answer the questions Mandy fired at him like a Gatling gun. Buck was doing a marvelous job of fielding them and tossing his nephew, to little Billy's delight, when they heard two rifle shots from the fort, still over a half-mile away.

Melton mounted, scanned the plain around them for a second, then said, "Uh-oh. Y'all mount up, get ready to fight. 'Bout twenty of 'em coming from the east."

Dobey brought up his telescope. "Kiowa. They're gonna try to block us from the fort, maybe ride right over us. Mandy, you and the baby get down, stay down."

Melton dismounted again. "First though, Mandy, hand me that Sharps and that cartridge pouch."

Melton took the rifle and leather pouch and strode ten yards toward the hard riding war party, now within 300 yards. He knelt and banged off six fast aimed shots, giving a running commentary as he fired and reloaded.

"Good thing the fort warned us." *Boom*. "Won't none of us paying attention." *Boom*. "Got one." A horse tumbled, throwing its rider. "Hold off with them carbines 'til they're closer." *Boom*. "'Nother one. Maybe a hundred yards, Cap'n?" *Boom*. "Dammit. They're splitting up. Cap'n, Ridges, watch them going left." *Boom*. "Got him, the son of a bitch. Buck, we'll take these straight on." *Boom*. "What you carrying there, Buck?" Melton stood, slung the rifle and ammo pouch, remounted, and drew his Spencer. "It ain't a Henry."

"Winchester carbine, Boss. Brand new." Buck gulped air. Melton had knocked down three horses, entangling a fourth, but now nine riders bore down on them, yelling and yipping, while another seven had veered to come at them from the direction of the camp. Ridges was standing in the wagon seat, facing the second smaller group, as was Dobey on his horse. As the Kiowa party veered again, toward the wagon, Dobey yelled, "Let fly."

Twenty bullets flew at both groups in twelve seconds, before the Indians came within arrow range. As the targets were horses, many of those bullets slammed home.

Only two warriors were knocked off their horses, but three more horses went down in each group. Other wounded ponies slowed and swerved away. At that moment, as Dobey's party ran out of carbine ammo and started to reload, the bray of a bugle cut through the yelling, and the fight was over. As a half-section of blue-coats thundered out of the little fort, the still mounted Kiowa quickly picked up most of their dismounted survivors, in some cases with three to a horse, and galloped back to the east.

Melton, the first to be reloaded, got off five more shots, knocking off one rider and hitting one pony in the rump. At fifty yards the blood and dust from the impact were clearly visible. The pony stumbled, but kept going.

"Nice shot, Jimmy." Dobey was still reloading the Henry. "Never thought I'd enjoy the sound of a Yankee bugle

sounding the charge."

THE CAVALRY RAN DOWN and finished three injured Kiowa and several mortally wounded ponies, but let the

Kiowa horsemen go, fearing a trap. They gathered up three ponies that were 'walking wounded', and led them back to the fort, to recover or wind up on the mess table.

Jimmy Ridges was the only friendly casualty. A musket ball hit the wagon seat and splintered it, putting a three-inch sliver in his upper thigh. Another ball smashed one of Buck's canteens and imbedded in his saddle.

* * *

FORTY-FIVE YARDS FROM THE WAGON, unnoticed by all, crouched Wolf Killer. He had broken his bow and his left arm, and his only weapon was a lance. He was surrounded by heavily armed men, who were shooting his wounded comrades. Having been a warrior for thirty summers, he knew his only hope to live was to throw down his weapon and beg for mercy. He stood up, took his lance in his right hand, and began running low and fast toward the wagon. As he jigged through the brush, he hummed his death song.

* * *

THE KIOWA WAS within ten yards of the mounted Dobey before Melton saw him. "Cap'n, behind you. Lookout!"

As Dobey started to turn his horse, the warrior let out a bloodcurdling scream and slapped Dobey across the shoulders with his lance, then turned toward Melton.

Dobey said, "What the hell?" and managed to shoot the warrior in the back before he could hit Melton, whose horse was bucking wildly.

Buck, still breathing hard, rode over and put another bullet in the Kiowa's head, while Dobey rode a quick circle around them, looking for more skulkers.

"There," said Melton, trying to swallow. "That weren't too bad."

Dobey said again, "What the hell? Why did he whack me, 'stead of running me through? He had me easy."

Cherokee Jim answered. "It's called 'counting coup.' You touch an armed enemy, maybe with a club or bow or lance, show how brave you are. 'Specially if you're the first to do it in a fight."

Melton spat. "Well, I wish they'd all fight that way. Somewhat easier to kill, if they ain't trying to kill you."

The cavalry section leader, a lean thirty-year-old corporal, rode over, threw them a loose salute, and drawled, "Y'all awright here? 'Bout ready to ride on in?"

"Yes," answered Dobey. "And thanks for coming. If they'd had twenty more fighters, they'd have ridden right over us."

The corporal stood in his stirrups and stretched. "Don't know 'bout that. 'Spect y'all woulda hurt 'em with all them pistols." He smiled, noticing the Lone Stars on the Texans' hats. "Texas cavalry, right?"

"Yeah," said Melton, on guard. "Eighth Texas."

"Rode with y'all in the Carolinas. Wheeler's Brigade. I was a captain in Hampton's Legion."

As they rode to the fort, Dobey asked, "Why didn't you go back to South Carolina?"

"Did. Weren't nothing nor nobody left. Not for me, anyways. I'm Bob Bridges."

"I'm Dobey Walls. This is Jimmy Melton, and in the wagon is Cherokee Jim Ridges, his wife Mandy, son Billy. You probably met Buck Watson there already. Mandy's brother."

"Yeah. He came out here with us."

"We need to get on to Santa Fe. How soon you think we'll hook up with a group heading west?"

"Train left not three hours ago, with an escort. They had oxen. With your mules, you'll catch 'em before dark. Problem is, the captain ain't gonna want to let you go."

"Why not?"

"Hell, you seen what just happened to you. Might be a bigger group of hostiles watching the west side. Might be you don't fight them off so good as you did these. Anyhow, that's what the captain's gonna say."

"But if they was watching, they'd have followed them that left this morning, right?" Melton joined in.

The corporal grinned. "Yep. You and me know that. Captain probably does too. Real problem is, he don't want to send out no escort with you, even for a few hours, 'cause he's nervous."

"Nervous? You mean scared?"

"Sad, but true. He don't want to leave these walls up here, and he ain't comfortable without a hundred men around him." They started up a small hill to the fort, protected on three sides by ravines. "We got two sections out now, one with that small train that just left, another one out to the east, looking for the main train, the one we was sent out to meet."

"I heard this fort was closed."

"Yep. Has been, probably six months. We're out of Fort Bascom."

* * *

FIVE MILES NORTHEAST, the Kiowa survivors of the raid stopped to lick their wounds.

"What happened back there?" Beeswax nursed his leg. "My horse went down, and then all I could see was smoke and fire from the wagon."

"There was a long-shooting buffalo killer with them. He hurt us first. But then I think they must have had men hidden in the wagon. They tricked us pretty good. Too many guns." Snake looked around. "Where's Wolf Killer? This was his idea."

Walks-At-Night looked back down their trail. "I don't think he made it. His horse was shot. I heard him yell when he fell."

"Horses don't yell. They scream."

"No, Beeswax, I meant Wolf Killer yelled. But that man with the little yellow boy-rifle shot my leg, so I left. That's when I picked you up." Walks-At-Night was sewing up his own wound. "That yellow boy-rifle was a fast shooter, with lots of metal cartridges. I could see the finished ones flashing in the sun as it spit them out."

"Well, we must get some of those guns, or just go back to killing farmers." Snake looked at his tacky old musket with disgust. "Forget about horses. We have plenty, and we can steal more, but we left many good men and boys dead in the dirt back there. There aren't many of us, and these Whites, they have no honor, killing at a distance like that."

"There seem to be a lot of them, too." Beeswax shook his head. "Enough to make me sad."

Chapter Four

"ALL RIGHT, Bridges, if this Yankee captain ain't going to want us to leave now, how do we do it? How do we deal with him?" Dobey halted just outside the old fort.

"I'd get your men to refill them water barrels quick, and be ready to roll. I'd go inside here, and tell Captain Moethe what you plan to do."

"Captain Who?"

"M-o-e-t-h-e. German. Pronounced 'Mer-tha'. He was back east during the war, but I don't think he fought none."

"And if he tells us no?"

"Tell him yes, right back. He ain't got no substance. Y'all ain't in the army. He'll have trouble finding me for a while. Meantime, y'all just ride on. You'll catch them others before late afternoon. Hell, soon as they see you behind 'em, they'll pull up and wait. And you can see five miles."

Dobey and Melton were kept waiting for twenty

minutes by Captain Moethe, as he drank coffee with several of his officers. Dobey decided that Ridges had had enough time to refill the water caskets, and stood to leave.

As he and Melton mounted, a lieutenant hurried over, and placed himself between them and the gate.

"Excuse me, gentlemen. The colonel would like to see you now. If you'll dismount, and follow me?"

Melton looked back at the gaggle of officers, now standing and staring at the Texans. "Colonel? What colonel?"

"Colonel Moethe, sir. We address him by his brevet rank. He, ah, desires that."

"Brevet rank?"

The lieutenant lowered his voice. "His wartime rank. Like many others, he was reduced to his permanent rank of captain after the hostilities ended."

"You think they've ended? You think I ain't still hostile?" Melton flared.

Dobey intervened. "Don't shoot the messenger, Jimmy. Let's just make this quick."

They dismounted again, tied off the horses, and walked with the hapless lieutenant to the conference site, a folding table and a few camp stools in the shade of one wall of the quadrangle. They carried their long arms.

The lieutenant looked askance at the Henry and Spencer, then noticed that each Texan also wore two revolvers.

"How shall I, uh, introduce you?"

"I'm Walls, and he's Melton. We don't use our brevet

ranks." The nervous lieutenant completed the introductions, and the Texans nodded to the heavy-set captain, who slouched on a camp stool.

"Quite a little dust-up out there this morning, gentlemen. It's a good thing we were here to bail you out." The captain smirked, while several of his junior officers laughed.

Melton tensed and started to say something, but Dobey touched his arm, and said, "We appreciate help whenever we find it."

"Well, I suppose you Rebs want to wait with us here for the next Santa Fe wagon train. You'll be safe enough now, and there should be one here within days. Make yourselves comfortable, and stay out of trouble, you hear?" He pronounced the last word 'heah', a slight mockery of the Texas drawl. The other bluecoat officers snickered.

Dobey stopped smiling. "We'll just ride on, now. Our mules will catch the ox-train that left this morning in a few hours."

"Well, you may not, sir. I forbid it."

"Forbid it, did you say?" Dobey's voice was soft, but menacing nonetheless. Melton's tension was palpable.

Some of the captain's smugness slipped away. "I cannot spare another escort, and . . ."

Dobey held up a finger to interrupt him. "We just came from the Canadian River, a hundred-fifty miles without your escort . ." Now Melton interrupted Dobey. "And it won't be the first time, neither. And I don't know what damn fight you was watching this morning, but ain't nobody bailed us out." He got

37

louder as he talked. "Ever."

Dobey touched his arm again. "Enough, Sergeant-Major. Let's mount up."

A trooper had brought their mounts up close behind them. As they swung into the saddle, Captain Moethe said, "If you disobey me, I'll have you arrested."

Melton cocked the Spencer and wheeled his horse, causing the officers to scatter somewhat. He glared at Moethe. "You can try. But me and the Cap'n, we've shot our way out of lot nicer places than this. You heah?"

As they turned and galloped toward the gate, Moethe yelled at his troop sergeant, "Arrest them. Do it now."

The old sergeant spat tobacco and wiped his chin. "You arrest 'em. Bridges tole me he recognized 'em. They was in Shannon's Scouts. And I seen 'em fight this morning."

As they cleared the gate, Dobey asked, " 'Nicer places than this'? When?"

"Hell, Cap'n, that whorehouse in Atlanta. Lots nicer than this. That paradise millpond, too."

"Oh. Yeah, you're right again. You ever get tired of that?"

* * *

BUCK WATSON'S heart was full, near bursting to be back with these people. His little sister Mandy, Cherokee Jim, and their new baby, of course, but mostly with the two Texans.

They'd saved his whole entire family, he was sure,

back there in Mason's Landing. Taught him stuff, too. Fighting, covering ground, taking care of women, being tolerant and open to new things and people, all that and more, on that long trip west a few years back. He was eager to reconnect with them.

Nervous on how to start, though. Boss Melton seemed a little agitated right now. Maybe worried about running into them Kiowas again?

Buck was riding in front of the wagon with Dobey and Melton, watching for the escorted convoy ahead of them.

"What happened back there in that old fort?" Buck finally asked.

Dobey smiled. "Mister Melton here kind of lost his temper with their boss man. Just put him down, I mean slammed him proper, without ever so much as touching him."

Melton snorted.

Dobey said, "You ain't really over it, are you? The war, I mean?"

"Cap'n, it's just that I see somebody like him, that fat captain back there, and I'm minded of that boy in Tennessee."

"Well darn, Jimmy, what boy?"

"From K Company, maybe. Yankees took him whilst he's off sparking. Having tea in a damn parlor, two girls and their auntie, weren't even sleeping with 'em. Hung him 'cause he had a little book. Sons a bitches." Melton glowered at Dobey. Buck shrank.

Dobey shook his head at the memory. "Oh, yeah...

how could I forget? Said he was a spy because of his diary."

Melton was trembling with building rage. "Spy. He didn't even know what the word meant. He weren't more'n maybe eighteen. Hadn't never even seen no slaves before he came to Tennessee to fight along of his friends and family. Just a boy. And they hung him."

"It was truly wrong, Jimmy. And we truly punished 'em, afterward. For months."

"Not near enough, Cap'n. Not near. I'd like to go back there right now, cut out that sorry fat bastard, string him up. Maybe a couple of them snickering, suck-ass other officers too." Melton jerked off his hat and slapped it against his leg, rubbed his forearm over his eyes, and snorted again. Sniffled? "They's just the kind of men as hung that boy."

Buck rode silently, scared to talk, almost sorry he'd brought it up. Is them tears, he wondered, from Boss Melton? No way. Ain't no way.

As if he sensed the question, Melton shot a look at Buck and grunted, "What?"

Buck shook his head and shrugged. "Nothing, Boss. I didn't say nothing. I didn't even think nothing. Honest."

Melton jammed his hat back on his head and glared holes in the horizon.

Dobey looked over at Buck, shrugged himself, gave him a 'Hell, I don't know' look, and tried to calm Melton again.

"Look it, Jimmy, I agree. I think that was maybe the worst thing I heard of in the whole war. But those sorry rascals back there didn't do it, and…"

"You don't know that," Melton exploded, his face almost black now. "They could'a been there. And it won't like they killed him in a rage. Nosir. They took him back to their camp, read his little book, had a fake trial. Took their time at it. Then they hung him. Hung him, Goddammit. I seen that little book. 'Had some roast and pie with the Joneses. Pretty young sister there. Tuesday stayed with the Tates again. Nice swing on the porch. Asked me to say Grace. Peach cobbler.' Spy, my big raw ass. Them murdering bastards."

Buck shuddered. Them Kiowa better hope they don't run into us right now, he thought. And ain't nobody in that cavalry escort up ahead better say nothing crossways about the war, neither. Buck decided to change the subject. He wore a pair of Navy Colts and had a Remington in his pommel holster. He patted it as they slogged west. "Bear's old Remington he loaned me. I can return it whenever we get back there. Got me another Navy in my saddlebags."

"You might want to give one of those Navies to your sister, 'til we get to Santa Fe. Just in case. And tell her 'bout the last two bullets."

"What about 'em, Cap'n?"

"One for the baby, one for her, if things go bad."
"Oh. Yeah."

"Then come back and tell us 'bout that shiny yellow carbine."

* * *

"IT'S A WINCHESTER, Cap'n. Same company that makes

your Henry. Same .44 rim fire cartridge, same action, but it loads through the side plate here, so's the magazine ain't got that open slot underneath, to let in dust and mud."

Dobey handled it. "I like this wood forearm on it, too. Hot day like this, or a hot fight, you need a glove on your left hand for a Henry. These new ones come in rifle size too, or just carbines?"

"Rifles, too. Seventeen rounds in the magazine." Buck passed the carbine to Melton for his examination. "One in the chamber, makes them eighteen shooters. The carbine is a fourteen shooter."

"Why'd you take the carbine over the rifle version? Or did you have a choice?"

"Naw, I bought it, Boss. They had both kinds. This one's just easier to handle on a horse, and as for the number of rounds it'll hold, well, it's real easy to top it off."

"Yeah. It ain't like reloading a Henry. You just pop 'em in the side here. But you giving up some range and bullet speed with this shorter barrel."

"Well, Boss, you ain't gonna hunt big game with either one of 'em, no how. I mean, it ain't a Sharps."

"Good answer." Melton handed it back to Buck. "Tell you what, though. I'll be happy when somebody brings out a pistol to handle them .44 metal cartridges."

"Amen," said Dobey. "You'd think that Smith and Wesson would have done that already. You know, a bigger version of that .32 Army like Honey has."

"The superstition gun," Buck grinned. "Ol' number five-fifty-five, right?"

"Yeah," muttered Melton. "She oughtta just throw it away." Buck winked at Dobey, then continued. "Well, anyhow, the

gunsmith at that store where I bought this Winchester? He said that Smith and Wesson was working on that exactly."

"Well, good." Dobey stopped, and glassed the area all around them. Putting away the telescope, he asked, "What do those Winchesters cost, anyhow? We were gonna buy a few Henrys for the camp."

"Forty, forty-two dollars, Cap'n. Not much more'n a Henry. And Cap'n, for twenny-five dollars, they had some Springfield central-fire rifles, .50 caliber breechloaders. Damn bullets looked like cigars. Ought to make a hell of a buffalo gun. They call 'em Trapdoors or needle guns."

"What?" Dobey frowned.

Buck said, "Breech flips up like a trapdoor. Firing pin must be five inches long, runs right through the whole breech. Like a needle."

Melton asked, "What makes a central fire cartridge so different?"

"Primer's centered in the base, 'stead of the rim. Better ignition, they say. Still ain't re-loadable, but they's a lot bigger than Spencer nor Henry bullets. I mean, a lot bigger." Buck nodded for emphasis.

"How much?" Melton was skeptical.

Buck said, "Henry's got twenty-eight grains of powder, and Spencer's what, maybe forty-five?"

"Yeah."

"Trapdoor uses seventy grains," Buck said. "Damn bullet itself weighs five hundred grains."

"It'll hit hard as a Sharps, then?" Dobey asked.

"Yes sir. Yes, it will. But faster to load. And waterproof."

It was sort of quiet for a while, as Dobey, Melton, and Cherokee Jim absorbed that.

Mandy spoke first. Well, actually the baby, Billy, spoke first, but he said the Cherokee word for 'hungry,' and only his father understood him. And ignored him.

Mandy said, "Buffalo hunters gonna love that."

They hadn't realized she was paying attention. Dobey said, "Jesus, you are right. This is a big thing."

"God almighty," said Melton. "It ain't been but six years since we was amazed by the rimfire cartridge. This mean they're obsolete?"

The baby said, "Comida."

Dobey said, "Yeah, I guess pretty soon. Soon as they figure a way to re-load the empties. These are just more powerful, for right now."

The baby seemed to think that Dobey was answering him and relaxed somewhat. He understood 'yeah,' 'pretty soon,' and 'right now.'

Cherokee Jim looked despondent. "What's gonna be obsolete is buffalo."

"Yeah," said Melton. "Whole bunch of ex-soldiers is gonna become hunters, and they ain't killing 'em for the meat."

Little Billy perked up again. "Carne!" He clapped and looked around, smiling.

"Well," said Mandy, "I guess it's good we're setting up

to trade with them hunters. Ain't that what we're in it for?"

"Faim!" shouted Billy, rubbing his tummy.

Mandy smiled and rubbed his head. "No, Billy, not fame. We're in it for the money. That's what storekeepers do. Now, ain't you about to get hungry, baby?"

Mandy handed out jerky to everyone. In Southern Cheyenne dialect, Billy said the phrase for 'thank you.' Everybody knew that one. Three nervous hours later, they spied the wagon train that they were chasing. Melton fired off a round to get their attention and slow them down, and the two parties were married up long before the sun dropped behind the mountains to the west.

Chapter Five
———————

"What are we eating here, Miz Watson?" Jimmy Melton was digging into his plate of meat, beans, tomatoes, and peppers. "This is mighty good."

"Dog meat," said Button, grinning. Melton spit it out.

Hazel whacked Button with the ladle, smearing sauce on his neck. "I've had 'bout enough of that joke, young man. No, Boss, it's prairie dog. Button shoots 'em in the head with that squirrel rifle. Ain't but thousands of 'em around. They's like fat ground squirrels."

The Watsons lived in a small adobe house with a shed, under trees on a creek a mile from the zocalo, or town center. On the plain along the creek were hundreds, if not thousands, of prairie dog holes. As it turned out, Button Watson and his father were running a thriving business of killing, cleaning, and chopping up the prairie dogs for food, and delivering the meat fresh to a dozen or so eating places in Santa Fe. It became so popular for chili con carne that some wealthy families were also on the delivery list.

"I started it. Didn't have nothing but that Sharps you loaned me, so I was shooting 'em to pieces." Buck laughed. "That's why we started chopping 'em up fine. Soon as I could, I bought me and Button some .32 caliber squirrel rifles. Hell, we might kill fifty a night."

"A night?"

"Oh yeah, Boss. Take lanterns out, set 'em up on the prairie, they come up to stare. Them beady little eyes is a perfect target. Use half-charges. Ain't much overhead."

Melton laughed. "What a business. How come you to quit?" "Made enough to buy them guns, supplies, and pack horse.

Guess I was hoping Doc would'a tired of Junebug by now. Guess he ain't, or you'd have said so." Buck's spirits sagged visibly, when no one corrected him. "Anyhow, Button and Daddy do fine at it. I still want to go back with you."

* * *

HENRY AND HAZEL WATSON were delighted with the visit of their daughter and grandson, though they understood little of what he said.

"Is that all Cherokee?"

Cherokee Jim smiled. "Very little of it." "Well, does he speak any American?"

"Mostly, he does. Now if you mean English, very little of it."

* * *

WHEN THEY HAD ARRIVED in Santa Fe, Dobey and Jimmy Melton were each wearing money belts with three hundred dollars in currency. When they left three weeks later for the return, both of them carried new Winchester carbines, as did Cherokee Jim.

Their old weapons were in the wagon, along with some new clothes. So were five new Winchester rifles, and ten new .50-70 needle guns, plus thousands of cartridges.

For the old Sharps rifles, there were also percussion caps, lead, bullet molds, powder, and linen cartridge paper. And there were condiments for Big William's kitchen. Buffalo hunters were going to love them.

The money belts were empty.

* * *

THE WOMEN'S tears flowed freely as the travelers loaded up to join the eastbound wagon train forming up on the prairie just outside town. Even old Henry clouded up a little.

"Well," he sniffed, "y'all have sure made a handsome baby. And Jim, it's clear my daughter has taken to you."

"And him to her, too," put in Hazel, sobbing.

"Yes. You know we wish y'all would stay here. You see we're making a good living. If things don't pan out there in Texas, y'all come back. We'd welcome you as a partner, Jim."

"Oh, please do, please do," Hazel wailed.

"Now hush, Hazel. They got to make their own way." Henry looked up at Cherokee Jim. "But I can see you're taking good care of her. Buck, you watch out, too."

* * *

THEY ALMOST MADE it out of Santa Fe without incident.

Though they'd bought new clothes, Dobey, Melton, and Cherokee Jim decided to get one more rough trip out of their almost threadbare gray uniforms. That shouldn't have been a problem. They sent Buck forward to represent them at the mandatory meeting with the commander of the cavalry escort, on the chance that it might be Captain Moethe again.

"We'll just try to stay lost in the dust, back here," said Dobey. A few minutes passed. Two sergeants galloped by from town,

apparently carrying messages to the escort commander. Dobey and Melton saw them coming, moved to the far side of the wagon, and dismounted.

"You think they saw us, Cap'n?"

"I don't think so, Jimmy. I'm pretty sure they missed us. Besides which, I don't recall them from Camp Nichols. Maybe these ain't dyed-in-the-wool Yankees."

Ten minutes later, the same two sergeants trotted directly up to the wagon, and halted.

"Well, well, and just lookee here. And I was thinking I saw some Rebels, as we come by. Faith, it must be too harsh for 'em out here, the darlings, do you think so, Sergeant Blitzer?" He gave the travelers a big smile. Not a trace of warmth in it. None.

"Ja, maybe dey go home to Carolina. It's safe dere, now Sherman's gone. Ja, I tink so, Sergeant Rather," cackled the pot-bellied German. He was somewhat cross-eyed. He tried to sit erect, hands folded on his pommel. Dominating. Fearless.

Cherokee Jim smiled at them, trying to comprehend the humor through the Irish brogue and guttural German. Dobey and Melton faced them, and moved away from the wagon.

"Gonna have to ask you to get down in the wagon bed again, and stay down, Mandy." Dobey didn't take his eyes off the two horsemen. He'd given up the shoulder holster. At Doc's suggestion, he wore the sawed-off Colt in a cross-draw holster on his left hip. He was even faster this way.

Mandy's jaw jutted. "I ain't scared, you know," she muttered, as she moved the baby to safety.

Facing the sergeants, Dobey asked quietly, "Is that other fat German, Moethe, running this escort?"

"No, he ain't, cracker. Captain Collins is. What's it to you?" "Oh, good," said Melton, "we get to piss off a new captain." "Hey, vait. Vat you mean, 'udder fat Cherman'?"

"He meant you and him, lard-ass." Melton's right hand was on the handle of his short Colt. "And make up your mind who you're looking at, you wall-eyed son of a bitch."

"That's it, then, you're under arrest." Sergeant Rather started to unsnap the cover on his holster.

The Texans drew, cocked, and covered the two sergeants before they could begin to draw their revolvers. Cherokee Jim, now comprehending that these men weren't trying to be friendly, also stood and covered them with his new Winchester. There was a triple click behind him, and he turned to find Mandy pointing a cocked revolver at the two soldiers too.

"You started this," said Dobey. "Now, we might have to ride back to Texas by ourselves, but we're not gonna be arrested over your foul humor. You do what you gotta do."

"Y'all can ride away or just die right here. You pick." Melton focused on the Irishman, as the German had raised his hands.

"We'll go, darlings, but we'll be back. Come on, Blitzer."

As the two sergeants raced back toward the head of the column, Cherokee Jim jumped down and asked, "What now?"

Dobey looked around. "I think we take our Winchesters and move over by those trees, near the creek. Mandy, if this doesn't turn out well, you just go back to your family. Jim, why don't you just take her and go?"

"No sir, Captain Dobey. I'm in this."

"Well, we can use you. Hope Buck gets back before they do." "May I approach, gentlemen?"

The Texans turned to face the speaker, who stood

between their mules and the next wagon. He was huge, at least 6' 2", about two hundred and fifty pounds, maybe thirty-five years old, with some European accent. He carried a Winchester rifle.

"These are my two wagons just in front of yours." He gave them a broad smile as if that explained everything.

"And? You're worried about your property? Well, we're gonna move away some." Melton shook his head in disgust as he turned to go.

"Oh. Oh no. Not my meaning, not at all." He held up one hand in a placating gesture. "I mean, I heard and saw your encounter. I think you'll have some trouble, yes?"

"'Spect so." Dobey stared at the man, as Melton stopped and looked back.

"Forgive me. I am Graf Gustaf Baranov von Konitz. From Prussia. I am called Count. I am hunting your large game animals, and have been a guest of the U.S. Army here for several weeks. Perhaps I have some influence. With their leader, here. Captain Collins." He nodded earnestly.

"Count? Like a duke, or baron or something?" Melton was skeptical.

"Precisely, sir. At your service."

"Thank you. I'm Dobey Walls, this here's Jimmy Melton and Cherokee Jim Ridges. That's his wife Mandy and baby in the wagon."

The count tipped his wide-brimmed hat. "Madame." Turning back, he said, "I believe you have another man up front for the meeting? I sent my, ah, associate to that, too. Perhaps they will be back before those two scoundrels return."

"Maybe. But there's likely to be a fight, if your influence don't work."

"In which case, I have this Winchester. I will stand with you. I'll leave my drivers with my wagons. I noticed the cavalry only have Sharps single-shots. We won't be out-gunned, but I have high hopes of a successful negotiation."

* * *

CAPTAIN JOEL COLLINS was eager to wrap up the pain-in-the-butt briefing with the attendant dozens of scared and stupid questions. These usually came from a few whiners, as most of the wagon leaders had made this trip before. Today was no exception. He handled them easily, having been a practicing courtroom attorney before throwing it away to join the Union cavalry in '64, back east.

"That should do it then. Keep your eyes open, don't wander off, shout out if you have a problem. We're not going to leave you. From what you tell me, we've got plenty of repeaters in the train. We'll be fine. Let's roll in fifteen minutes."

As the representatives of each wagon family rode off, Corporal Bridges tapped Collins' arm, and pointed.

"Don't know what this is about, Cap'n. Here comes them two sergeants back."

"Can't be good."

* * *

BUCK COULD TELL something was wrong as he rode up. The Texans and Cherokee Jim were well away from the wagon, near the creek. A big stranger stood with them. They all had Winchesters. *Wonder if this has something to do with them two soldiers who just pounded past?*

Melton spoke. "Tie off by the wagon, and bring your carbine over here."

As Buck dismounted, another young man rode up and stopped.

"Graf Baranov, what gives here?"

"Willi, put your horse there, and bring the shotgun. And buckshot."

"Ja, mein Graf."

Introductions were made, and Buck and Willi were briefed. Dobey agreed to let the count do the talking, whenever the cavalry returned.

Less than three minutes later, Captain Collins thundered up with a half section of ten troopers, Corporal Bridges, and the two sergeants.

"That's them, Captain. Look's like they's got reinforced." Noticing the shotgun and five Winchesters, Sergeant Rather pulled back some. "Draw carbines, boys," he shouted.

"I'll give the commands here, Sergeant Rather. You men just hold what you got," Captain Collins countermanded, then faced the Texans' party.

" A fine good morning, Captain Collins."

"Count." Collins saluted. "You know something

about this?" "I do, Cap'n," Corporal Bridges spoke. "They's the ones I

told you about. The fight at Camp Nichols?" He smiled and waved to the Texans. "Can't stay out of trouble, can you?"

"Seems like it." Dobey smiled back, but kept his eyes on Rather.

Baranov stepped forward. "I witnessed the incident. Those two sergeants there, they desired to insult these men, to treat them as cowards, to demean their uniforms and service. When these civilians responded in kind, your sergeants attempted to arrest them, and these men refused to be arrested."

"They drew on us, Captain." Sergeant Rather was still fingering his revolver.

"Your sergeants attempted to draw first," Count Baranov was firm. "I can assure you, this entire event was unnecessary, and was entirely precipitated by your two sergeants. In my regiment, these two would be reduced to privates in disgrace. Possibly hung. Certainly shot."

"I don't have to listen to such shit from no foreigner," shouted Rather.

Captain Collins was livid. "That 'foreigner,' Sergeant Rather, is a visiting dignitary from a friendly government. Consider yourself under arrest. Sergeant Blitzer, take his pistol, and take him back to headquarters. Tell Colonel Sussman that the train's departure will be delayed while I write up this incident, and that blame will fall to you two as well. I'll send the report by messenger before we leave. Dismissed." He dismounted as the two shocked sergeants rode away. "I apologize, all around. Those two are normally harmless. Pretty worthless, but harmless. I'll bet you have some paper, Count. If I can have a piece, I'll write this up, and we'll get this show on the road."

Chapter Six

"COUNT, when we stop tonight, we'd like you and your party to eat with us. Mandy's got this big iron pot, and she'll make a big mess of chilis and beans."

"Why, Captain Walls, how delightful. Willi and I will be happy to join you."

"What have you got, four others? Go on and bring them too. She'll make enough for a section."

"Section?"

Dobey laughed. "Cavalry term. Twenty men. I just meant she'll make a lot."

"Well, then. Good. Perhaps tomorrow we can return the favor? My Mary Belle is a wonderful camp cook, and Willi was schooled as a chef, before I convinced him to join me on this adventure."

"How did you meet him?"

"Willi?" Baranov pronounced it as 'Villi.' The count reversed his 'V's' and 'W's', and broad 'A's became soft 'E's, so he "vas heppy to be on this edwenture, that he had conwinced Villi to choin." He now hesitated to respond.

Dobey sensed it, and apologized. "I shouldn't pry."

"Well. I think you might as well know. I am forty-two. Twenty years ago as a Captain of Hussars, I courted a lovely Jewess, Sara Lang, and Willi was the result. I was married, of course, but I have always provided for them. Sara died a year ago. I loved her very much. Willi is what I have left."

"Oh." Dobey was shocked by the honesty. "You have no other family?"

"Oh, yes. Two fat daughters, married to two fat diplomats. There was three sons. One killed in a duel, one killed in battle, one priest. As I said, Willi is all I have."

"The countess? She's gone too?"

"Ah. Well, she's still there. She was always there. Indulged by her physicians, and psychics, and priests. Card readers, hair dressers, such persons as that." He paused, smiling at a memory. "One large African, who had visions. He told of one in which we went to Africa, I became a king, and made him my general."

Dobey smiled too. "Did you consider it?"

The count snorted. "I told him to envision me putting a boot up his arse, and going to America instead."

* * *

AS MANDY FINISHED PREPARING her chili stew, Dobey walked to the count's wagons to let that party know that soup was almost on the table. The count made introductions.

"This is Willi Lang, whom you've met informally." He hesitated. "He is my son." As Dobey already knew that, and Willi was visibly startled, Dobey assumed that Willi was not expecting that admission. Willi flushed, glowed, and stammered. Dobey thought, *if he had a tail, he'd wag it.*

There were also Hannity and O'Reilly, mule 'skinners' who were also real buffalo skinners and back-up hunters for Willi and the count. "Irishmen," said the count. "Former soldiers, now run from a brutal ship's captain in San Francisco. Fair brutal in a fight themselves. We watched them clear a cantina in Santa Fe." He smiled. "I believe some one suggested that they were English."

O'Reilly nodded. "That they did, too. And learned from it. But the running, Captain, that were years ago. This ain't our first hunt, me and Seamus."

"No sir," added Hannity. "We've knocked down bear, buffalo, Indians, elk, and everything in between, we have."

"What do you use?" Dobey looked around.

"Sharps .52's, the long ones, there, for me and Colin. The count has a bloody beautiful .44. It hangs there." He pointed to a full stocked Colt sporting rifle, with brass furniture.

"I've got something y'all might want to see after dinner," Dobey said. He thought, *might sell one or two of these needle guns before we get home.* He turned to the large black woman in an apron. "I'm Dobey Walls." He shook her hand, obviously surprising her, and repeated the process with the silent black man behind her.

"Yassuh. I's Mary Belle White, the cook, and that there is George Canada, the handyman." George nodded and grunted. "He got no tongue. He run to Canada, 'fore the war, but Indians there, they got his tongue. Had to run again, didn't you, George?"

George smiled ruefully, and nodded again.

"Well, shall we go? I am starved, and have been smelling the meal for an hour." The count stood and moved toward Dobey's wagon.

As the four white men left with Dobey, Mary Belle and George returned to their chores.

Dobey stopped. "Count, I meant for them to come, too. Plenty of food for them."

"Oh. But I thought, …"

"It ain't that way, Count. I mean, we ain't that way. I'd appreciate it if you'd have 'em join us." He thought, *Honey would cut me off if I cut them out.*

"How wonderful. Yes. Mary Belle, George, the captain wishes us to eat together." He turned back to Dobey and added, "As usual."

DINNER WENT WELL. When the count's party returned to their wagons, they carried two new Springfield Trapdoors, plus four hundred rounds of .50-70 ammo. Fully paid for. Full price.

* * *

THE NEXT EVENING Mary Belle served everyone rice laced with onions, raisins, and chunks of salt ham, covered with red-eye gravy, and accompanied by the best biscuits Melton could remember. "Gonna be a better trip than the one to get here," he said.

The count brought out his technological counter-point to their 'central-fire' Trapdoors: a breech-loading shotgun, utilizing reloadable central-fire copper cartridges. "A twelve-bore," he said, handing it to Melton. "English-made."

"God almighty, Dobey, this would be even faster'n my old Colt shotgun, in a fight."

"A fight?" Baranov looked bemused.

"Yes sir," said Dobey. "Jimmy thinks in those terms, as opposed to hunting."

* * *

BEFORE THEY LEFT THE MOUNTAINS, O'Reilly nailed a nice stag using the count's Trapdoor. "Two hundred yards. Dropped the bugger like a sack of potatoes, it did," said Hannity.

"More the like of a hundred-fifty, Seamus darling, but it was a marvelous shot, too. He'll feed us a while. I truly love the gun, Count." O'Reilly turned it in his hands, caressing it as he talked.

* * *

BACK AT CAMP NICHOLS, Dobey trotted up to the count's party. "We've enjoyed your company, but tomorrow we'll follow our old tracks home to Canadian Fort. Just want to wish you luck and safe passage, sir."

"Well, then, you can help with those things." Baranov grinned.

"What things?"

"Luck and safe passage. I have decided to go with you to this Texas, and see what nice big animals you have for me to kill."

Next morning, three well-armed wagons left the train, heading south and east. Shortly after noon Dobey halted the convoy for rest, food, and water beside a small rock outcrop. As everyone else stretched and walked, he climbed the rocks to glass the countryside. Finding no movement, he closed the telescope and stood a moment, lost in thought.

Willi noticed him, grabbed some sort of board from his wagon and sat on a rock to begin scribbling furiously.

"What the hell is he doing, Count?" Melton was watering his horse with his hat.

"Willi? Oh, he is a wonderful artist. I think he captures your captain in his heroic pose on the little hill. Let us go and look, ja?"

Willi had sketched an incredible likeness of Dobey, carbine over his left forearm, gazing off to the south. All the details were there: holster, hat, uniform, boots, spurs, scope, knife, Winchester, his pensive expression.

"Damn. I mean, that's pretty good. You had some training, ain't you?"

Willi flushed, and stammered, "Yes. Yes sir, Boss Melton. Do you really like it?"

"Hell, you can tell it's him. I mean, it ain't just some soldier, it's Dobey hisself."

"Show him the animals, Willi." The count was beaming with pride. "He really is very good at this."

There were bears, cougars, elk, pronghorns, white-tails, and turkeys, almost photographic in their accuracy. Melton clucked approval.

"It is my hope, that with Willi's pictures, my skins and skulls can be transformed into realistic representations for my Museum of Natural History in Prussia."

"You mean, like stuffed? I seen a stuffed bobcat once, back east. Hey, y'all," Melton shouted to the others, "you got to come see this."

As the others marveled over Willi's work, Dobey asked, "Just where is this museum, Count Baranov?"

"Just now? Just here." He pointed to his head.

* * *

THAT NIGHT AT THE FIRE, Buck got up enough nerve to ask about Junebug again.

"So, Cap'n Dobey, is Junebug still hooked on that old dentist?"

Dobey took a sip of brandy, and winked at Melton. "She hangs out with him. I think she cares more for him than him for her. But she's convenient."

Melton poked the fire. "You still hoping to get between them? 'Cause you want to be real careful around that old dentist. Hell, he's faster than the Cap'n here."

"I ain't forgot, Boss. I's just hoping…"

"Look it, Buck, he's thirty year older than she is, and he don't seem to need her much. Don't take a detective to figure out that you got a chance, long as you don't make him shoot you." Melton grinned at him.

Buck raised his eyes to the stars and said softly, "Oh, sweet Jesus Christ."

Dobey stared at him and said, "Buck, what's wrong? He's trying to tell you that you got prospects."

"No, Cap'n, it ain't that." Buck was clearly agitated. "It's what he said about detecting. I was supposed to tell y'all something important, and I clean forgot 'til just now, when he said that. See, there was some detectives come through Santa Fe two months ago. Pinkertons. Looking for some people that stole a Yankee army payroll back in Mississippi, right at the end of the war."

"And?" Dobey's voice was hard and his eyes were boring into Buck's.

"Said they could have been Yankee deserters who done it, but they thought it was a couple of Rebels traveling with some darkies or breeds, heading west up the Arkansas. Said they heard I come out that way, and wanted to know if I'd seen some people like that." Buck swallowed hard, and his eyes flicked back and forth from Dobey's to Melton's.

Melton suddenly stood over him. "Well, Goddammit, what'd you say?"

"I said, yes I had. Boss, I had to get 'em away before they found my family. My ma ain't bright enough to lie." Buck swallowed again. "I told 'em y'all got off the boat in Fort Smith, and was going on up to Fort Dodge and Buffalo City, while I come on west."

"They buy that?"

"Not right off. Said they'd heard y'all was from Texas, and they was tired of being lied to. Said some marshal had already steered 'em wrong, cost 'em two years at least."

"That fat bastard Fetterman." Melton jabbed the fire with a stick. "Knew I should'a killed him."

Buck nodded. "Yes sir. But maybe not, Boss. He did steer 'em wrong, and I told 'em y'all couldn't come back to Texas because of the law, and that I's pretty sure that Fetterman was in cahoots with y'all, and y'all was going into business up in Kansas."

"Shoot. You did? You told 'em that?"

"Yes sir. I figured Fetterman might be looking for y'all too, and now maybe if these Pinkertons run into him again, they'll just kill him."

It was quiet for a moment. Melton spoke first.

"Sweet. That's just By-God sweet, is what it is." He grinned at Dobey. "Not bad, for a dumb-assed child."

Dobey stood now. "So far, so good. What happened next?" "Cap'n, I think they bought it. They caught the first east-

bound wagon train, and I caught the next one, and here I am." Melton looked at Dobey. "Bother you that Fetterman might

just be still out there hunting us?"

Dobey pulled at his moustache. "Thing is, him and those Pinkertons been after us this whole time, and we didn't even know it. It's like, I don't know, we just been lucky. I don't like this hanging over our heads."

"Yeah. Buck might've shined them detectives on past

us, but I don't think I'll sleep good 'til I know Fetterman's dead." Melton stooped, picked up a small log, and slammed it into the fire, showering the others with sparks.

"Judas Priest, Boss," Buck sputtered and jumped up.

Melton put his hands on his hips, grimaced, and shook his head. "It just don't seem right. We work hard, fought good, got lucky with our women, and put together a pretty good outfit. Got some good money put back, and trade is starting to pick up, and still we can't ever just lay back and enjoy it. Always something bad out there, just out of range."

"Cap'n, seems to me these folks wouldn't be so interested unless they's a lot of money involved."

Dobey nodded. "Well, Buck, could be there is." "How much trouble are we in, Cap'n?"

"About seven thousand dollars worth."

"God almighty. There ain't that much money in the whole entire world."

Dobey shrugged. "Well, there is in Canadian Fort. See, we just happened up on this little store, and these three Yankees was trying to, uh, to take Honey by force…"

"Already had her pants down," said Melton. "Done killed her daddy. He was a old white man. Would'a killed Anne-Marie and Bear too, maybe worse."

"So you saved 'em, like you saved us at Mason's Landing, 'cept for Momma getting used badly." Buck shook his head. "I hope Honey and Anne-Marie don't ever have to go through something like that."

Melton nodded. "They would of, too, 'less we got

there just then. And then we found the money they'd stold. No way to give it back to nobody. I mean, you see how they got it figured now? Pinkertons and all? Yankees would'a shot us down or hung us all, Anne-Marie and her fambly too."

"Yeah," said Dobey, "so we took stolen money. Don't know how that works out, legal wise. Don't know how to give it back, don't want to, and now don't know how to get Fetterman and them Pinkertons off our tails. But you sure helped, Buck, and we wouldn't have even knowed, wasn't for you."

Melton nodded again. "Sure weren't no good like it was."

Chapter Seven

"You MIND DO I have some more coffee?" Without waiting, Fetterman poured himself another cup, then smiled at the two hunters. "So, you seen anybody like that?"

The older man frowned. "It ain't like that coffee grows on trees, you know."

"Hush up, Charley. We'll get more when we sell these hides, and I ain't had no real conversation for a month now." The younger man turned his attention back to Fetterman. "Charley don't say much. When he does, it's just to piss and moan. Fact is, that's about his only exercise, other'n shooting. I has to do all the skinning." He paused. "Lemme think. You know, you could be talking about them folk at Balliett's Post, up on the Canadian. Three used to wear gray uniforms , though one's a Injun. Couple of niggers and mex's, maybe one or two breeds. We've traded with 'em."

Fetterman had trouble containing his excitement.

He'd been looking for these people for over two years. "So, you headed there now?"

"Naw, we was gonna try and sell this load in Fort Worth ourselves. Sort of cut out the middlemen. Have a little sport, huh, Charley?"

Old Charley just grunted, apparently pouting over this marshal taking such liberty with the coffee. They were sitting beside the buffalo hunters' wagon, south of the Red River. About noon, it was still cold. He stirred the fire. "What month is it, anyhow? Is this damn cold weather here to stay?"

Fetterman smiled again, despite the stench of these two men and their wagonload of hides. "Prob'ly not. It's just September, Year of our Lord 1867. Listen now, where is this Balliett's Post? Can y'all take me there?"

"Don't know as we can afford to, even did we choose to. Hell, we ain't lawmen." Charley snorted. "Now, mind you, Little Eddie here might be interested, as he admires talking more than profit."

Little Eddie said, "It's about the same distance, but why would we want to go up to the Canadian River, 'stead of on down to Fort Worth? I mean, ain't much up there 'sides this trading post, and buffalo, and Injuns. No whores at all." He frowned. "And like I said, we can get more for these hides in town."

Fetterman said, "Maybe not. These sound like the folks I'm after. If it's them, I'll need help to take 'em. We'd split the reward, of course. Be more'n you'll get for them hides."

"Reward?" Little Eddie's head bobbed. He punched Charley's leg several times. "You listening?"

"Cash. Substantial."

"We got to take 'em alive? For the reward, I mean?" Now Charley was interested.

"Nope. Probably just pick 'em off, with them Sharps rifles of your'n." Fetterman looked up. "Jesus, is this snow? In September?"

THE SNOW HAD STOPPED LATE the previous day. After a cold fitful night and thin coffee with their breakfast jerky, the half-dozen bandits set out toward the northwest again.

Bobby Joe Jackson saw the wagon tracks first. "Hey, Red," he yelled to their leader. "Lookit this over here."

The other five horsemen angled left through the scrub to where Jackson's pony stamped nervously. The white steam of breath from the men and horses was almost thick enough to cut.

"See here? Wagon tracks. Heavy loaded, too. Two horses pulling it. Or mules maybe. 'Nother horse riding beside it. Horse shit's on top of the snow, too. Ain't too old. You reckon they's going same place as us?"

A second rider dismounted and picked up some of the manure. He broke it apart, then dropped it and wiped his hands on his pants. "It ain't solid, Red. Must've been last night. Probably not far ahead, though. Like Bobby Joe said, probably buffalo hunters going to that camp, like us."

Red glanced up at the tracks disappearing over the next hill. "Don't make sense to me, Penn. This far south, why take hides back up to the Canadian? Why not Fort Cobb, or Richardson? Fort Worth, even?" He rubbed his thick red beard. The others looked at each other and shrugged. He wasn't really asking them. "No, I'll give you that they's heading for Adobe Walls like us, but not likely hauling hides. That'd be like, I don't know, hauling water to the river."

"Coals to Newcastle," said Robbins, grinning, proud of his contribution.

Red glared at him. "Where do you come up with shit like that? No, I think these boys is taking supplies to that camp at the Walls. We'd best overtake them, relieve them of their burden. Ought to start us off on the right foot too, once we find that camp. If we's the ones as bring in the supplies, I mean."

* * *

"HOW Y'ALL DOING? Looks like we's all heading for Balliett's Post. Might as well ride together. Plenty of red Injuns around. Y'all hop down, have some coffee. I'm Little Eddie, that there is Charley, my partner, and the big feller is Marshal Fetterman." Little Eddie's head bobbed as he chattered.

Red stared down at the three men standing at the midday fire beside the wagon full of hides, then smiled. "I'm Red. We's heading for Adobe Walls. Heard they's a bunch of buffalo hunters show up there each spring now. Killing hundreds and hundreds of 'em."

Little Eddie nodded. "Heard that too. We hunted south

of there. Buffalo all over the place. We was gonna take these to Fort Worth, but the Marshal here convinced us to take 'em to Balliett's Post instead. He's, ah, got some business there." He jumped as Fetterman prodded him in the back. Frowning at the marshal, he continued. "Anyhows, it's on the way and y'all probably needs to stop there first, and buy y'all some long Sharps rifles, like our'n. Them old Enfields you got will do the job, but they is slow."

"Well, you're right. We got to get 'em somewheres." Red looked over his shoulder at Penn and Robbins, and nodded toward the two hunters. Turning back to the fire he pointed his Enfield at the marshal. The click-clack of it going on full cock in that still air brought everyone to attention.

Penn and Robbins cocked their rifles too.

"Why'nt you slip out of that nice overcoat, Marshal?" Red gestured slightly with the tip of his rifle. "Hang it over the side of the wagon there."

FETTERMAN'S MIND RACED. *This can't be happening. Not now. Not this close, after all this time. Shitfire. Have to share with these thieves too. Just pray them Rebels ain't spent all that money yet. Got to be careful now. Can't just give them the coat.*

In the pocket was an official looking arrest warrant for the two Rebels. He'd taken a real one from a drunk lawman, copied it, and paid a printer to make one up for his two fugitives. *That's going to be real handy now.*

Little Eddie stared stupidly at Red. "You want me and Charley to take off our coats too?"

"No need," said Red. "Who else would wear 'em? Stinking rags." Turning back to the marshal, he said, "I done ast you nice. Take it off."

Fetterman held up a finger. "Just hold on, now. There's something you don't understand. I'm the law, and I got something to show you right here..." As he pulled the thing from his coat pocket, Red shot him.

The heavy slug knocked Fetterman around and into the fire on his stomach. From a great distance, he heard Red say, "Oh, I understand, all right. You boys pull him outta there afore that coat's burnt up. And be careful. He was trying to pull a hideaway gun."

Fetterman wanted to respond. He was face down in the cold slush of melting snow. The warrant would explain everything but it was pinned under him in his right hand, which was burning like hell itself, and his legs wouldn't move. He wanted to say several things. Like, he didn't even have no hideout pistol, and there'd be plenty to share, and now his crotch and stomach was burning too. They should hurry, he tried to tell them, but he just coughed up blood.

As his hand melted under him, the bogus warrant turned to ashes. Someone pulled him through the fire by his heels, out of it, into the cool snow. God, that felt good on his stomach. He heard talking, then two more shots. Smoke got in his eyes. He closed them. The pain eased and he slipped away, into the clouds.

Chapter Eight

RED and his gang were approaching Balliett's Post at Canadian Fort for the first time. The two buffalo hunters had given them directions shortly before the gang murdered them for their Sharps rifles, hides, wagon, mules, food, and supplies. A third man had perished with the hunters.

"Red, you think that fat one was really a marshal?" Bobby Joe Jackson squeaked as he rode beside Red.

"Not so as it matters. Didn't you look at his badge? It said, 'Town Marshal,' for some place in Arkansas." Red pulled a tin star from his coat pocket and looked at the back of it. "Mason's Landing. Whoever heard of that? He didn't have no standing here." He stuffed the badge in his saddle bag.

"Why you keeping it then?"

"Hell, it fooled you, didn't it? Might just come in handy some time. Judas Priest, it's gotten hot again.

Probably ain't gonna need that marshal's coat for another month."

Baldwin said, "Are we gonna be there soon, Red? My butt is killing me. This wagon seat is jes' murder."

Baldwin and Clooney were the drivers, and had whined most of the way from Fort Worth. It worsened when Red assigned them to drive the stolen wagon.

Now Clooney started again. "Yeah, Red. This ain't like sitting a saddle. Damn seat is hard. And I been 'bout throwed off a dozen times."

"Christ, you sound like young'uns on a trip." Red remembered the long wagon ride from Alabama to Texas twenty years ago, with his younger brothers and sisters. "Are we there yet, Daddy? I got to pee, Daddy. Are wild Injuns gonna kill us, Daddy?" He'd been ten years old and the miserable memory was still crystal clear.

"Well, I'm gonna have blisters for sure," Baldwin whimpered.

"Well, I ain't your Goddamn daddy," Red exploded. "If your ass hurts, fold one of them buffalo furs and sit on it, you stupid bastards. And don't let me hear no more about it."

They'd seen him kill a Raider for less. They'd better let him brood in silence.

Red's Raiders, Red thought. *Red's Ragamuffins would be more like it. Childish, dumbass, Ragamuffins.* "Who the hell named us, anyhow?" he fumed, not realizing he said it out loud.

"Why, that was Boxer, Red, I think. Weren't it Bobby Boxer, Clooney?"

"Yes, it sure were, Alfred. Back before you kilt him, Red." "Well, it was one more good reason for that stinking bugger

to die. We had too many Bobbies, anyhow."

Bobby Boxer's flatulence had been a terrible problem, and Red had warned him to stay downwind. Twice. When Boxer pretty well ruined a good buzz one night, drinking around a campfire, Red simply said, "That's it," and shot him.

Bobby Joe Jackson's head nodded fervently. "You did the right thing there, Red, for sure. We's all better off without him." His high-pitched voice never failed to irritate Red. Bobby Joe was certainly better off. He'd gotten Boxer's Starr carbine, and no longer lived in dread of being blamed for something the other Bobby did, just because they had the same name.

Penn and Robbins, the least stupid of his gang, were riding out front. Robbins stopped suddenly and yelled, "Hey, Red. Smoke off to the left front. You reckon that's the place?"

Red nodded, and they changed direction slightly. He thought, *No, Sean Robbins, it's probably some other large town out here in the middle of nowheres.*

Penn yelled back, "Hey, Red. You think maybe Comanches done burned 'em out? I mean, it's too hot for a damn fire."

"Why, no, Tim, I think they might be cooking, or washing clothes. Maybe smoking some meat, or making corn likker."

"Oh. Yeah, could be. Well, I hope it ain't Comanches. I hope they got whores and likker."

"Hold on, now. All of you listen." The little convoy ground to a halt. "I told you, and I mean it, we ain't here for mischief. If this buffalo hunting business works out, we may need to trade with this camp, rather than making twenny-day trips back and forth to Fort Worth. For now, we're just gonna scout 'em out."

* * *

UNSEEN, almost a mile to their east, Weasel and nine Dog Soldiers continued to track them.

"You were right, Weasel. They are going toward Balliett's Post. These men may be dangerous to our friends there. They killed the other hunters, robbed them. Shouldn't we attack?"

"No, Striker. We'll get closer. As they get closer to the post, they will become careless, unafraid. But maybe the men they killed were bad. These men may be friends of our friends at the post."

"Besides," said Tree Bender, "they are six with many guns. We are only ten, with three guns."

"Bah," said Rain-On-His-Face. "We are Cheyenne Dog Soldiers. We can fill them with arrows."

"Maybe. Of course, I cannot tell you what to do. You must follow your own noses. If you follow the nose of Rain-On-His-Face, a very brave warrior, just remember that his nose has only been sniffing for sixteen summers." Weasel paused. "My old nose tells me to get closer, make ourselves available if our friends need us. Maybe we don't have to go against those guns."

* * *

IF IT HADN'T BEEN for that mean mustang filly, the gang might have surprised the camp.

Bear stepped off the fence into the saddle, found the stirrups, and said, "Let'er go."

Tad Walls snatched off the blindfold, and the mustang went wild, bucking, jackknifing, twisting until she launched Bear over the fence. At the height of his arc, the young black man noticed the approaching riders.

As Tad tried to get another rope on the mare, Bear brushed himself off and said, "Leave her, Tad. I seen some riders coming from the southeast. A wagon, maybe seven or six men."

"How far?"

Bear picked up his hat and slapped it against his leg. "Most of a mile."

"Let's get everybody to the store. Probably just buffalo hunters, but let's don't take a chance."

Their weapons leaned against the corral. Bear handed Tad the old Paterson sixteen gauge, then took his Spencer and jogged to the main house to get his mother, sister, and their children.

Tad limped to Doc's adobe, interrupted his siesta, then hurried on to the store. By the time he got there, Big William had seen the riders too. Bigger and darker even than Bear, Big William ruled the kitchen. He rang the dinner bell repeatedly.

That was their danger signal, other than at meal

times. If trouble appeared just before lunch or supper, the bell was rung only once, another clear signal.

When her son, Tad, came in, Annette Walls Balliett was already in the store, her duty post during daylight, lo these last many years. Carmela Walls and her younger sister, Manuela Gomez, worked with Annette or in the garden, and tended the goats, cows, pigs, chickens, and babies. Shelly normally sat in the smithy with old Ignacio Gomez, learning 'Mexican,' when she wasn't babysitting too. She had been a translator, an Osage slave of the Cheyenne chief Black Kettle, and aptly named 'Serenity Killer.' He finally got tired of her chatter and gave her to Cherokee Jim Ridges, who freed her and changed her name to Shelly.

Big William spent most of his time in the kitchen, cooking or smoking meat. When he was caught up, he helped in the smithy or played with the children. Just now, he put an apron on over the Dragoon Colt and stood in the door between the dining porch and the kitchen. The Avenging Angel, a ten gauge Colt revolving shotgun, was just inside the door. He wiped his glasses.

Doc Thomason and Junebug slipped in the back door. Tad handed him a sawed-off ten gauge double and said, "Sorry 'bout your siesta."

Doc in turn handed Junebug his little Colt, and said, "Why, Tad, it's just fine. We were only sleeping." Junebug had been the old dentist's assistant and girl-friend since they met in Mason's Landing, Arkansas.

Bear walked in carrying the sleepy Mikey and Millie, closely followed by his sister, Honey, and their mother, the quadroon Marie-Louise. He handed the children to Carmela and Manuela, kicked aside a buffalo rug and opened the trapdoor to the storm cellar. The Gomez sisters hurried below with the children, followed by Junebug.

Bear looked at Annette Balliett, who hesitated, canteen in one hand, a .31 Colt pocket model in the other. Bear glanced to Tad, who said, "It's all right."

Bear shrugged, unslung his Spencer, and walked outside to join Ignacio and Shelly in front of the smithy at the opposite end of the store from the dining porch. Ignacio rested a twin of Doc's ten gauge on his worthless left forearm.

Tad said, "They're almost here, Mama. You know the drill. I need to close and hide this door. You need to go on down now."

She sighed. "I know. I just hate it. You're all my babies. I'll go. Give me the Twins."

The Twins were a pair of 1855 Springfield percussion pistols, .58 caliber, loaded with buck-and-ball. Lanyard rings on the butt of each pistol were connected by three feet of leather thong. Tad draped the leather around her neck, leaving the large pistols hanging at her waist.

"You checked the caps?"

"Yes, Mama. Watch your head." He put the floor door back in place, recovered it with the bulky rug, and went to the window.

* * *

OUTSIDE, Shelly eased up closer to Bear. Her duty as translator for the camp kept her out of the cellar. "They are almost here. Their leader must be that big man. He is smiling, but his beard looks like red clay. Or fire. Why do you never come to my bed?"

Bear said, "You never stop talking."

"I see you looking at me. Don't you see me watching you? You are a powerful man. You need a woman. Will we fight these men?"

"Merde. I will fight you, if you don't shut up."

"I cannot shut up, but for you, I will slow down."

Something in her tone made him look down into her eyes. *Like a fawn*, he thought.

She stared back, nodding. "A lot."

"You, I won't need here. Not with these men. Go inside." She nodded, and went inside. Her silence startled him.

* * *

INSIDE, Shelly picked up a big knife and smiled at Bear's mother and sister. *I think he wants me*, she thought. *Maybe his babies will live.*

Tad, Marie-Louise, and Honey stood at the front window, watching the approach of the strangers. Tad was oblivious to everything else, but the women were disconcerted by the lack of chatter from Shelly.

Marie-Louise looked back at her. "You all right, Chere? You're very quiet."

"Bear say to talk not so much, so I try. I think he wants me. I don't think he knows it."

Marie-Louise was startled. "You want him, Cher?"
"Oh, yes. Ver' much."

"Hmm. Chere, that knife, it ain't much. You see, I have this Colt, my Honey-Marie, she have her little superstition pistol. Let's get you something."

Marie-Louise went behind the counter and opened a drawer. She handed Shelly a cut-down Navy Colt. "There, Chere. More better. My Honey's man, he has one jus' like this one. You put her back when these men leave, non? She stays here to keep the store."

Shelly nodded her thanks. "But why do you call Honey's gun a superstition pistol?"

"Ah, Chere, it is one she got from a man who tried to ruin her, a Yankee captain. It is numbered five-fifty-five." Marie-Louise smiled as if that explained everything.

"And that is an evil number, or a good one?" Shelly looked more confused.

"Well, neither one, exactly. But my Jimmy Melton thinks it is bad." Marie-Louise looked to Honey for help.

Honey patted Shelly's arm. "Boss Melton thinks it is the same as six-sixty-six, which is a bad number. But he's wrong about this one. This number is all right."

Shelly frowned. "And what happened to the Yankee captain?"

"Oh, my Dobey shot him, and Boss Melton let me kill him with this pistol," she added, holding up the little Smith and Wesson Number Two Army. "His very own, the bugger."

"Maybe Boss Melton is right. It was not good luck

for the Yankee, was it?" Shelly smiled brightly, and it was Honey's turn to frown.

Tad walked out, the Paterson shotgun cradled in his left arm. "Top of the day to you, gents. How can we help?"

The leader had a disarming smile and manner. "Heard y'all had a oasis here in the desert. Cooked food, supplies, even a medico. We hoped to water up at the river, catch a good meal, maybe start a trade relation. We'll be hunting on upriver, hoped we could sell and trade hides here. Any chance?" He grinned. "We even got a few hides now."

Tad smiled back. "Go 'head and water up. We'll get some grub on. We can talk terms later."

"Much obliged. By the way, I'm called Red. Go figure." Everyone laughed. He wheeled his horse. "All right, boys, take 'em down to the river. Whoa. What's this? Comanches?" Weasel and his warriors watched from a small hill, a quarter mile away.

Tad said, "Nope. Cheyenne Dog Soldiers. Friends. You can relax. Shelly, come out here and signal them Cheyenne that ever'thing is all right. See do they want to join us."

They didn't. After a few minutes, Weasel led them away.

* * *

"SO, how long y'all been here? Good while, from appearances. I mean, you got the start of a nice little town."

Tad said, "Seven or eight years, I guess."

"It's closer on ten. We came here in August '58," Annette corrected him.

Red gave them his warmest smile, one of total admiration. "Good God. How'd y'all manage to keep your scalps? There ain't but thousands of Kiowa, Comanche, Cheyenne all around you."

"Yep, and Arapahoe. We're sort of protected by Black Kettle and his Cheyenne now, being on the edge of his stomping grounds. We trade honest with 'em, Doc treats 'em if he can, and to be honest, they're a little scared of one of our fighters, Cherokee Jim, who ain't here just now. And before them, the army was here off and on."

"Whoa, Nellie. Back up. The Cheyenne is scared of one man?"

"Well, it's his uncle. Stand Watie."

"Oh. Jesus, I see. Well, we're sure glad you're here. You said one of your fighters weren't here? Where's he?"

"Him and his woman and baby went to Santa Fe to see her family. Hoping to bring her brother back with 'em. They rode there with my brother, Dobey, and his partner, Boss Melton. Those two kinda run things here."

Red stretched, then leaned on his saddle horn. "We heard there was three former rebels here. Would that be them?"

Tad said, "Dobey and Melton was with the Eighth Texas, and Cherokee Jim rode with his uncle."

Red nodded approval. "Eighth Texas. Terry's Rangers. Good bunch. Me and young Penn there, we rode for the South too. So, y'all got women and likker here too?"

"None for rent or sale. Mama won't stand for it. Used to sell likker, but it got her husband and her horse breaker killed. We're looking to do something along that line across the river there."

"So, y'all got a regular family business here."

Tad smiled and shook his head. "Sir, you just don't know. How right you are, I mean. See old 'Nacio there, the blacksmith? I married his oldest girl. Bear here? My brother Dobey's married to his half-sister, and Bear's mama is Boss Melton's woman."

Red sat up straight in the saddle. "They's married to niggers? I thought it was still against the law in Texas. Nothing personal, boy." He nodded to Bear.

"Ain't much law up here," Tad said. "And they ain't dark like Bear here no how. Honey's whiter'n me, and her mama's a light quadroon. Main thing is, I'd like to see anybody tell Dobey and the Boss that they had to undo things."

Bear just snorted and rolled his eyes.

AFTER A SIMPLE HEARTY meal of buffalo steaks, beans, and cornbread, Red's men slept around their wagon. When they headed upriver the next morning, there was a general feeling of warmth, security, and prosperity over the camp. It was apparent, and Red thought, *this is good*.

Penn kicked his horse up beside Red. "Who the hell

is this 'Stan Way-tee' y'all was talking about? Some Cherokee muckety-muck?"

"Chief Stand Watie. Or better, General Stand Watie. Had several regiments of redskins that fought for the Confederacy. Did good, too. Never was beat, so they say. Last to surrender, too. Shit, Penn, you rode with the Third Texas, same as me. You never heard of him?"

"I might've not paid attention."

THE FEELING of warmth was general, but not unanimous. After Red's group departed for Adobe Walls, several of the denizens of Canadian Fort gathered for breakfast. When Junebug commented on what a nice smile Red had, Doc replied, "I'd like to pull every one of his nice white teeth. The man is a snake. Smarmy bastard."

Bear simply said, "Him, you could like. But he is dangerous. His men were stupid cutthroats. I hope they don't return."

But Tad said, "Hell, Bear, who do you think we trade with out here? People along the Canadian ain't gonna be plaster saints. These mighta been a cut above normal."

TWO HOURS LATER, Dobey and his group rode in from Santa Fe. As Tad and Bear led the horses away, Annette rubbed Dobey's arm and smiled at the newcomers.

"Son, it seems every time you wander off, you come home with a load of strays. Now, who are these nice folks?"

"Momma, this is Count Baranov and his son, Willi, from Prussia. They're here on a long hunt, and those two hard cases there are their shooters and skinners. Short one's Hannity, and the heavy one's O'Reilly. On the second wagon is Mary Belle White, their cook, and George Canada, the handyman, who can't talk. The Count helped us out of a tight spot as we was leaving Santa Fe. His men have kept us in fresh meat, and Mary Belle there did most of the cooking. I invited them to hang out here a while."

Melton added, "All y'all got to see Willi's pictures that he drawn, people and animals. You ain't gonna believe 'em."

Dobey said, "True. And here's Mandy's brother, Buck, again, who I guess you remember from two years ago."

Annette had shaken hands with each of the count's party. She hugged Buck. "Welcome back, Buck. Your baby sister surely missed you." The hug almost caused Buck to stop staring at Junebug.

1868

———————

Chapter Nine

1868 BEGAN WELL for the inhabitants of Canadian Fort and their Cheyenne neighbors in the Washita grasslands. Red and his band as well as other hunters brought in hundreds of buffalo hides. The remaining Trapdoors and the old Sharps were quickly sold or traded for hides, and there was demand for more.

In the spring, Dobey borrowed the count's two wagons, and with his own, took a load of hides north and east, up the Santa Fe Trail to Fort Dodge, Kansas. Willi stayed behind to continue his sketches of wildlife and of the Cheyenne, but the rest of the count's party went with the wagons. Big William drove Dobey's wagon, which seemed to please Mary Belle White to no end. Big William showed a proprietary interest in her as well.

Bear scouted for them. Shelly wanted to come, but Bear insisted the trip would be too arduous for her at four months pregnant.

Count Baranov would ship his skulls and hides and Willi's sketches to Prussia "for their reassembly." Dobey and Big William would re-stock hardware, ammo, and condiments, after selling the buffalo hides. All of them were expecting to be somewhat amazed, as Buffalo City outside Fort Dodge was already becoming somewhat of a cow town.

* * *

FORTY MILES southwest of Fort Dodge they came upon an abandoned stage station, corral empty, gates down, outbuildings burned weeks earlier. Five miles later they picked up on distant gunfire, ahead of them.

"That shooting, it gets closer, Cap'n Dobey. Maybe two miles, maybe less. What you think?"

"I dunno, Bear. I guess we keep moving toward it. No place to run or hide. Y'all listen. If we're attacked we'll circle tight, animals inside. We'll hobble the mules, and fight from the wagons. Mary Belle, you and George re-load. Let's move."

The gunfire slackened, but got closer quickly. Within ten minutes, a stage raced into view, six horses pulling it straight toward them. Six cavalrymen rode hell-for-leather with them, flinging occasional carbine shots at the forty or so Kiowa chasing them.

"Circle up," shouted Dobey, then saw it was a wasted command. Hannity was already turning the lead wagon left, while O'Reilly and Big William were swinging right before pulling hard left into the little circle. Before they fully stopped, George and Bear were hobbling the animals, tying their back legs together.

"Gimme the Trapdoor, Big William. I'm gonna see if I can spread them out some." At a half-mile, Dobey began banging away with the .50-70 at the bunched hostiles. With seven shots, he dropped one rider and one horse. As they got closer, the count and O'Reilly joined in, knocking down three more horses. The Kiowa pulled up a little, allowing the stage and troopers to close on the little wagon fort.

"Can you open up?" The stage driver was sporting two arrows in his right leg. The shotgun rider was missing.

"No," yelled Dobey. "We're hobbled. Pull in tight on the backside."

The troopers followed the stage to the far side of the triangle, and dismounted, grabbing Spencers and shot tubes. None but the sergeant carried a pistol.

"Help the driver hobble them lead horses, Billie. Boys, we'll fight 'em from behind the stage. Better yet, from inside it. Git them passengers out and inside this wagon circle." The sergeant had to yell, as Bear and the count opened up rapid fire with their Winchester rifles when the Kiowa came within two hundred yards.

Dobey switched to his carbine, and O'Reilly and Hannity picked up their Spencers. Big William knew his Avenging Angel was no good at that range, and Dobey signaled the Irishmen to wait, too.

"Hold... Hold...Almost...All right, now!" Dobey and the Irishmen opened up at a hundred yards, and the charge split to encircle them. As the Kiowa passed to the rear of the triangle, only fifty yards from it, the six cavalry Spencers began to hit them, plus fire from a Henry in the hands of a stage passenger.

Eleven ponies were down, several others were hit, and at least five Kiowa were shot from their mounts. The charge blew on past, out to perhaps three hundred yards away, where the Kiowa circled and huddled to consider another charge.

As Mary Belle and George stuffed cartridges in the Winchesters, Baranov, Dobey, and O'Reilly picked up their Trapdoors again and moved to the back of the stage. Hannity grabbed his old Sharps, climbed to the top of the stage, and assumed the prone firing position.

As one huge chief incited the party for another charge, Hannity aimed a yard over his head, added a little right windage, and knocked the top of his head off. Sprayed with his blood before they heard the boom of the shot, several prominent warriors voted to go elsewhere.

O'Reilly whistled. "Hell of a shot, that one."

Hannity reloaded, and gave him a sheepish grin. "And just so's you know, I was aiming for his horse, I was."

* * *

WHEN RIFLE FIRE hit two more of the stationary horses, the war party pulled away to four hundred yards, split, circled wide, and rode back to whence they came, picking up several survivors. Their consensus was, roughly translated, "Damned buffalo guns. Damned yellow-boys."

One warrior, unable to contain his rage and frustration, peeled away from the group and came racing at the wagons, screaming his hatred. Everyone turned to watch. He kicked the pony into a lather and shook his lance at the whites. At one hundred and fifty yards, a few carbine shots were flung at him, as he settled in low along his pony's neck and began to jig right and left through the low brush.

THE OLD SERGEANT YELLED, "Quit wasting shells, boys. Let him get closer."

At the same moment, Dobey shouted, "Hold fire. Hold fire. Big William, bring your Angel, get up on this wagon."

George Canada pulled Big William up into the nearest wagon, as the crazed warrior came within a hundred yards. Canada picked up the count's English double and stood by Big William, a burning hatred in his own eyes, unnoticed by all but Big William.

At forty yards, Dobey looked up at Big William and raised his eyebrows. Big William said, "I got him, Cap'n." He and Canada fired together.

THE PONY WENT DOWN on its chest, flinging the attacking Indian at the wagons. Hit multiple times, leg broken, the warrior staggered to his knees and tried to cock the pistol hung on his chest by a neck lanyard. The scatterguns roared again. His last fractured thought was, roughly translated, "Damned shotguns."

* * *

THEY ALL RODE together to Cimarron Crossing, twelve miles closer to Fort Dodge. As they rode they collected the bodies of the coach shotgun rider and three troopers, mutilated and each filled with ten or more arrows. They also picked up Corporal Jim Bob Daniel, who hailed them from some rocks. Wounded, horse killed, he'd killed the two warriors left to finish him, grabbed a canteen from his dead horse, and started walking back to Cimarron Crossing.

Happy to be alive, he was hard to shut up. "I'll tell you, boys, these fellows ain't easy to kill. I emptied my Spencer at 'em, finally knocked one down, and the other'n charged me. Whoooee. I hit him twice with my pistol afore it jammed, damn Remington, and he still managed to whack my foot with his hatchet. Damn if it don't hurt, too. Had to beat him to death with the pistol butt. I think a spent cap was stuck in it."

He paused to take another sip of the count's brandy. "Whoo-dawg. Good stuff, here. Thankee. Well, Ol' Jim Bob is still the last man standing, and I lifted both their scalps. Uh, don't need to say nuthin' 'bout that to the major, Sergeant Boye. I just wanted to piss off the other redskins."

"Actually, it's believed to be a sign of respect among warriors," Dobey told him. "That's why they usually don't scalp women. Unless they put up a fight."

"You don't say. Well, ain't no way I can put 'em back on. Just leave things as they is, I guess."

Dobey smiled. "I guess."

* * *

THE SEVEN CAVALRYMEN were riding on to Fort Dodge with Dobey's party, and Sergeant Boye was riding between Dobey and Count Baranov. They left the stage at the crossing to wait for a new crew. The driver had died from loss of blood on the return trip.

"You won't get to meet Lieutenant Colonel Custer, our illustrious leader, or the general, as he likes to be called. He's pretty damn illustrious." Sergeant John Boye spat. "But he was court-martialed here last September, for shooting deserters, and then for leaving his own post. Relieved his illustrious ass. He's setting out a year without pay."

"I've met him," said Dobey. "He was just starting when I finished at West Point. In '58. And again last year, on my last trip here."

Sergeant Boye withdrew somewhat. "Oh. Y'all friends? You served with him?"

"No. I just know him. I was with the other side. Didn't quite make it to general. Just a captain, Eighth Texas Cavalry."

Sergeant Boye said, "Bless your heart. I only made it to lieutenant. Wade Hampton's Legion. We rode alongside of you boys some."

"You surely did. I met another man from the Legion, but now he's out of Fort Bascom. Was a captain during the war, name of Bridges. Now a corporal."

"Hell, yes. I knowed Bob Bridges. Tough, mean little son of a bitch. Good man. I'm glad he made it. He was hurt bad outside of Columbia."

"Yeah, we lost one of our boys there. Drowned, trying to cross that last river, just ahead of Kilpatrick's cavalry." Dobey said. "Anyhow, your friend Bridges seemed all right now. I guess there wasn't much to go home to in South Carolina?"

"Not much at all. Besides, I been doing this, riding and fighting, since I's sixteen."

Dobey said, "Sixteen. That's how old General Hardee's boy was when he was killed in our last charge at Bentonville, North Carolina. Our last charge, his first ...and last."

Sergeant Boye said, "You might not've knowed this, but the boy weren't killed outright like everybody said back then. He were still barely alive when we picked him up for the general after your charge. We tooken him to the general's sister's place, I think it was, over to Durham. He died the next day. Didn't have no chance, nohow. I could see how y'all thought he were kilt. Anyhow, the thing of it is, he's mortal wounded in his first action, and you and me, how many did we get through?"

Dobey had to think on that. "Eighth Texas was in

way over forty scrapes. I was in at half of 'em, at least. You?"

"About the same. 'Course, I guess you got a scratch or two, just like me." Boye grinned.

Dobey gave him a rueful smile. "Yeah. A couple." He thought, *six, actually.*

Boye said, "Well, I can count a couple on your face. I 'spect you had more'n that, but we made it is the main thing. And damn lucky we are, too. So you knowed Custer."

Dobey rode quietly for a while, remembering his last meeting with Custer.

"THOMAS 'DOBEY' WALLS, Class of '58. Well, well, well." Custer clasped Dobey's shoulder as he shook his hand. Custer was effusive, and resplendent in a non-regulation blue jacket, knee boots, yellow scarf, and curls. He was a full six inches taller than Dobey.

Dobey was grimy, tired, irritable, and saddle sore. "Autie Custer," he nodded.

Custer darkened slightly. "Well. I heard you went with the other side. How did things work out?"

"Oh, just great, Autie. I'm retired on a good pension. I spend time collecting stamps, tending my garden, writing memoirs, such stuff. What about you?"

Custer stiffened. "I don't believe sarcasm is warranted, Walls."

"I apologize. I thought it was a sarcastic question, Colonel."

"No. Not intended to be." Somewhat mollified, Custer continued. "I meant, I heard you were fearless. I'm happy you survived. Did you get a regiment? Division?"

"Not exactly. And I'm pretty cautious actually. I think that's why I've survived."

"Ah. Well, where are you now?"

"We run a trading post on the Canadian River, west of the Washita grasslands, northwest Texas." He walked to Custer's map. "Just here."

"My God. How have you survived there? Aren't the damned Indians all around you?"

"They're close. In the winter, Black Kettle's Cheyenne are here, along the Washita." Dobey again pointed to the map. "We trade with them, treat 'em fair. I think that's why the Comanche and Kiowa have left us alone. We're on the border between your army districts, and on the edge of Black Kettle's hunting grounds. He thinks he's an American, by the way. Still doesn't understand why he was attacked in Colorado in '64."

Custer stood and posed, rubbing his chin. "Because he's a damned savage, like the others. Vermin. Cannot be trusted. I wait for the order to wipe them all out."

"Colonel, Black Kettle keeps things kind of level where he is. The Cherokee call him Old Woman. There are plenty of hostile Comanche and Kiowa around here to keep your attention. Black Kettle might make a good ally."

"Walls, I find your attitude to be one of a storekeeper. You're worried about losing a trading partner. Good day, sir. I have a regiment to run."

* * *

THAT HAD BEEN A YEAR AGO. Now, a handsome young major named Joel Elliott was acting commander of the Seventh Cavalry. And Dobey and Count Baranov were having drinks in a Buffalo City saloon, a few miles outside Fort Dodge.

"So. You met the famous General Custer. What did you think of him?"

"Positively illustrious. A legend in his own mind." Dobey stretched and downed his whiskey. "I'm gonna get a bath and go buy some guns."

* * *

LATER, Sergeant Boye joined them in the saloon, and introduced the regimental sergeant major. "This here is another wayward Rebel. Walter Kennedy was a officer in the Virginia cavalry before he came here to make my life miserable."

With a drink in him, Boye loosened up. "We know General Custer is coming back, 'cause all his dogs is here."

"Dogs?"

"Yep. He's got a mess of 'em. Even one greyhound who talks."

The Count said, "You jest."

"No sir. He'll tell you he served with Sherman and Sheridan, rode with Custer against Jeb Stuart in the Blue Ridge fight, and even ripped out the throat of a murderous Arapahoe to save Custer's life. Tracks

Indians and deserters, trained all of Custer's other dogs, so he says. He'll flat talk your head off, but I wouldn't have him, myself."

"Really."

"No sir." Boye's eyes twinkled. "Damn dog lies about everything."

* * *

SERGEANT-MAJOR KENNEDY and Sergeant Boye met Dobey and the count for lunch the next day.

"I got a story about you Rangers you might not have heard," offered Boye. "About Shannon's Scouts, in particular. You know who I mean?"

"I've heard of 'em," smiled Dobey. He pushed away his food. "Some called them Shannon's Raiders."

"Yeah, I heard of them too," said Kennedy. "Chewed at Sherman's flanks all through Georgia, up into the Carolinas, right?"

"That's right." Boye spat out a piece of gristle. "Killed hundreds of deserters, rapists, murderers, looters. Sherman got so damn mad, he shackled sixty prisoners, sent word to General Hampton he was gonna execute 'em, if Hampton didn't shut down Shannon. Hampton called for a truce and met with Sherman on it."

Dobey leaned forward. "You know this?"

"Well, Dobey, I was there. I was part of Hampton's escort. This was before Columbia, see, and Hampton was still willing to speak to ol' Billy Sherman."

Kennedy interrupted. "Columbia. South Carolina? What did Columbia have to do with it?"

"Oh, hell, Walter, after Columbia burned and Sherman blamed it on Hampton, there couldn't have been no truce. After that, you mention Sherman, Hampton had a conniption fit." Boye took a sip of beer. "Anyways, we met 'em, and right off, Sherman says Shannon was operating 'outside the rules of land warfare,' and Hampton should be ashamed for tolerating it. Hampton come right back at him, said Shannon was only executing criminals and Hampton was not tolerating it, he was encouraging it. Said Sherman was the tolerant one, allowing his men to rape, murder, pillage, and burn houses with people in 'em."

Kennedy said, "I know y'all hate Sherman, and we didn't see him in Virginia, but be fair. He had sixty thousand men in his army. He couldn't control all of them."

Boye smiled. "That's just what ol' Billy Sherman said. Hampton come right back at him, said, 'Well, then, we'll have Captain Shannon and his boys continue to help you with them fringe elements.' I thought Sherman would bust wide open."

"You know, we took a lot of prisoners, a whole lot more than we executed. We only killed the bad ones. From both sides." Dobey spoke softly as he remembered.

"You was there?" Boye's jaw dropped.

"Me and my partner, Boss Melton. We were with Shannon, start to finish."

"I be damned. Hell, you probably already heard all this." "No," said Dobey. "Honest, I ain't. I want to hear the rest." "Well, Ol' Billy got his back up, said he had them sixty men,

some of 'em Terry's Rangers, ready to be hung if it didn't stop. Hampton stood up and said, 'Very well. But I will shoot two of my prisoners for every man you hang. And we'll let your officers die first.' No, wait. He said, 'We'll give first preference to officer prisoners.' That's exactly what he said, and he was steaming."

"I'll be go to hell. Did he really?" Dobey was grinning. "You sound just like him."

"Yes, he did, and Sherman couldn't mistake but he was serious. Hampton flat called his bluff." Boye turned toward Sergeant-Major Kennedy. "See, we was taking lots more prisoners than Ol' Billy was."

"So, Sherman didn't execute none of 'em?" Kennedy asked. "Hell, he went back and released 'em. Not just unshackled

'em. He sent 'em back to us without waiting for an exchange." Dobey said, "I remember them coming back. I mean, I wasn't

there, but I heard they came in all mad at Shannon's Scouts, saying we almost got them hung. Wasn't long afterwards we got sent back to the regiment."

Boye took another pull. "Yep. I still think that's why Ol' Billy blamed the Columbia fire on Hampton. I mean, he was gonna burn it anyways, but it made it double sweet to say a South Carolina man did it."

SERGEANT BOYE MET Dobey and Count Baranov for

breakfast the next morning just before the Texan started his party on the trip home. After johnnycakes, bacon, and coffee, Dobey and the Count stood to leave.

"Dobey, could you give me a minute? You'll have to pardon us, Count, this is personal, sort of."

The Count left as Dobey sat back down. Boye ordered more coffee. "Was some Pinkerton agents through the fort yesterday. Sergeant-Major Kennedy heard 'em out, then called me in and said I should handle 'em. Gave me a big wink as he turned 'em over to me." Boye took a sip. "Seems they been after some half-darkies or breeds, might be traveling with a couple of Rebs who was wearing white stars on their hats. Seems this gang killed a payroll team, took the payroll, back in '65 in Mississippi. Headed west."

Dobey started to say something, but Boye stopped him. "Also seems maybe the Yankee payroll team was going in the wrong direction when they was killed. Might've had their own ideas 'bout heading west, what with the war over and all."

Dobey had eased out his short Colt and held it under the table. "Why you think I'd be interested?" He went on high alert.

"Your man Big William talked some about your 'family' back there in Texas," Boye smiled. "Listen, ain't no problem. I told these Pinkertons I'd seen some folks just like they's looking for, heading for Wichita on their way to Abilene, then Saint Looey."

"They still around?" Dobey's stomach knotted. He looked past Boye into the street, then out a side window.

"Nossir. I helped 'em hook up with a stage crew, and they left for Abilene late yesterday. Didn't wait for the cavalry escort. Took a couple of bully-boys with 'em, said they was gonna order the stage to get moving right away."

"They can do that? No escort?"

"Hellfire, yes," said Boye. "They's By-God U.S. Government agents. Showed me their papers. Got reward money, too." He spat sideways. "Right much."

"How come you and Kennedy didn't steer 'em toward us? What with this fat reward and all, you ain't sold us out?" Dobey glanced over his shoulder toward the back door.

"They didn't ride for the Bonnie Blue Flag, did they? Nor save my ass a couple of days ago." Boye made a soothing gesture. "Take it easy, Dobey. Sure, the money looked good, but I don't owe nothing to no dog-assed Yankee Pinkertons, now do I? And Kennedy don't, neither." He grinned. "You ain't gonna shoot me now, is you, for repaying a favor?"

Dobey stood and re-holstered the Colt. "Listen, I ain't saying... see, it could be that payroll team was killed to stop an outrage. A rape." He locked on Boye's eyes. "Maybe the payroll wasn't found 'til they was dead. Maybe it wasn't a robbery after all. And they had stold it and was deserting. Ain't no question there, not at all."

Boye shrugged. "Who knows? I don't think Sergeant-Major Kennedy even thought about none of that, nor cared. He just thought you was a former Rebel like him, who saved some of his troopers. I guess it was enough for him. It was for me."

They were interrupted by Corporal Jim Bob Daniel, who hobbled in on one crutch. He nodded to Dobey, then leaned in close to the sergeant.

"John Boye, that special stage didn't make it to no Wichita," he whispered loud enough to be heard in Wichita.

Sergeant Boye rolled his eyes at Dobey, then gave Daniel the come-on sign. "You can talk, James, my boy. Surely you remember Dobey Walls here, who bailed out our sinking ship just a couple of days ago?"

Daniel touched the brim of his campaign hat and nodded again. "Oh, but not so clean and smooth then as now. But I sees it's you, all right." Turning back to his sergeant, he said, "Here's the thing, John Boye. Patrol just come in, said they found the stage, forty miles east. Horses gone, driver and shotgun rider dead, along with four passengers. All cut up, stripped, full of arrows, o' course. Funny thing was, there was paper money blowing ever'where, caught in the bushes and all. Some of it stuffed in one of 'em's mouth. Them Dog Soldiers must don't know what it is, or just don't care for it. But they's lots of it. Most ever'body got some. Do they got to give it up?"

Sergeant Boye had straightened up as Daniel's report unfolded. Now he folded his hands on the table as if in prayer, and touched his forehead to the tips of his fingers. "Faith, they do, James. The money is evidence. Probably stolen. Collect it all, and I'll get it to the sergeant major. I'm sure there'll be a small reward. Off with you now, afore they have a chance to blow it. And tell them not to talk about it outside the troop, or everyone will want to share it. The reward, I mean."

As Daniel stumped away, Boye winked at Dobey. "Strange how things sometimes work out, when you try to do the right thing, ain't it?"

Chapter Ten

MARIE-LOUISE CAME in to interrupt Dobey's coffee and was deep into her role as grandmother. "Little Mildred has really missed her father. She has been sad, Chere, sure you were all finished off, never coming home. I think you should spend a little time with her."

Dobey yawned. "Why, Mama, I'll do just that. Soon as I finish this coffee." The convoy had gotten in from Fort Dodge late the day before. There were various celebrations. Honey's and Dobey's had ended about 3:00 a.m.

"Tha's good. Me, I like to see my granddaughter smiling. You take her down to the river. She likes to look on them turtles, she does. Her little life should be happy, no?"

Dobey stretched. "Yes, Mama." He strapped on a pistol belt, picked up his carbine, and went outside. Millie immediately left her game with Mikey and Billy and ran to hug his leg.

"You are not leaving, Papa?" She spoke with the lilting Cajun twang of her mother and grandmother Marie-Louise. Though she didn't talk until her first birthday, she had become conversational by age eighteen months. Dobey frequently forgot she was now

only two, as her speech and comprehension were well ahead of her years.

"No, Millie. Not soon, I hope. I thought you and I would stroll down to the river and see what we might find."

She squealed. "Goody. Do we got to take Billy and Mikey?" "Not this morning. Let's just you and me, uh, you and I walk

and talk. All right?"

"Oui, Papa." They started down the gentle slope to the river crossing, a half-mile away. "Those boys, they are a lot of trouble."

"Now you don't come down here by yourself, ever. You understand?"

"Yes, Papa. Only with a grown-up, with a gun. Don't want something bad to get me. Like that big hawk. You see him? Can you kill him, Papa? So he won't kill no more rabbits?"

"Baby, the hawks have to eat, too. There are lots of rabbits. Just remember those hawks also kill some rattlesnakes."

"Oh. Then they can stay. Me, I don't like snakes none." "Well, some of them are good, too, but 'til you can tell the

difference, you just stay away from all of 'em. Now, tell me what you been up to, while I was gone."

She was quiet for a moment, then hung her head. "Well, I have been really sad, Papa. There have been lots of darkness over me."

"Say what?"

"Oui, Papa. My life has been full of black clouds, while you was gone."

Dobey scooped her up, and strode back up the hill to the main house. Marie-Louise came onto the porch as he came up the steps, but recoiled somewhat at the look on his face. He thrust his daughter into her arms and said, "Go get her something sweet. Down at the store. Leave us be here a minute."

Without breaking stride, he went inside to the kitchen. Honey looked up from her biscuit making and smiled. "Good morning, my Chere. Oh. What is it? What is wrong?" She still had a sleepy glow from their long night of lovemaking. She was lighter-skinned than the darkly tanned Dobey, even though she was an octoroon.

"You tell me why our child tells me her life is full of dark clouds." Red-faced, his jaw jutted, his eyes bored into hers.

"Wha…? Why, Dobey, Chere, it has rained here for three weeks. Why? Wait, wait a minute here." Now, her nostrils flared. She shook a rolling pin at him. "Jus' what did you think she meant?"

He backed out rapidly. "Nothing, Honey. Really. I knew that. I was just messing." Passing Manuela on the steps, he muttered, "Be careful. She's touchy as all hell this morning. She may be fixing to start."

Manuela grinned and said, mostly to herself, "Probably just wore out." As she watched Dobey hurry away she thought, "He's a good man. I need one like him. Just wish Boss Melton was free. Buck is free, but he don't want nobody but Junebug."

"HAD a visit from a man named Palmer, while you was off gallivanting around," yawned Jimmy Melton. He and Dobey were having coffee on the store porch with Tad and Annette. "He wants us to sort of organize a reaction force for the area, seeing as our Yankee governor won't send no one out here. Says folks is setting 'em up in each county. Says the Comanche and Kiowa been hitting 'em hard, south and east of us, since the army's been pulled in."

Dobey sipped. "Governor ain't a Yankee, but he might as well be. Won't let none of us ex-rebels serve in government, the police, or the Rangers. I guess we got to do something. I guess we'll be Minute Men, like before the Revolution."

"Ain't no good like it is."

* * *

OCTOBER 1868 BROUGHT several signal events to the community, at least in the mind of Shelly. The first was the birth of a son to Shelly and Bear. Bear named him James Thomas, for Boss Melton and Dobey. The Cheyenne called him Black Dog. Three days after his birth, his mother was back at her chores, and two weeks later she strapped the baby to her chest and took him for a short ride. With Bear, of course.

A single rider approached them riding hard, but slowed to a walk when he saw them. At fifty yards, he and Bear squared off, both of them cocking their carbines.

"You running from something?" Bear shouted.

"Nope. I'm riding to take a warning to that there trading post up ahead. Indian trouble." He stared at Shelly for a moment.

" Ah, Comanche trouble, I mean."

"We're from there. We'll ride back with you."

"Thought maybe I'd seen your woman there on my last visit. Name's Foxy Palmer. Don't remember seeing you before."

"Yessir. I'm Bear. Heard about you coming, I did. I was up to Fort Dodge with the Cap'n."

"Your leader. I wanted to meet him anyhow. Let's ride. A Mex trader come through, said the Comanche is all stirred up, planning a raid before the snow."

TWO WEEKS LATER, Foxy Palmer visited again, and it wasn't social. Pulling a spare horse, he pounded in at midmorning. "Can you help us now? Comanche hit Pete Jackson's place, killed 'bout everyone, tooken his livestock, and pushed 'em southeast. Got to be a major raid, out of the Palo Duro. We'll try to be between them and their camp, whenever they start back."

Dobey nodded, thought for a moment, then said, "I

won't take all the men. They might swing north instead, come back through here."

Palmer said, "No sir. I wouldn't ask you to. Just bring who you can. We'll meet some others on the North Fork, head south 'til we cut their trail, then try to bust 'em up when they try to go home."

"You got other places to go, or can you wait twenty minutes and ride with us?"

"I don't know of nobody farther north than you. I'll be glad to rest for twenty minutes."

Tad said, "We'll feed him, put together some trail food for you. Who'll go?"

Dobey did a quick take on the question. "You think you'll be all right with Doc, Big William, George Canada, and Willi?"

Tad nodded. "With the women, we can stand watch, fort up here in the store every night. Any buffalo hunters come in, we'll ast 'em to stay. We got Ignacio, too."

"Right, then. Count, Hannity, O'Reilly, y'all are guests. Can't tell you to come, but we could use you."

"Of course. We go with you."

"Good. Bear, Cherokee Jim, Buck, two canteens, two horses, extra ammo, at least two pistols. Pick me and Melton out a couple of spare ponies too. Meet us here in fifteen minutes."

Twenty minutes later, a nervous-looking group of stay-behinds watched them ride south. When Dobey would recall it much later, he'd think, hell, they had every reason to be nervous.

* * *

"GLAD TO SEE your boys all got them new Henrys. Most of the boys we'll join got Sharps or maybe just shotguns or Enfields." Palmer was at least fifty, chunky, though not at all fat.

"Yessir," said Dobey. "The new ones are called Winchesters, by the way."

"Same cartridge, though, right?"

"Yessir. Forty-four rim fire." Dobey held one up.

"Well then, you may be happy we've got them Sharps and Enfields."

"Oh?"

"Yup. Kiowa and Comanche're using tough shields, dry buffalo hides double thick, and they might soak up Colt or Henry bullets. Now, a Spencer, Sharps, or Enfield will pass right on through'em. Shield, man, horse. Knock 'em right on their back-side, too." Palmer spat. "'Spect you seen that though, ain't you?" Dobey answered. "I guess we did, but didn't know what we were looking at. Last couple of fights we were in, up on the

Trail, the hostiles seemed to duck a awful lot of good shots." "Yeah," said Melton. "Maybe we didn't miss so many after

all." He thought a minute. "Guess we'd better focus on their legs and heads, next time."

"Yup," Palmer nodded. "Expect so. You watch, they'll sling them shields over their backs after they pass by you. Cover their backside as they ride away."

Dobey snorted, "I'll be go-to-hell. I saw 'em do just that." Melton said, "I should'a kept my old Sharps."

Dobey smiled. "So much for progress."

Palmer smiled. "Hell, just shoot their horses. You boys know that. One of their partners will surely pick 'em up, but they don't fight worth a damn with two on a horse."

Melton groaned. "God, I hate shooting horses."

Dobey looked stunned. "I ain't never noticed that, Jimmy." Melton shrugged. "Well, I worry, you know? One day, I'm

gonna be hard pressed, gonna need to get just five more miles or just one more spurt from one of those beauties, and they're gonna look at me and say, 'You're the one who shot my momma.' "

Chapter Eleven

RED and his men pushed east along the south bank of the Canadian as hard as they could, given the wagon being slam-full of hides and what with Indians on the prowl. Two hunters had come into the Adobe Walls camp the week before, reporting a huge war party leaving the Palo Duro Canyon, far to the south.

"You reckon they got likker and whores at Balliett's place now, Red? They still didn't have none, last trip. Sort of a dugout, across the river, but no regular cantina yet. Maybe they've finished it."

"Well, Baldwin, I dearly hope so. You're starting to look right nice to me, it's been so long." Red was half-drunk.

"Why, thank you, Red. I guess." Baldwin immediately regretted the comment, as he didn't want to encourage the unpredictable Red. He'd heard things about being in prison and such. He shuddered.

* * *

RED SHUDDERED, too, remembering those women at Canadian Fort. They better have brought in some whores, or who knew what might happen. A man could only wait so long.

They closed Canadian Fort just after dark. Red halted the wagon downhill, and rode in for a scout.

Everything was dark and quiet, except for the main store. Lots of activity down there. Something was going on. Then he noticed the lights in the main house. He trotted up, dismounted, and tapped on the doorsill.

A smiling Marie-Louise approached the door carrying a lantern. Behind her, Red could see her daughter, the one called Honey.

"We're through, now, Cher, don't worry. I tole you we'd be there before you know it. Come along, Honey, someone has come to hurry us."

"Why, I'd never rush two pretty ladies like you-all." Red gave them his best smile.

"Mon Dieu! You have give me the heart failure. Is it Mister Red?"

"Yes, Ma'am, it surely is. Ya'll having a fandango, or something? Down there at the store? You finally brought in some loose women, for us poor lonely men?"

"Non, Mister Red. The wild Indians are loose, raiding. Most of the men, they go to chase them. Rest of us, we all stay in the store at night. Honey and me, we are just going down there. Where are your men?"

"They'll be right here." As Marie-Louise started to step through the door he held open, he grabbed her neck with his left hand, then drew his revolver right-handed and clipped Honey with it. As she fell, he clubbed Marie-Louise too, grabbing the lantern as he hit her, then placed it on the floor in the dining room.

He walked to the edge of the porch closest to the river, and whistled. Thirty seconds later, Penn and Robbins rode up.

"Tell the others to come up and cover that store. Anybody comes out, kill 'em. Then you two come on in. We're gonna have a little fun."

Penn directed Clooney, their best shooter, to set up with his Trapdoor to cover the store.

"Make your stand here. Cover the front door. Anybody comes this way, shoot 'em. Otherwise, stay quiet. Baldwin, Bobby Joe, y'all back him up."

"Who put you in charge, Mister High-and-Mighty?"

"Red. You want him to explain this to you? I'm sure he'd be thrilled."

"Oh. No, that ain't necessary, Tim. Don't be so damn touchy."

Inside, Red and Robbins carried the unconscious Honey into Marie-Louise's bedroom and tossed her on the bed. Red pulled off his gun belt and suspenders, and said, "Y'all take her momma, and make do in there. You want to share with them other idgits, that's your call. But don't make a bunch of noise and we might have time for seconds before we go after them in the store. I'm sick of hunting, and there's got to be money hid in there."

Robbins was already tearing off Marie-Louise's clothing.

The bedroom was dimly lit by the lantern in the dining area. Red left the door open. *I want to see this*, he thought, as he cut away Honey's pantaloons. She lay on her back, arms flung wide, out cold. He pushed her meddlesome skirt back over her face, and started to mount her, but noticed the bowl of water on the washstand.

"No, darling, let's have you awake." He poured the water on her face and stomach, threw the bowl aside, pinned her arms, and entered her. Honey woke up, struggling. Her wet skirt covered her face, her arms were pinned, her stomach and the bed were wet. " Am I bleeding? Am I drowning?" She twisted. "I'm on a bed? Who are you? How did you...Red!" She remembered, and screamed.

Red head-butted her, and she was knocked stupid. Her eyes filled with blood.

"Red, this is like screwing a dead person. You didn't kill her, did you?" Penn shouted from the dining room.

"I don't think I did. Throw some damn water on her, if you want her playful. But I'll kill you, you interrupt me again."

Robbins walked to the bedroom door and asked, "Where'd you find the water?"

"Don't make me come out there, Goddammit!"

Penn, kneeling on the floor between the legs of the nude Marie-Louise, whispered, "Sean. The rain-barrel. Out by the porch. Don't provoke him."

* * *

COLD WATER WAS SPLASHED on Marie-Louise's face and breasts. She coughed and stirred.

She was in a painful haze. She felt the crunch of the back of her skull on the floor and dimly realized it was fractured. The cold water only partially revived her. A bandana was tied around her mouth, someone was holding her arms and biting her breasts, and someone else was between her legs pounding her. She could not comprehend it. Where was Jimmy? She struggled.

"Oh, that's better, you nigger bitch. Oh, yeah." Penn finished. "Your turn."

She tried to turn over, as they changed positions. Penn slugged her, and said, "No, you don't."

Robbins said, "Naw, let her roll over. That'll be fine." She passed out again, mercifully. For a few minutes.

Outside, Clooney strained to hear what was going on in the house. Baldwin punched his arm and said, "Lookee there." A man had come out a side door of the store, with a sawed-off shotgun on his arm. As he trudged to the outhouse, Clooney centered the Trap-door's sights on the middle of his back.

"Go 'head," whispered Baldwin. "Get him afore he gets to the privy."

Clooney lifted his head from the butt stock. "Nope. Penn said shoot 'em if they was coming at us. He's going away. Prob'ly just got to piss or something."

* * *

HONEY SWAM UP from unconsciousness again, and

began to moan and struggle. It was enough to finish Red. He pushed off, and stood up.

"So. Liked it, didn't you, girl? You get undressed now, give me a few minutes, and we'll try something different." He tucked himself in, and walked to the doorway to watch Penn and Robbins.

Behind him, Honey pushed her skirt and apron down, and struggled up onto one elbow. She wiped the blood from her eyes. She drew her little Smith and Wesson from her apron, sat up and cocked it.

Red heard the snap-click, and turned back in time to take the first bullet in his right shoulder. As she struggled with both hands to cock it again he yelled and lunged at her.

As Red landed on Honey, she screamed and fired again, hitting him in the thigh. He snatched the pistol away, hit her with it, and pushed back off the bed, yelling with pain as he put weight on the wounded leg.

THE MAN with the shotgun must have heard the shot. He burst out of the privy and began running toward the main house, shouting, "*Señoras. Señoras. ¿Quien es? ¿Quien es?*"

Clooney, having turned to the sound of the shots, lost the man in the darkness for a moment. By the time he remembered his duty and re-located his target, the man was forty yards away and closing fast.

* * *

SEAN ROBBINS EXPERIENCED the worst case of interruption one could imagine: nearby gunshots and yelling during the short strokes. He shriveled, withdrew, and rose to his knees, looking back at the bedroom. Penn released Marie-Louise's arms, and stood.

Honey's scream made it through the fog into Marie-Louise's tortured brain. She rolled over, grabbed the only weapon available to her, and swung it with her last ounce of strength.

The lantern hit the kneeling Robbins in the side of his head, and broke. He exploded into flames. He screamed, and grabbed the curtain to try to stand. The curtains ignited too. His pants tripped him and he fell. In the other room, Red screamed, "You witch!" and shot Honey with her own .32 as she tried to sit up again. At the same moment, Penn shot Marie-Louise, jumped over the burning Robbins, and fled. Red limped after him, stuffing the .32 in his belt. Robbins crawled onto the porch.

THE FLAMES ILLUMINATED the main house as old Ignacio ran toward it. In front he could see several horses, a wagon and mules, and some men kneeling on the ground. There was a flash and a boom, and he was knocked backward. He heard yelling from the store and looked up to see a woman in a white apron run by him. There was another flash/boom, and she went down. Ignacio could not breathe. He could not sit up. Though he would never know it, the five hundred grain slug had blown out his right lung and left a gaping hole in his back. He saw the house burning, and thought, *I have failed*. He felt the sawed-off ten gauge under his right arm, picked it up one-handed and fired it at the men by the porch. He missed. He hit the mules, and they bolted. He thought, *I have failed again. Consuela, I am coming. Roberto, Pedro, Manuelito, Romero, Tomaso, your one-armed failure of a father is coming*. He joined them, with a sigh.

* * *

THE RAIDERS, minus the still-burning Robbins, raced after their runaway wagon, east into the vast grasslands.

Behind them, Tad emptied a Winchester into the darkness in their direction, while Doc, Big William, and Willi pulled Marie-Louise and Honey from the blazing house. Canada threw a robe on Robbins, rolled him off the porch and finally extinguished his personal oil fire, then dragged him away from the searing heat. He didn't get far. Doc stopped him.

"Leave that miserable piece of meat, George. Make certain he doesn't have a weapon to finish himself with, and leave him. Help us get these women into the store. The house is a goner."

They found Annette near Ignacio's body. Canada put his fist in his mouth, and moaned. Doc said, "Oh, my God."

Chapter Twelve

THE HOUSE MADE a worthy pyre for itself, though few humans marked its passing. The surviving residents of Canadian Fort were busy tending to their wounded and burying their dead by the firelight.

Weasel and his Cheyenne hunting party could have easily seen it, had they not been sound asleep since dusk. They were only twenty miles east. Their slumber also caused them to miss Red's gang passing nearby in the dark.

Dobey and his men could have made out the glow thirty miles to the north, were they not being drenched by a steady rain.

"Damn. That give me a cold chill down my back." Melton shuddered.

"Me, too," said Dobey. "I want us to get up early and press on home. I worry we didn't catch those Comanches."

It had been a long patrol. To make it worse, Honey

had been blessed with "the monthlies" when they left. For Dobey, that by itself had made the trip much longer.

* * *

THE LITTLE CEMETERY at Canadian Fort had long held four head markers and three residents. The oldest was a soldier who'd shot himself in 1859. Tim Balliett and Tomaso Gomez were the other two occupants. The fourth cross marked an empty grave for Annette's daughter Becky, who was actually buried outside the abandoned Fort Motte in Colorado.

The rain stopped before dawn. The Minutemen, as they thought of themselves, quickly noted that there were three new markers on the little hill, and they broke into a gallop. They were moving fast anyhow, having smelled the smoke for miles. Now they saw why.

The main house was gone, with nothing but smoking blackened timbers in its place.

Buck said, "Oh Jesus. Indians. Oh, no."

Bear said, "No. Not Indians. The livestock, they are still here."

Dobey had trouble speaking. He finally choked out, "Spread out."

As they approached the store, Big William eased onto the eating porch, carrying the Angel at high port. He spoke back through the door, and others started to come out slowly: Tad and Doc, then Shelly carrying little Black Dog, Mandy with Billy, then Carmela and Manuela with Mikey and Millie. The older children squealed and fought to get loose to run to their fathers.

Dobey, Melton and Buck could not swallow. Who were those crosses for? They clattered to a walk, then stopped, the horses blowing and snorting in the cold air.

Willi, Mary Belle and George Canada came out, then Junebug pushed by Big William and joined Doc. Buck tried to stifle a smile, as he nodded to her. Bear dismounted, as Shelly brought little Black Dog to him.

Doc tried to speak, but couldn't. His bloodstained clothes said a lot.

Melton got his voice first. "Where's Marie-Louise?"

Doc said, "You just passed her, Jimmy. On the hill. There was nothing I could do."

Melton choked back a sob, then looked around fiercely, daring sympathy. He got down and joined Bear, who stared at him, tears pouring down his face.

Dobey said, "Honey?"

"She's inside. She's hurt, shot through the neck, but she'll survive."

"Who did this, Doc?" Melton picked up little Mike, as Dobey dismounted.

"We don't know. We have one of them, but he is not recognizable, and cannot talk. He was burned."

"Well, don't make me drag it out of you, Doc. Who are the other two crosses for?" Dobey's speech was strained. He picked up his daughter and hugged her.

"Ignacio." The Gomez sisters wailed, as Doc tried to finish. "And the other, well, your mother, she…"

"Mama, too?" Dobey pushed past the stammering Doc and stepped inside, to find his mother sitting in her blackened rocker. She gave him a sweet, sedated smile.

"Old George saved my rocker, Thomas. Weren't he nice? Couldn't save my arm. Buried it up there by my Becky's marker, beside my Timothy."

It was only then he noticed her left sleeve was pinned up, almost empty.

From behind Dobey, Melton said, "Miz Annette, you got to try to tell what happened."

From the bed behind her, Honey groaned.

Chapter Thirteen

THE BURNED MAN WAS SCARED. Not so scared as he had been last night, when he heard the animal near him. Or animals. He could tell it was daylight now, had been for a while, but his eyes were so burned he couldn't make out shapes.

He'd wanted to yell, to tell his captors he was about to be eaten alive, but his throat was burned too. He was sitting on the ground, tied to a tree or a post, maybe, with the rope around his chest and upper arms. His hands were free, but his fingers were gone or fused together, or something. No hope of untying himself, and his damn pants were down around his ankles.

He'd kicked at the animal noise, and managed to scoop up some dirt and fling it, but it was probably his subhuman groans of fear which saved his life. But that was last night.

A group of riders came in a few minutes ago. It was probably late afternoon, but no one had brought him water, or spoken to him, since they left him here last night.

Scared now because someone was approaching, his mind struggled. Never very sharp, he was sensible enough to realize that whoever tied him and left him out here last night, cooked meat ready to be eaten, was probably not coming to nurse him

back to health. He tried to whimper, but it came out a rasping wheeze.

* * *

THIRTY MILES east of the trading post on rocky ground along the headwaters of the Washita River, Penn told Clooney to halt the wagon.

"Why the hell are you stopping?" Red growled from the back of the wagon.

"We need to talk, Boss." Penn raised his eyebrows and, nodding briefly toward Baldwin, Clooney, and Jackson, shook his head sideways, ever so slightly.

It took a moment for Red to comprehend. When he did, he muttered, "Jesus. All right. Baldwin, ride up that little hill and look behind us. Clooney, take Robbins' horse, cross the creek, and go look over the ridge over there. Bobby Joe, you go off to the left."

Clooney climbed down, untied the horse, and mounted. "Well, all right, Red, but what am I looking for?"

"Fort Goddamn Worth, you stupid bastard," Red exploded. "Though I doubt you'll see it for several hundred miles yet. I ought to cut off your head and piss down your throat." Seething with frustration and pain from the bullets in his shoulder and thigh, he flopped back on the buffalo hides.

Penn intervened. "Y'all just ride out, have a good look, be back here in ten minutes and tell us what you seen."

Baldwin and Jackson were already riding away. Clooney started, then turned back and said, "I didn't mean to make you mad, Red. It's just, I'd hate to ride into a batch of wild Indians, or something."

Red sputtered, "That's it," and struggled to haul out his Colt and cock it.

Penn, who had dismounted, reached up and placed his hand over Red's pistol, putting his finger between the hammer and the cylinder to prevent it from firing. "Then don't do that, Clooney.

Go up there careful, and keep all of us from stumbling into a mess of hostiles. Go on, now."

As Clooney jumped the stream and rode away, Penn decocked Red's pistol and handed it back. Red's face was as red as his beard. Left handed, he held a little Smith & Wesson storekeeper against Penn's temple.

"Easy, Boss. Easy, now. Lemme talk."

"Talk good. Fast. You don't just take a gun away from me while I'm making a command decision. I need to just shoot the dumb bastard."

"Yessir. Yessir. But Boss, you're eat up with pain, and we got to do something different, and soon. And we don't need no gunfire."

"Go on." Red decocked the storekeeper.

"All right. We ain't made over thirty miles. Somebody is gonna be coming after us. I'm thinking, if you can ride, we leave Clooney here with the wagon, keep going downstream 'til we find somebody, trade 'em the wagon and hides, sight unseen, for fresh horses."

"Yeah. Them mules ain't going to last much longer no how." "Yeah. Maybe get you some help with them gunshots, but

anyhow, put some distance between us and them two Rebels. After what we done to their women, they're gonna come after us."

Red frowned in agreement, at the memory. His half-drunk decision to have a one- sided orgy with the women of the two absent ex-Rebels didn't rank with his best. "They don't know who did it, and them women are dead."

"They got Robbins, Red, and he might not be dead. They might make him talk."

"No way. He were burnt to a crisp."

"It don't matter, Red. They'll be following this slow-ass wagon. We got to leave it, and ride on."

Red thought Penn was right about the two mules. Having each been hit by several buckshot the previous evening, they were about played out. Even had they been healthy, they were pulling a wagon packed with buffalo hides, and had now hauled them over fifty miles of rough ground. First from Adobe Walls to Canadian Fort, then to here, as fast as they could be driven. Shit-fire. " All right, then, we'll change. Ain't no good like it is."

* * *

THE FOOTSTEPS CRUNCHED around him for a few minutes; Robbins could tell it was just one person. He could hear just fine, even though one ear was burned off. He tried to pull up his pants again, but his hands were so damaged he couldn't grasp them firmly enough to get them over his knees.

He gave up and put his trembling hands over his privates. They were burned, too. How could one lamp hold so much oil? Every movement, ever so slight, caused the rope to bite into his blackened chest and upper arms. He shivered, and it wasn't just from the cold wind.

The visitor spoke. "You, you're the one called Robbins. I know them hob-nailed boots. You know me, Cher?" The voice was soft, but chilling.

Robbins knew. It was that big black man, the Frenchy, the tracker. *Oh God. Oh God, oh God, oh God, that must have been his mother last night. Half-breed Nigger bitch hit me with the lantern. Oh God.* He shook his head side to side, shuddering.

"No? Oh, I think you know me. Robert Weathers. Bear. Here, someone ruined my Mama and sister last night, then shot 'em. Killed Mama." The voice was close; the man must be squatting. The voice moved away, as he stood again. "You and me, we got to talk, Cher. I go get you some water." The footsteps crunched away.

* * *

"YOU STAY WITH THE WAGON, because you let them

mules get shot, Clooney. I told you to kill anyone coming at us." Penn helped Red to mount, as he spoke.

Clooney started to protest, but Red drew his Colt again. "You're staying because I said so, Clooney. Dead or alive. You choose."

Clooney scuffed the ground with the toe of his boot, and nodded. "Yessir. Yessir, Red, but y'all don't forget me, now. I'm sure I'll be scared here."

Penn mounted. "Just hide the wagon in one of these gulleys, climb in the back and get comfortable, Clooney. We'll be back soon as we have fresh horses or mules. And if any them others shows up, fight 'em. Hold 'em off. We'll hear the shots and hurry back. But if you're taken, whatever you do, don't tell 'em we've gone to Fort Worth."

Clooney had never felt more lonely or afraid than then, as they rode away downstream. As he lashed the sluggish wounded animals into the creek and turned back upstream, he shouted, "These here is valuable hides. Valuable. Better not forget 'em." No one heard him. "Or me," he muttered.

A hundred yards upstream, a dry creek bed merged with the stream, and Clooney turned up into it. He didn't notice the ground had changed to red clay, and within twenty yards the wagon was thoroughly mired.

Clooney pushed, tugged, and whipped the poor mules for twenty minutes, but only managed to exhaust them and get the clinging red muck all over himself. He finally leaned some branches against the wagon to camouflage it, then climbed in and slept like a dead man.

* * *

ROBBINS HEARD FOOTSTEPS RETURNING, but there were more of them. Maybe three people, this time? A cup of cool water was poured on his head. Robbins turned his face up so that some of it went in his mouth.

"So this is Robbins? One of those buffalo hunters who rode with Red?" That was the doctor speaking. Maybe he would help.

"Is him, Doc. I know them boots, for sure."

"I think your mother hit him with a lantern. She still had a grip on the handle, when I pulled her out. Her hand was burned, too."

A boot suddenly stamped on one of Robbins' hands, grinding it into the dirt. He tried to scream, but only made a gagging sound. He heard a pistol being cocked.

"Don't shoot him, Boss Melton. Him, I need to talk with." That was Bear. He must have brought the water.

"He can't talk, Bear."

"Him, he can tell me things, though. You watch." The voice got closer; he must be squatting again. "Robbins, you know there was a badger here, last night? And a coyote?"

Robbins nodded.

"You, Cher, you are gonna answer me some things. Just use your head. Do it right, and me, I don't drag you out on the prairie tonight, for to feed those animals. Eh?"

Robbins nodded slowly. Yes.

"And Red, did he help you ruin my Mama last

night?" Robbins hesitated. Something cold and sharp probed his

groin. He shook his head, side to side. "My sister? Did Red outrage her?" Robbins nodded again. Yes he did.

* * *

FIFTEEN MINUTES LATER, Bear looked up to Melton and asked, "Anything else, Boss?"

When Melton shook his head, Bear cut the burned man's throat, stood, and spat on him. "You can finish Penn, Boss, when we catch him. I know she was your wife, but first, she was my mama." Robbins' body jerked with spasms for several moments.

"I just hope the Cheyenne ain't already killed him, or the others. We better brief the Cap'n, and get started after 'em."

As they walked back to the main store, the original Balliett's Post, the three men saw Tad Walls limping down the hill from the ruins of the main house, carrying two small sacks. He beat them to the store by a minute.

As they walked up, Tad came back out with his older brother Dobey. They stopped and looked to Melton expectantly.

"It was Red and his bunch, Cap'n. Had Penn, Clooney, Baldwin, and that boy, Bobby Joe Jackson. The burnt one was Robbins."

"Was?" Dobey asked. "He's gone?"

"He didn't make it, Cap'n. It was Red who, uh, did

138

Honey. Beat and shot her too. Penn and Robbins did Marie-Louise."

The hard old ex-sergeant took a deep breath, and looked away for a moment. Honey was Dobey's wife, Marie-Louise had been Melton's. "Robbins said Red was hit. Honey shot him, 'fore he shot her. He thought Penn shot Marie-Louise after she set Robbins and the house on fire. Said Clooney probably shot Ignacio and your Momma. He didn't know if any of the others in Red's bunch was hit."

Doc added, "Ignacio got off both barrels before he died. We found blood up there by their wagon tracks. A good bit of it."

"Their mules was hit, Cap'n, but I don't know about the men. Blood might just be from them mules."

"All right. A good report, Jimmy. You stay a minute, talk with me and Tad. Doc, tell Big William to get us freshened up with food and water. Bear, we'll need horses for you, me, Boss Melton, and Buck, and some spares. Pack us at least one Trapdoor."

"I'll be going too, Bear. I'll help with the horses." Doc said it simply and started inside.

"Whoa, Doc, hold it. You need to stay here with the camp. You know, the kids, Honey and all."

"You hold it, James Melton." Doc turned back and held up a finger to the big Texan. "I saw what they did here. I'll be going."

After an awkward silence of several seconds, Melton shrugged and said, "I don't think I want to know what you saw."

"No. You don't. We need to get moving."

Doc went inside, but Bear held back. He said, "I think Cherokee Jim, he will want to go too, Cap'n. The Count and his men will be here, and Big William and Tad. We will be chasing at least five men, and they may split up. Cherokee Jim is not as good as me, but he's a better tracker than the rest of you."

Dobey nodded. "All right. Makes sense. That it?"

"Well, no, Cap'n. Shelly, I want to take too. We may need her languages. She can ride, and she can pull the pack horse."

Dobey looked at his old Sergeant Major. Melton shrugged, so Dobey said, "Do it, but don't let her pull the spare. Hell, she just had a baby."

As Bear left, Tad finally spoke. "I know y'all are hot to get after 'em, but I thought you'd want to know that I pulled the hearth stones, and your money is all right. I think we should hide some of it here, and some in Doc's place."

Melton said, "Whatever," and started inside.

Tad said, "Y'all listen. I ain't gonna bury that man, Robbins, with the others. Wouldn't be right."

Melton turned back, his face flushed, and jabbed a finger at Tad. "No, you ain't, for a fact. You ain't gonna bury him nowhere. You have somebody drag him a mile away and leave him."

Tad sagged, head down, and mumbled, "Sure, Jimmy. That's what I was …," but Melton had stomped off. He suddenly turned back again.

"And don't let our pigs eat none of him. They was sniffing around him last night, but Bear tole him it was a coyote or something to make him talk. If they do get to him, kill them and don't let nobody eat none of them." And he was gone.

Dobey grasped Tad's shoulder, and said, "He doesn't blame you. Take care of what's left, and we'll get back as soon as we can."

As Dobey started away, Tad said, "I thought we'd put up a palisades, when we rebuild. Put things closer together."

Dobey stopped and looked back. "All right, little brother. Don't you blame yourself, either. Oh. You didn't find that little superstition pistol, did you?"

"What?"

"Honey's storekeeper .32. It was serial numbered five-fifty-five. Melton always thought it was bad luck."

"Oh. Like triple six. No, Dobey, it weren't there. They must have tooken it."

Chapter Fourteen

"So, you are friends of my friends at Balliett's Post?"

"Chief Black Kettle, if you mean the people at Canadian Fort, the little trading post, why, yes we are. Matter of fact, that's how I was hurt." Red pointed to his two wounds, just recently stuffed with some wet weeds by a Cheyenne woman.

A Mexican trader translated for them. Several Mexicans made the dangerous trip regularly, trading guns and goods for hides.

When Black Kettle signaled he didn't understand, Red expanded the lie. "The men at the post, our friends, yours and ours, was out with us looking for Comanche raiders, but some of the raiders doubled back, outraged some women, killed some folks, and stold a wagon full of our hides. We chased 'em, caught 'em, fought 'em. That's when I was hit. But we run 'em off, recaptured the wagon."

Black Kettle clucked approval, and passed the pipe.

"Chief, I just want to trade you the wagon full of hides for some fresh horses, and for the food and medical help you've give me here." Red puffed on the pipe. "We left it back up this here creek, 'cause the mules was hurt."

Black Kettle nodded. "You mean Lodge Pole River."

Red looked confused. "I mean this damn little creek." He turned to the translator, who laughed.

"You Yanquis call it the Washita River. To the Cheyenne and Arapaho, it's the Lodge Pole. For because there are so many lodge poles here in the winter. There is a lot more water in it when the snow melts."

"Oh. Well, if you Mex's and these Injuns want to call this cheap-ass creek a river, it don't matter to me. Anyhow, not even one good day's ride upstream is a good wagon full of hides. It's yours, or the Chief's here, if we can just get four good horses. You can translate that or not, Pedro."

The Mexican continued smiling, but his eyes hardened, and his voice changed. "My name, Senor, is Manuel. Manuel Rosario. The Chief don't want no hides, but I do."

"Whatever. We need them horses, and we need to be off. To, uh, Fort Worth. And you, or these Injuns, whoever's gonna get that wagonload, better get moving afore them Comanches come back. There was some white men, Comancheros, with 'em too. You see them, you'd be doing us all a big favor by just killing them."

* * *

AFTER A HARD NIGHT'S RIDE, Dobey's party followed the wagon tracks into a rocky crossing of the Washita River, only a shallow stream this close to its headwaters and in late Fall.

"Four horses, they come out the other side and go downstream, Cap'n." Bear looked puzzled. "The wagon and mules, they go in, but they don't come out."

"Then the wagon stayed in the stream. Can you tell which way it went?"

"Too rocky, Cap'n."

"Can't be too far 'til it's gotta come out. It's close on ten o'clock. Let's break here, eat, rest a while. You go downstream. Cherokee Jim, you go upstream. No noise. Come back quick and tell us what you find."

A HUNDRED YARDS AWAY, Clooney had finally awakened, to find things worse than he thought they would be.

One of the mules had died. The other, snorting with fear and pain, was trying to remain upright.

"What the hell am I supposed to do now?" he muttered, trying to unhook the dead animal. As he did, the other mule bit him savagely in the back. Clooney yelled, mad with fear and pain himself. He drew his Remington Navy and shot the creature in the head. It snorted at him. He fired again, and again. Its brain was an elusive target. Clooney realized this and shifted his sights to the mule's chest. On his fifth shot, the mule, braying, red eyes blazing its insanity, lashed out with a foreleg. It knocked the pistol from his hand and broke two fingers.

"I won't tolerate this, Blacky, not from no ignorant mule." Clooney struggled through the mud to the wagon bed, drew his Trapdoor, stepped away from the wagon, and shot Blacky through the lungs and heart.

Blacky dropped. *Just like a buffalo*, thought Clooney. Then, *What have I done?*

"Now, look what you made me do, you dumb-assed mule," he wailed, pounding the dead animal with the rifle butt.

Still sobbing, he sensed rather than heard the riders behind him. Turning, shielding his eyes against the midmorning sun, he saw they were not Indians. *Thank God.*

"That you, Penn? Y'all are back sooner than I thought. Is Red all right?"

The riders closed in some.

"Had to, uh, put down ol' Blacky. Just hurt too bad. Gray Man, he died in the night …"

Some of the riders on the ridge above him still had the bright sun behind them, but the one to the north looked like the big buck from the trading post. Clooney swung toward the creek. Another one there. Confederate jacket, but an Indian. *What the heck?*

"Hey. Y'all ain't …"

"No, we ain't. Toss that there rifle away, and lay down on your face. Doc, you got them little pliers with you?"

* * *

SHORTLY AFTER DAWN the next day, Bear raced back to the posse to announce some riders were coming directly toward them from downstream.

"Fast? How many?"

"Coming slow, Cap'n Dobey. Six of 'em. Mexicans, I think. Got some extra horses, they do."

"May be the ones we want, in different clothes, coming back for the wagon. You see any of Red's men, Bear?"

"No, Cap'n, but I ain't sure. There's a place just ahead, the trail is through some cottonwoods on the riverbank, and a nice bluff above it. We could ambush them there, trap 'em, Cap'n, try to talk to 'em. Shelly, she speaks Mexican."

LAURENTINO GUTIERREZ WAS A CHEERFUL, huge man. Over six feet tall, maybe two hundred and eighty pounds, with an immense belly. He was also old, somewhere over forty. One might occasionally see an old vaquero out here, but an old fat one? Unheard of; the times, the country were simply too harsh. Yet, here he was.

Everywhere he went, people realized Poco Tino needed more, and they seemed to delight in giving him extra portions. He never had to ask.

As he rode beside his young friend and boss, Manuel Rosario, his stomach growled. He said, "Jefe, you must have believed those Yanquis about this wagon. Do you think we'll have to fight for it?"

"I think Red Beard was truthful about this wagon, Amigo. On other things, I don't think so. They were running, not chasing."

Rosario had an uncanny sixth sense about things. He halted. "We must be very careful."

"At the wagon, Jefe?"

"No. Right now. Something isn't right." Manuel Rosario and his men were traders, mainly, though occasionally bandits. He had lived thirty-two years in dangerous occupations, in a deadly country, by being careful. There was no real reason to be afraid just now, but the hair on his neck was rising. As he realized it, a young Indian woman stepped into their path, forty yards ahead.

"Damn, Manuelito, how do you do that?" Poco Tino drew his carbine.

"Hola, Jefe. I hope you are understand my talking your language. There are many men around you. Yanquis. Many guns, good fighters. They do not wish to fight you. They just want to catch and kill four Yanquis who came this way, yesterday. Have you seen them, Jefe?" The woman spoke passable Spanish.

"Maybe. Maybe we have seen some Yanquis. Why do they want to kill these other men?" Rosario kept twisting in the saddle as they talked. He couldn't see any fighters, but he knew she was not alone.

"Those other Yanquis, they have raped and murdered family people of these fighters, Jefe."

"They didn't steal no hides or wagon, did they?" "No, Jefe. Why do you ask me?"

"Because, Senorita, we just traded four good ponies

for some hides and a wagon, from some Yanquis. Maybe you have seen it?"

"Si, si, Jefe. Let me talk to my Jefe." She spoke English to someone in the bushes above her, then turned back to Rosario. "It is waiting for you, behind us one half day, just beside this Lodge Pole River."

"This is very strange, Senorita. Your friends, they want these other Yanquis, but not their buffalo hides?"

"No, Jefe. Just their blood."

Switching to English, Rosario said, "And your amigos here, they are not Comancheros?"

A man stood on the bluff above the woman, holding a Winchester carbine at the ready. "I guess the one with the red beard told you Comancheros were chasing him." The man wore a white star on his hat.

Rosario smiled. "No, Senor. He said he was chasing Comanches and Comancheros."

"Did you believe him?"

"No, Senor, for some reason, I did not." Rosario laughed. Another man, larger than the first, appeared on the bluff,

above and slightly behind Rosario's band. "Mostly, we just shoot Comanches. Now Comancheros, them we'd hang." He also had a white star, and a Winchester.

"*Rinches*" whispered Poco Tino. "Rangers. I know those hats, Jefe. Maybe we fight them from the riverbank?" He nodded to his right.

Rosario glanced toward the river, just as two more Yanquis stood up there; a large black man with a Winchester rifle, and ten yards from him an old gringo with a sawed-off shotgun.

Smiling, Rosario nodded to the men by the river. The Mexicans' horses, sensing the riders' nervousness, began to dance a little. Poco Tino clucked, and Rosario turned back to see two more men stand up on the bluff. He whispered, "Maybe we don't fight them at all."

To the gringo leader, he yelled, "Those men you want, I'm sorry to tell you, I gave them fresh ponies in trade for their wagon of hides. Half a day behind us. Black Kettle's camp. They were going to ride south."

"Four of 'em? Any of them hurt?"

"Si, Senor. Their leader, the Red Beard. Shoulder and leg. Said Comanches shot him."

"My wife ain't a Comanche. Y'all can pass on by, then. The wagon's a half day behind us, other side of the stream, just past a rocky crossing."

The big ranger added, "We left a man hanging around there, near the mouth of the gully where it's hid. He'll help you find it."

"Gracias, Senor. We will be coming back to the Cheyenne camp. Do you want us to bring your amigo back with us?"

"Don't worry none about him. He'll be fine, on his own." "Will he fight us for the wagon?"

"Not likely."

* * *

FIVE HOURS LATER, the Mexicans found a man swinging beside a thirty-foot cottonwood, on the riverbank. His shirtfront was covered with blood. The rope led from his neck over a branch, then laterally up into a gully, where it was tied off to the wheel of a wagon. Near the wagon were several human teeth, clearly visible on the red clay. A large cut square of buffalo hide was pinned to his pants leg with his own knife, and on it was inscribed his epitaph: 'He didn't mean to do it.'

Chapter Fifteen

"HE IS CALLED LITTLE ROCK, and he is chief of this small band of Cheyenne. Most of his band left this morning with Black Kettle's camp, going back up toward the Cimarron River. Many of his fighters left before them, with Dog Soldiers from several camps." Shelly paused, thinking about all she had just heard. "Oh, and the men we want? They rode out the other way." She pointed south. "These people all thought they were our friends. Red Beard told them he and his men were ..."

"Yeah, we know." Melton cut her off, impatient as he was to ride. "Is he mad at us? Why is he yelling?"

"No, Boss. He's, uh, nervous. Not scared, but nervous. He remembers me as Serenity Killer, old Black Kettle's foot warmer. And he knows Cherokee Jim is Chief Watie's nephew." She smiled at Cherokee Jim, who blushed.

"Why did Black Kettle go back north? His tribe just got back down here from Kansas."

After some more yelling, she turned back. "Chief Little Rock says there was much raiding up in Kansas this summer, along the Trail, and the rivers you call the Solomon and Sabina. Mostly Dog Soldiers, but some of his young men and some of Black Kettle's was with them. Him and Black Kettle was worried about the Bluecoats coming after them for revenge, so they come down here for a while. Now they go back up there for a while."

"How come he ain't gone, too?"

"His daughter is going to have a baby soon. Her name is Meotzi. She taught me Cheyenne talk." Shelly nodded to a very pregnant, very pretty girl behind the chief. "Anyhow, he told them Mexicans he'd watch their wagons and goods for a day or two."

"Ain't that like a coyote guarding the henhouse?"

"Chief says some Bluecoat chief told the Indian agents they couldn't trade any more guns to the tribes, nor ammo. So they need to keep trade open with those Mexicans, as well as with us. They'll all be back down here in a few weeks, for winter."

AS THEY TRAILED Red and his men southeast, Melton said, "I guess I don't understand this Dog Soldier business. I thought that's what you called all Cheyenne warriors." They were walking beside their horses, for a brief rest.

Dobey said, "No, it's some different. Any of y'all heard of the Knights of the Round Table?" No one had.

"Never mind, but it was an old warrior society, like the Dog Soldiers are. Other tribes have brotherhoods, likewise. Matter of fact, there's a lot of Lakota Dog Soldiers, as well as Northern Cheyenne."

Doc said, "Lakota? You mean Sioux?"

"Right. They don't agree to any treaties. Want to fight us coming into their lands and stick to the old ways. That about it, Shelly?"

"Yes, Cap'n Dobey. And now, since so many peace chiefs was killed at Sand Creek four winters ago, many young Cheyenne and Arapaho want to ride with the Dog Soldiers. The Dog Soldiers, they do not want old Black Kettle to even camp near them. Threatened to kill his horses." She paused. "My man is coming."

Melton said, "You think he found 'em already?" Dobey said, "Mount up."

* * *

FROM A SMALL HILL a half-mile to their right, Red and Penn watched their pursuers walk past. As they watched, a rider joined the posse from the south, and they quickly mounted and followed him back down the trail Red and his men had left the previous day.

"Must be their nigger tracker, Red. Must have found where we cut into the river."

"Yeah. Well, let's ride. We need to catch up to that cattle herd, stay with them 'til we get to Fort Dodge."

"You don't think them Rebs run into them?"

"Ain't no way they've met. Them Rebs is hot on our

old trail. They would'a missed each other by forty mile. Anyhow, we'll shave these beards tonight."

"How long afore you think Baldwin and Bobby Joe figure out we ain't coming back?"

Red laughed. "Them dumb-ass children? Maybe never. But if they stay on the back-trail of them cattle, they might get away. Even the buck nigger will have trouble tracking 'em."

They rode north. As they crossed their old trail, Penn snorted, "Yeah, I can just hear that squeaky Bobby Joe now: 'I'm skeered. I wonder where Red and Penn is. I wisht I was with old Clooney. I'm hungry.'"

"He'd best be careful what he wishes for."

* * *

"THIS GOT to be the Red River, Cap'n. They went into it here. I rode down a ways, and they ain't come out. But they could come out on one side while I'm checking the other, maybe ambush me, non? So I come back." Bear stopped to see if they followed his thoughts.

"Good thinking, Bear. So now we can track down both sides, and keep moving."

"Yes, Cap'n. I think they come out on the far side, head southeast to Fort Worth. I think you and Cherokee Jim and Doc ride the far bank. Boss, Buck and Shelly ride on the left side, and me, I go down the middle. Maybe I see some sign in the water."

Four miles downstream, the river turned east. The tracks of hundreds of cattle and several riders crossed the river to the left and headed north. The posse halted for a conference.

"What do you make of it, Bear?"

"Cap'n, ours could have gone farther downstream, maybe go out the other side, you know, to split up. Or …" Bear looked away, and bit his lip.

"Or they could'a doubled back up river, heading north the whole time we been following this river south. Hell, they could be trailing us, now." Melton pulled his brass telescope and glassed the area behind them.

"Looking to ambush us?" "Maybe. Your call, Cap'n."

Dobey stretched, and rubbed his eyes. "All right. I think they're still ahead of us. Their man Clooney really didn't want to tell us they was heading for Fort Worth."

"Yeah, it was like pulling teeth," Buck grinned. "Hen's teeth." Dobey glared at him, then went on. "The man I want is hit, twice, and probably looking for a doctor. I don't expect him to

double back, anyways."

Melton settled it. "Cap'n, you take Doc and Cherokee Jim, follow the back trail of this herd, I'll take one river bank, Buck the other, Bear and Shelly can stay in the river. We don't see sign of anyone pretty soon, we'll pull out and catch you. If we do find sign, I'll send back to fetch y'all."

* * *

FORTY MILES SOUTH, riding hard, Baldwin said, "You

think we ought to slow down? Red and Penn gonna have trouble catching us."

"It ain't them catching us which worries me. I wish we was in Fort Worth already. I'm hungry."

"Well, my ass hurts from pounding this saddle. Wish I was back on our wagon with Clooney."

One half mile later, Baldwin's mare stepped into a badger's hole and snapped her leg, throwing Baldwin. He threw out his arms to break his fall, and broke his arm instead.

Bobby Joe Jackson pulled up, turned and trotted back to Baldwin, curled up. and groaned on the ground. "Judas Priest, Baldwin, what've you done? You best move afore that horse kicks you silly."

Baldwin scuttled away from his mare as she flailed her hooves, trying to regain her feet. "I think she broke my arm, Bobby Joe. Hurts like hell. Help me get my coat off and see is it bleeding."

Bobby Joe dismounted, pulling his carbine from its scabbard. "First things first, I always say." It took him two shots to kill the mare.

"I ain't never heard you say no such thing. Never. You just made that up. 'Sides, the damn old mare could'a waited. She's the one as stepped in the stupid hole." Baldwin winced as Jackson pulled the jacket off over the damaged arm and rolled up the shirt sleeve.

"Whooee, Baldwin. It's broke alright. Feel the lump there? Least ways no blood. Lemme see can I set it here." He twisted, and Baldwin yelled.

"Damn, Bobby Joe, that hurts. How'd you like it,

somebody did that you? Just strap a stick to it and let's get moving. I'll set up behind you."

"Oh, now you're in a hurry, Mister We-Need-To-Slow-Down-So-We-Can-Be-Caught. Now that you done killed your horse. I'm telling you, you ain't right. Take off your kerchief so's I can make you a sling."

* * *

"WE KEPT GOING FIVE, maybe six mile, Cap' n. Bear says ain't nobody been in the river along there. Figures they's still ahead of us, tryin' to hide in this herd's back trail."

Dobey said, "I was about to send back for you. Cherokee Jim found sign of some of 'em heading south on top of these cattle tracks."

"Just some of 'em?"

"Hell, Jimmy, look at the mess that herd left. Could be all of 'em. Least we know some of 'em is ahead of us."

"Yeah. Let's push."

* * *

THE HERD of longhorns blundered into quicksand at the Canadian River. The confusion and delay allowed Red and Penn to catch the herd much sooner than they expected, and to make themselves useful in completing the crossing. The cowboys saved most of the cattle, but one of the supply wagons was lost.

Before being lassoed and pulled free, the cook threw clear several bags of beans, one of coffee, and a box holding salt and peppers. Later, when it was nip and tuck as to whether he should be fired for negligence, those final actions saved his job but not his reputation.

The foreman rode up to Red and Penn. "Thanks for the help there, friends." He took off his hat and rubbed his face, then gestured at the hapless cook who was searching the river shallows for anything that might have floated loose. "That worthless son of a bitch. He weren't my wife's cousin, I'd shoot him. Either of you done any cooking?"

Red nodded. "Did some for my section during the war. Third Texas Cavalry. And we could use some work."

"Bunk down and eat with us tonight. I owe you that. But you help with the meal, and I'll think about jobs for both of you."

* * *

THE NEXT DAY was a magnificent fall day. It was a Thursday. Red and Penn were hired by the trail boss, Red as a cook's

helper, Penn as a cowpuncher.

Baldwin, riding double behind Bobby Joe, was delighted to see a wagon full of pilgrims crossing the cattle trail, heading east. He bummed a ride with them, and Bobby Joe rode on, hard bent for Fort Worth.

Dobey's posse found Baldwin's dead horse, and pressed on harder.

Tad, Big William, George Canada, and Hannity began cutting wood along the Canadian for the new house and palisades. O'Reilly stood guard.

Mary Belle fed soup to Honey, while Junebug changed the dressing on Honey's neck and on Annette Balliett's stub. Carmela and Manuela cared for the animals and the four children.

Manuel Rosario and his men finally started their return trek to Mexico with their three wagonloads of hides.

Graf Baranov sat atop the main store, scanning the horizon. In the shade of the dining porch, Willi touched up his sketches.

George Armstrong Custer won his effort to return to functional command of the Seventh Cavalry, having been court-martialed and suspended from active duty the previous year for gross misconduct. Of these various people, only Lieutenant Colonel Custer knew it was a Thursday. Most of the denizens of north Texas and the Indian Territory simply didn't give a tinker's dam; 'Autie' Custer had a Thursday appointment with General Sheridan, and was chafing at the bit.

Chapter Sixteen

THEY'D STOPPED to water the horses and stretch when Bear came riding back to them. Riding hard.

"Now there's only two of 'em, Boss." Melton was Bear's second 'stepfather', and Bear invariably reported to him, which apparently bothered Dobey not at all. Dobey's former sergeant was older and more imposing, and he and Dobey were almost silently synchronized anyhow after years of combat together.

"You know which two?" Melton wasn't pleased, but he didn't blame Bear. He just didn't bother to let Bear know.

"No, Boss. Now only one rides the horse toward Fort Worth. The other, he got on a wagon that crossed going east. Maybe that one's Red, 'cause he's wounded?"

Dobey broke in. "As good a guess as any, Bear. Good work. Good report. Jimmy, y'all push on after the rider. I'll take Cherokee Jim and Doc and go hard after the wagon."

"Yeah. You oughtta catch 'em 'fore dark. Prob'ly see you in Fort Worth, 'less we catch this bastard sooner." Melton turned to the others, having already dismissed his partner from his thoughts; Dobey had his own mission, and would handle it. Melton could focus entirely on his own.

"All right, girls. Fun's over. Now we're gonna do some riding."

* * *

"WELL, sir, Mister Baldwin, I can't tell you how happy I am to have an experienced hunter and lawman riding with us," Odell Peterson said, and Baldwin thought he was right truthful. Old Peterson was not at all sure how happy he was. Baldwin didn't blame him; Baldwin himself was pretty scruffy, had managed to break his arm and lose his mount, and was bent on impressing Peterson's sixteen-year-old daughter back here in the wagon. Peterson twisted in his saddle to cast another worried look at his new passenger. "You sure you don't want to trade with my son? Ride his mule?"

"Aw, no sir, Odell, I can watch our back trail better from here. Fight better from the wagon, too, case them Comancheros catch up to us."

"Well, I wisht you'd tole me sooner that you was being pursued. Got my family to worry about." It didn't take a genius to see why the old man was concerned; Peterson's wife was also openly studying young Baldwin.

"All the more reason to have an extra shooter,"

Baldwin said earnestly, winking at Mrs. Peterson on the wagon seat, and squeezing Kate Peterson's thigh. The girl giggled, and insinuated her bare foot between his legs.

"Well, keep your eyes open, and keep your mind on our safety."

"Yessir. Oh, yes sir." Baldwin faced the rear, closed his eyes, and concentrated on Kate's footwork.

An hour later, Mrs. Peterson ordered her daughter to trade places so the mother might rest. Two hours after that, having been relieved of his tensions by both mother and daughter.

Baldwin nodded off. He was still sound asleep when Dobey ordered them to halt.

He was wide-awake when Dobey pushed him from the back of the wagon. The noose almost snapped his neck, but there was some give in the limb of the cotton-wood tree. He danced and strangled instead.

Mrs. Peterson and her daughter, each two dollars richer from their brief encounter with Baldwin, sobbed as he died. The father whined that Baldwin owed him for food and transport.

"Then deduct it from the goodwill you owe us, sir," said Doc. "He'd have murdered you all tonight, or tomorrow. Perhaps used your women rudely first."

"I doubt they'd have stood for it," huffed Peterson. "They ain't tramps, you know."

* * *

BOBBY JOE JACKSON had been unable to extract his

heart from his throat for the good part of a week, until now. He still fretted over where Red and the others were, but he was sure he'd made it now.

Now the pinto was re-shod, and he was bathed, shaved and wearing a new shirt. Bright red, double-breasted. Nobody would recognize him now. Hell, he'd surprise Red hisself, whenever he got here. He still had seven or eight dollars, and Fort Worth was a good place to be with some real spending money.

The fat young whore had cost him two dollars and the whiskey another three bits, but now he was as mellow as he'd been since before he'd started riding with that damn Red. He patted the sleeping whore on her butt, took another swig, and walked out to find a good place to eat. Not a care in the world. Good old Fort Worth.

On the street, a large black man was examining the right rear hoof of Jackson's horse. Bobby Joe shifted the whiskey bottle to his left hand, drew his Colt, and stepped close behind the man.

"Stand up, nigger. Slow and easy. How'd you find me?"

"Stables, Cher. Told the blacksmith my old massuh had thrown a shoe, and I had to catch up and give him a message." Bear turned, hands up low in front of him, and smiled. "You shoot me, Cher, and that lawman across the street, he be on you real quick. Maybe my friends, too, eh? So, what we do now?"

Bobby Joe glanced around. The lawman was dozing on the porch. The only other person nearby was an Indian woman shuffling down the street behind him.

"Get the hell away from here, Squaw." He waved the bottle at her, keeping Bear covered. She smiled, obviously uncomprehending. "Dumb-assed Injuns are everywhere," he muttered, dismissing her. "Come on, Darky. We just gonna ease back down this alley and have a talk."

As he started to turn, a lightning flash coursed through his right rear side below the ribs. Shelly twisted the knife on the second strike, staying behind him as he tried to turn to face the attack.

Before she could strike a third time, Bear snatched the Colt from him and pushed him down. "Don't kill him, Cheri, if you haven't already. Go get Boss." He dragged the moaning man between the horses and into the alley. Across the street, the lawman snored.

BUCK STOOD at the mouth of the alley, partially blocking it with his body. Boss Melton had simply said, "Don't let no one come down here," then disappeared with Shelly.

He hadn't told Buck how to keep them out, exactly. Boss was like that. Mission-type orders, he called them. If Buck had asked him how, he'd have said, "You'll figure it out," if he said anything at all. More than likely, he'd have just glared that "What kind of idiot are you?" glare of his, or maybe let him have his, "Do I have to do everything?" look.

Buck levered a round into the chamber of his Winchester, then carefully lowered the hammer to half-cock. Anybody but the sleeping lawman, he decided, I'll just tell 'em the alley ain't available for passage. Do the lawman wake up and act interested, I'll fire off a shot up the street and yell, "They're robbing the livery stable," it being over two blocks away.

A few minutes later, Melton joined him. After checking the quiet street, he nodded toward the sleeping figure across the street. "How was you gonna handle him?"

After Buck explained, Melton snorted, "Hell, your idea is a lot better than mine. I was gonna just try to wing him. All right. Take the pinto, right there by the bay, pull him round back and help Bear tie that little son of a bitch on him. We're gonna finish questioning him outside of town. Cap'n might want to speak to him, too, do he live so long. I'll watch here."

"What about our horses?" Buck was sorry the second he asked the question. Melton gave him his, "Just how damn stupid do you think I am?" look.

Buck shriveled a little. "Oh. I bet you done sent Shelly to get 'em or something. I'll just shut my trap and take this horse on back ..."

TEN MINUTES LATER, Bear and his woman watched as Melton and Buck rode off pulling Bobby Joe's horse; Bobby Joe was trussed face down across his saddle, and was not a well man.

"You know, Cheri, his blood is on your hands." He squeezed the back of her neck. Fondly.

"No, Bear, I am too careful. Look." She showed him, extending her palms then turning them down.

"Not what I mean, Cheri. He'll die, because of you. Instead of me. Get the other horses and meet me in front of the hardware store." Bear started away.

Shelly tugged at his serape. "Hard-where store?"

"The gun store. You seen it. Me, I get you something better than that knife."

The gun store was more than Bear bargained on. It was more than an hour later before he and Shelly joined Melton, Buck, and the dying Bobby Joe at their camp northwest of town.

Chapter Seventeen

"I've TOLD you all I know, fellers. I doubt I'll make it through the night, without medical help. Won't you take me back to town?" Bobby Joe was tied to a tree, hands behind it, sitting in a small pool of blood. He had not gotten better.

Melton turned to glare at him for a moment, then returned to his instructions to Buck.

"We won't be long. I got to buy some of these guns and set something right. See if the Cap'n got by us and is waiting back there. You watch for him. You and Shelly take turns watching this piece of dirt. He starts making noise, cut his tongue. Do we start a ruckus in town, and you hear a lot of shooting, move into them rocks and cover us as we ride in. Kill him first." He nodded at Bobby Joe.

Buck and Shelly nodded earnestly. Both mumbled, "Yes, Boss." Seemed like no one who knew him wanted to disappoint this 'Boss' feller.

Bobby Joe, not really knowing him, yelped, "Hey, Boss, take me with you. I can ride. I think."

Melton stared at him a moment, then walked behind the tree and kicked his hands where they were tied, breaking two fingers and a thumb.

BobbyJoe heard them crack, distinctly, and said, "Nnnnnnnngh! Ah! Ah!"

Melton squatted in front of him. "Listen, shit-for-brains. Only reason you're alive is my Cap'n might want to ask you something else. Y'all outraged my wife and killed her. Outraged the Cap'n's wife, and shot off his mama's arm. Killed ol' Nacio. You ain't gonna live through this. But you could make it worse. Mmh?"

It is not easy to accept death as a done deal. Bobby Joe finally did just then, and his brain began to shut down.

* * *

AS THEY RODE BACK into Fort Worth, Melton said, "All right, Bear, run it by me again."

"Boss, I ast did he have a cartridge pistol, like that little Smith and Wesson Honey had. For me to give Shelly, you know."

"The superstition gun." Melton turned his head and spat in disgust.

Bear nodded. "Yessir. Well, he did. Pointed it to me. Same .32, but a six-inch barrel. Then he said he also had big ones."

"Big Smith and Wessons? How big?"

"Nossir, Boss. Remingtons. Like mine, but .46

caliber rimfires. Five shooters. Showed me the bullets. Me, I said 'How much?' He said, 'It don't matter, 'cause I'll not sell to no nigger nor no Indian.' So we come back to camp."

"Damn his eyes." Melton glared straight ahead. "You seen the bullets. Did you see the gun?"

Bear nodded again."Me, I did. Seen three of 'em, Boss. In the case. He was wearing one, too. Showed me how it worked, so's I'd know what I was missing, I guess."

"Tell me how."

Bear thought a moment. This was all new and he really wanted to get it right. "All right. It has a loading slot on the right side of the cylinder. Load 'em one at a time, from the back. Or, you can pop the cylinder out, put in a fresh loaded one, do you have it. Just like my old ones."

Melton nodded. "Big difference is copper cartridges, just like the Henry, Spencer, Smith and Wesson. Winchester. Don't get wet. Fast loading. Damn."

They rode on in silence, shaking their heads. 1868 was becoming a hell of a year for changes.

BEAR THOUGHT the hardware store was much like one he'd seen in Mississippi before the war. Walls covered with farming utensils, saddles and harnesses, axes, shovels, picks, and brooms. Tins of coal oil, barrels of nails and horseshoes, and fishing gear. The Franklin stove had it right toasty, and added the smell of wood smoke to the blend of oil and leather. The proprietor, thin and balding,sat playing checkers with an old bearded fellow as he had during Bear's earlier visit. Bear pointed to a glass-topped counter along the right wall. It displayed an assortment of knives, watches, and pistols, including three new blued Remingtons. Melton marched straight to it, tapped it, and said, "Anybody work here?"

The store owner pushed away from his game and took his place behind the counter. "And what can I..."

"Lemme see one of them metal cartridge Remingtons," Melton interrupted him. He took the pistol, cocked and decocked it, snapped the hammer once, then half-cocked it and spun the cylinder.

"Well, sir, I can see your boy retained a lot of what I showed him. You handle the Remington like you'd already seen one."

"Cartridges?" Melton glared at the owner.

"Yessir." The proprietor opened a box for Melton's inspection. "Hits 'bout like a Henry."

Melton loaded the Remington. "How'd you know he was my boy? You think we look alike?"

The storekeeper laughed. "Oh, no sir. Not what I meant. I just ..."

"Cause he is my boy, you know. My stepson."

The storekeeper looked confused, then concerned. "Well, sir, I never ..."

"Yes, you did. In front of his woman. Turned him down. There was a witness, too. Some other man. Was that you, sir?" Melton waved the Remington generally toward the other man, still sitting in front of the checkerboard. The man paled and nodded slowly.

"Come here, then. You'll want to see this, too."

"See what, sir?" The bearded one stood and eased slowly to the counter, holding both hands up waist high.

"This man's going to sell my stepson that little Smith and Wesson for his wife, and these three Remingtons, and all the bullets he has. Ain't you, sweetheart?" Melton laid the loaded Remington on the counter-glass, and pushed it toward the proprietor, who started to pick it up. In one fluid motion, Melton drew his sawed-off Colt, cocked it, and placed the barrel against the storekeeper's forehead, then jabbed him with it. Just a little.

"Ain't you?"

The man nodded, slowly, and pushed the Remington back toward Melton.

"And the one you're wearing, too? Belt and all?" The man nodded again, carefully, like he really didn't want to bump that Colt. He placed the other pistols and eight boxes of cartridges on the counter.

With his left hand, Melton pulled out a handkerchief full of paper bills and laid it in front of the proprietor. "Take your cut, and don't even think about the shotgun you got back of the counter."

Bear strapped on the proprietor's pistol belt, then walked behind the counter to pick up the short scattergun. He decapped it, then turned it upside down and banged the barrels on the floor to dislodge the charges. Nothing happened.

"This thing even loaded?" Bear asked.

The storekeeper nodded, and the second man said,

"Oh, it's well tamped. I seen him load it. 'Bout fifteen number four buck in each barrel."

Melton said, "Re-cap it. We'll give it to Shelly." Turning to the proprietor he lowered his pistol. "Take another five dollars for that, but we'll need a possibles bag with the mixings for it, too. Throw in holsters for these pistols too."

The storekeeper finally let out his breath and said, "Yessir. Can I get you gents anything else?" He didn't seem to dislike Negroes and Indians as much as he did ten minutes earlier. Melton had that effect on people.

Melton stared hard at him for a moment. "Listen. I don't think you and me are gonna be friends. But if I don't have to kill you or that dozy lawman out there and burn your place down, then I might need to do more business with you." He let that sink in. "We run a trading post, up on the Canadian. Need another source for Trapdoors and ammo, outside of Santa Fe. Buffalo trade."

"I got two left. A .58 rimfire, and a .50-70 central fire. Plenty of cartridges for both and I can order more."

"Get 'em. I got enough there to cover 'em?"

"Oh, yes sir." It was probably not a good time for gouging, Bear thought, as he watched, grinning. The storekeeper added, "Some left over, too."

Melton asked, "Either of you know of a woman by the name of Kathleen Melton? May have been called 'Little Bit'? Might have been a drinker?"

The other visitor said, "Hell, she's probably the madam over to the Gilded Lilly. Weren't she a Melton, Al?"

The proprietor squinted in thought. "Yep. I think you're right. Before she took the sheriff's name. He dried her out. She ain't no little bit, though. Goes by Big Kate. The boys, some of 'em, call her Planet Kate. Kind of broad across the ass. I, uh, hope she ain't a relative, sir. I mean, not that being a madam is a bad thing, …"

"She might be my sister. Let me ask you something else – do you ever take your foot out of your mouth?"

The second man laughed. "No, he don't, often. If she's your sister, she's around the corner, to the left, one block. She's a Jackson, now."

"Is he this sleepy law down the street?"

"Nope. Former sheriff. He was kilt, maybe two year ago. Yankee soldiers. Drunk."

Melton said, "Well. Bear, you settle up here, get this stuff loaded. Keep a eye out for the Cap'n." And he was gone.

Bear gave the proprietor a big smile. The man cleared his throat, stared at his feet for a moment, then said, "I, uh, I ain't never done something like this before…"

"What's that?"

"Apologized to no nigger. But, here goes." He stood tall, and looked Bear in the eye. "I was wrong. I didn't know who you was, and I turned you down, cold, in front of your woman, and you had legitimate business. I'm sorry. My name is Sharpton." He held out his hand.

Bear ignored the hand. "Wish my woman could hear those words." And he thought, if it weren't for the business part, this wouldn't be happening.

At that moment, Dobey walked in. "Hear what?"

Chapter Eighteen

SURPRISING AS IT WAS, the heavy rain brought warmer temperature along with the lightning. The crack and blast of a nearby strike caused the children to squeal, and Junebug to spill some coffee.

"Sweet Jesus!" She shuddered.

"Yeah. Here." Tad wiped the spill, then poured more for her and for Honey. They sat on the dining porch, taking a breather from the children trapped inside. "I just hope this stuff ain't striking no big trees. We having enough trouble finding wood for the new house, as it is."

Junebug took a sip and grimaced. "You should've let Big William make the coffee. You ain't never gotten no better at it. And I ain't seen no big trees since we left Arkansas."

"It won't do," whispered Honey.

"Why Honey, I'll just get Big William to make some

fresh right now. He weren't here yet when I made this, so..."

She shook her head, twisting the bandage on her neck and causing her to wince. "Not the coffee. The house. I won't live in no wood house. Not ever again." Her tears welled over.

"But Honey, we been cutting and hauling two weeks now..." Tad was dumbfounded.

"Hush, you fool." Junebug patted Honey's arm. "I was in a fire. Our house burned, afore I run away. I know what she means."

Carmela had heard it all, chasing a chicken out of the store. "My father, he taught us how to do the adobe. Manuelita and I helped him to build the bunkhouse and Doc's place."

Manuela joined them. "Si, and the ones we had back across the Rio Grande."

"Well, I guess I could use all this cut wood for the palisades then," Tad scratched his chin.

"We will need much of it for the roof, but it don't matter 'cause we can use the adobe for your old fort walls, too."

"That gonna be better, then, Honey?" Junebug patted her arm again.

Honey nodded and tried to smile, but suddenly threw up. "Sweet Jesus," Junebug said again. "Another baby."

Carmela and Manuela nodded solemnly, while Tad just looked confused.

Chapter Nineteen

"WHERE Y'ALL CAMPED?" Sharpton followed them out to the hitching rail. Mounted, Melton signaled silence to the others with a low hand, away from Sharpton's vision. "East, maybe four miles. Why?"

"Well, long as you're not northwest you'll prob'ly be all right. There's a man-eater up there."

"Do what?" snapped Melton.

"Bear. Three hundred fifty, maybe four hundred pounds. Ty Thoggen winged him when he kilt a goat, but he got away. Damn if he didn't come back and take one of Ty's boys. Ate him, mostly."

"One of his ranch hands? It's a poor hand who can't scare off a bear, even a big one."

"Nossir. His eight-year-old boy. Last week we heard yelling and hollering and he took a Mex girl, sparking down by the river. Her boyfriend weren't armed. It's like the bear can't hunt regular with his busted leg."

"Why the hell ain't y'all tracked and killed him?" Melton's agitation was frightening.

Sharpton shrank back. "Well, a few of the boys did try. First night out, one of 'em went in the bushes to do his business, and then, ker-pow, it happened."

"Bear got him too?"

"Naw. Others heard him, thought he was the bear, shot him up pretty bad. But they seen the bear trailing them, as they came back here. Now, folks is scared. It's like he's magical now, you know?"

"Magical, my raw ass. Bear just smelled blood. Let's ride." North of town, they crossed the river and turned slightly west. "Thought you said east?" Dobey asked, as he spurred his

horse to keep up.

"I lied, all right? And that damn Bobby Joe is sitting up there in a pool of blood."

THE SHADOWS WERE ALREADY STRETCHING FAR down the east side of the hill when Buck and Shelly heard the horses pounding toward them. They were already on full alert. An hour earlier, something had startled some grouse west of them, and a trio of deer had bolted from the same area, running straight uphill toward the camp. Buck had grabbed his carbine and muttered, "Fresh meat," but Shelly had pushed the barrel down and put her finger over her lips.

"No," she whispered, "Something scared them."

The deer, smelling blood, had suddenly veered away.

A tense hour followed but the incident was all but forgotten now, as the horses approached fast.

Buck handed Shelly his Winchester and picked up Bobby Joe Jackson's Sharps. "I think that's our friends coming. Still, let's get behind them rocks." He looked at the shivering Jackson. "You make a sound, I'll have her finish her knife work on you." When Jackson gave him a weak nod, he turned back to Shelly. "They's a round in the chamber. Go on and cock the hammer, but don't fire 'less I do."

Seconds later, he grinned. "This is our folks." "How you know?"

"Unless they's some other big black man riding around in a red and blue serape out here, your Bear is the third one back." He stood to wave.

Behind them, the other bear worked his way closer. A light rain began falling.

* * *

"Y'ALL SOME kind of generals, or something, with all them stripes?"

"I'm Sergeant Boye, and this here is Sergeant Major Kennedy of the Seventh Cavalry. You the cook who just came off the trail?"

"I ain't no cook, but I was helping one on the drive. I ain't full strength yet. Recovering from a gunfight."

"How's the other feller?"

"My partner? Hell, ain't nothing wrong with him. He's just upstairs getting his tensions relieved." They were in the bar of Brady's Bordello in Buffalo City, outside of Camp Dodge.

Boye spat, "Naw. I meant the one you was in a fight with." Red smiled, "Oh, them. They didn't make it." "Congratulations," said Kennedy with a sour smile. "We were told you needed to talk to somebody high up?"

"Yeah, Colonel. You help us find some escort toward Santa Fe and I can tell you where them Cheyenne plans to spend the winter."

* * *

DOBEY DISMOUNTED, handed his reins to Buck and strode straight to where Bobby Joe Jackson was tied. He drew his new Remington as he walked.

As the others dismounted, Melton said, "Let's get a fire and some coffee going, afore everything is soaked. Y'all ain't seen no bear, have you? I mean a real one?"

Shelly shook her head. "But something spooked some deer and birds, back side of this hill, maybe one hour ago, Boss."

"Might be him. Bear, give her the shotgun. They's a big one, wounded, somewhere around here. Turned man-eater. He ain't likely to try us, many as we is and with a fire, but don't wander off to do your business alone. We don't know how hungry he is." Leaving the others to set up for the night, Melton joined Dobey, who was already questioning the dying Jackson.

"We talked with Baldwin, Clooney, and Robbins before we killed 'em, so I think I know who did what to who, but I want to hear it from you. Straight and

184

simple. Do it right, I might have the Doc try to give you some relief." Dobey pushed Jackson's head back with the barrel of his pistol. "But you try to shine me on, you'll wind up dinner for some crazy bear that's ranging around here."

Jackson whined, "I didn't do nothing, and I done told him," he nodded at Melton, "ever'damn thing I knowed."

Melton drew his own Remington and broke Jackson's nose. "Didn't you hear a damn thing the Cap'n said? He wants to hear it from you. Straight and simple, he said. You got it now?"

Jackson snorted blood and gasped, "Nnnnh. Oh, jeez. Nnnnh. All right. Ohhh. Gimme a second." He choked.

Melton re-holstered. "We ain't got all night."

Jackson nodded and started. "We got to your place right at dark. Red told us to wait, and he rode up to the big house first, then called us up. Took Penn and Robbins inside with him. Told Clooney to make a stand with his buffler gun and kill anybody coming from the store." He snuffled some. "We could hear 'em inside going at them women, then some old man come out of the store, but he was headed away, so we didn't shoot him. Then there was yelling and shooting in the house behind us, and a fire and screaming…"

"How many shots?"

"Four, maybe five, pistol shots." "Who screamed?"

"Robbins, I think. Penn said the half-breed nigger went upside his head with a lantern..Nnnh. Oh, Jesus."

Melton had kicked him in the ribs. "She was my woman, stupid."

"I know, but I din't do nothing," Jackson wailed. "I mean, I'm sorry. Anyways, that woman set him on fire, and he bumped the curtains or something. Then Penn shot her, and here come Red limping and bleeding from the shoulder and leg, and some ol' Mex come running up hill at us yelling too, and Clooney shot him." Jackson took a breath. "Let's see. Then Robbins rolled off'n the porch, burning all over and screaming, and some woman charged us from downhill, and Clooney shot her too. 'Bout that time, somebody shotgunned our mule team, and they took off, and us after them."

"You didn't shoot no one? You didn't share those women?" Dobey's voice was soft, but ominous.

"Cap'n, I never fired. And I never seen them women that night. Don't take me wrong, now. I knew there was women in there, but I didn't know who, and I never seen 'em."

Melton snorted. "Don't let that innocent feeling overcome you. You had other choices." He turned to Dobey. "It's what he told me, too. Fits with Clooney, and what Bear got from Robbins."

Dobey shrugged. "Yeah, Baldwin too. What about Penn and Red?"

Jackson winced. "They turned back along the Red River, said they was gonna ambush y'all. Said if we was caught, make sure none of us told you we was meeting here in Fort Worth. But Cap'n, I think they lied."

"Yeah?"

"Yessir. I think they cut us loose, headed north for Camp Dodge behind some cows."

Dobey said, "You're prob'ly right. Jimmy, tell Doc to

give him something for pain so he doesn't keep all of us awake tonight. We'll hang him in the morning."

"Oh, Cap'n, please don't hang me. All I done wrong was to ride with Red. I must have just lost my head to have hooked up with him." Jackson began sobbing, as Dobey and Melton walked away.

AT THE FIRE, Shelly handed them tin mugs of coffee. "Beans and bacon be ready soon," she said. "And Buck, he helped me pull your saddles and bedrolls. They under that lean-to yonder."

Buck finished rigging a lean-to for Doc and joined them. "Got Doc set up, and Cherokee Jim will rack out with me. He's checking the perimeter and horses with Bear. Thank you, ma'am." He accepted coffee from Shelly. "What about the prisoner, Boss?"

"Doc'll throw a blanket on him after he gives him something for pain, though I ain't too worried about his particular comfort. Y'all figured out guards, yet?"

"Doc's got it from ten 'til midnight, then me and Cherokee Jim 'til two, you and the Cap'n 'til four, and Bear and Shelly from four 'til six. Bear set it up, Boss. Said he'll wake ever'body around five-thirty, if'n it do suit you."

Doc eased in beside the fire and Shelly handed him a plate of food. "Much obliged, Miss Shelly. I'll pass on the coffee. Might squeeze in a couple of hours of sleep before ten, while you young pagans chatter like birds."

Dobey nodded back toward Jackson. "You think he'll make it to morning?"

"You forget, Captain Walls, I am but a lowly dentist. That aside, I gave him enough laudanum to seriously dampen his heart rate. He just may live long enough for you to hang him, though you may not be able to tell."

"Tell what? Your fancy talk takes me in circles," said Melton. "Whether he's alive enough to truly appreciate the hanging. Perhaps I should have indulged myself with a dose; my ancient

bones ache from the hard ride over here."

Bear joined them. "Yeah. We come so fast, we couldn't talk. You gonna tell us 'bout your sister, Boss?"

"Not much to tell. She runs a whorehouse, and she stopped drinking and got big. Seems prosperous."

"Not too big," said Doc. "Voluptuous is the word for her. And damned pretty, to have such a scar-faced cossack for a brother. And I would hazard she carries some Hispanic blood." He lifted an eyebrow at Melton.

Melton stared at him. "If that means part Mex, you'd be right. Maybe one quarter. Same daddy, different mommas. So, you seen her."

"Not only did I see her, I proposed to her."

"Proposed what?" Buck tried for nonchalance, but spilled some coffee.

"After I re-stocked my medical supplies and purchased some condiments for Big William, I inquired about a brothel and was sent to the Gilded Lilly. You, Melton, must have just left. Not knowing Big Kate was your sister, I proposed she abandon this wretched cow town, bring several of her ladies, and join with me and Big William in our planned endeavor."

"Endeavor?"

"Project. Plan. You all know we intend to establish a sporting place, with gambling, ladies, good food and liquor. Across the river, so as not to offend Dobey's mother."

"What did she say to your 'endeavor'?" Dobey grinned.

Doc smiled. "I believe her exact words were, 'Do I look like some kind of God-damned idiot?' This left me somewhat apprehensive about my chances of success. When I told her where we were heading, and she realized I was riding with the Cossack here, it was all settled."

"So she's coming, after all?"

"Never in one million years, or so she said. And she explained that I was the God-damned idiot, rather than she, and said I should take my scrawny ass back to north Texas and rent out pigs, should I actually discover any horny men there with money or items to barter."

As the laughter died, Cherokee Jim came in for coffee. "Horses is a little nervous, but this drizzle is helping to calm 'em."

Dobey made Bear repeat the story of Melton bullying the storekeeper and the storekeeper's apology, and Melton insisted on hearing the details of Baldwin's capture and execution.

As Dobey finished, Cherokee Jim laughed and said, "As I slipped the noose over Baldwin's head, he whispered that we ought to try out the wife and daughter of the pilgrim. Said if they hadn't worn him out, we'd have never caught him sleeping like that."

Doc snorted, "Just a pair of fine, upstanding ladies, according to the pilgrim himself. Which proves again that man's reputation is always at the mercy of his woman. Well, I must begin my rounds. You children sleep soundly, as the old dentist watches over you, not unlike the Archangel Michael."

Melton grinned at Dobey. "Damn, he talks as good as you. Doc, you want my carbine with all this rain?"

"Thank you, Melton, but no. I'll keep my gun slung barrels down, and under my cape. Never fear."

THE BLOOD SMELL was diluted by the rain, but the noise of the rain allowed the bear to get close enough to strike. As his jaws crunched the neck of the newborn fawn, the exhausted doe sprang up and bolted away.

The bear ate the snack-sized morsel, and slept for a while.

THE PAIN WOKE Bobby Joe Jackson before dawn. His nose was killing him, his head throbbed from the laudanum, his side and stomach burned. He was soaked and cold to the bone and could not stop shaking. The squaw who had cut him was fussing over food and coffee at the fire. The rain had stopped.

"Hey," he whispered, not wanting to wake up and piss off the big Ranger.

"What you want, Cher?"

Jackson swiveled his head to the right and up to find the black man standing over him with a brass-framed rifle. "Food. Water," he rasped, "maybe some more of that stuff the doc gave me."

"Doc's asleep, Cher. Food or water, they might kill you with that cut gut. Don't want to miss your hanging, do you?" Bear smiled down at him. "Tell you what. I'll have my woman damp your mouth some, soon does she finish the food. Mean time, you should scoot you-self around to other side this tree, watch them woods down there, look out for the other bear. Me, I got to go check the other side of the camp."

It took Jackson ten minutes to slide halfway around the tree, and then he fainted. He woke to find something cool and wet on his face and lips. As the squaw withdrew the cloth, he said, "Help me get slid around so's I can watch for the bear."

She grabbed his belt over his left hip, and with two grunts had him facing down hill. He fainted again, as fresh blood soaked his pants and side. A cold gust of wind blew over the hill, and the bear woke to the scent of smoke, bacon, coffee, and blood….

* * *

SHELLY TOOK a cup of coffee across camp to Bear as he stood near the horse picket line. "Will you watch over me now, as I make water?"

"Merci, ma Chere. Is good, this coffee. Yes. You go there to those close bushes, you see? Maybe you come back, you stand here and help me wake up, no?" He took her hand and rubbed it on his groin.

Shelly squeezed him and said, "I will be quick before others wake." She hurried to the bushes, pulled off her coat, lifted her deerskin dress, and squatted. At the same moment, the bear attacked.

* * *

JACKSON DREAMED he faced a huge wild-eyed, pig-faced, open-mouthed nightmare. *Bad dream,* he thought, but then the nightmare took his head in its mouth and tugged, trying to turn and run. Jackson screamed. The ropes held.

Bear, running around the picket line, was kicked senseless by Melton's rearing, bucking bay. As the others scrambled out of their shelters on their knees, searching wildly for guns, boots, or consciousness, Shelly raced back through the camp carrying her coat and shouting, "Bear. Bear." She ran by her unconscious man, unnoticed in the darkness.

The bear, having taken Jackson's head in his mouth, could not open his jaws wide enough to release him. Wild-eyed, grunting, the bear pushed against the tree with its right forepaw, while he shook his head violently, trying to pull Jackson loose.

Shelly ran right at him, waving her coat and shouting, "Shoo. Shoo."

With his left forepaw, the bear swatted her,

knocking her down. Her right breast was nearly torn off.

Doc was closest, and when Shelly went down, he had a clear shot. Still kneeling, he got off both barrels of the ten gauge almost together. The first load hit the bear in the chest; the second was a direct hit in the neck… of Bobby Joe Jackson. With one more mighty wrench, the bear grunted and lurched away into the darkness.

Doc struggled to his feet, dropped the shotgun, and fired two rounds from his little Colt into the rump of the disappearing intruder.

Melton stepped up beside Doc, Winchester at the ready, but pushed down Doc's pistol. "He's gone, Doc."

Doc took a sharp breath. "Damnation. He just did not want to release our young Mister Jackson, did he?"

"He didn't," said Melton. "Prob'ly couldn't." He nodded at Jackson's twitching body.

A small red and white carrot jutted from the body's shoulders, where the head had been.

"Hurts," said Shelly.

Chapter Twenty

"ALL RIGHT, children, listen up. You've all heard the officers talking about some of this, and you've all heard or done some bitching about it. Here's the bottom line. Pretty soon, middle of November at the latest, the Seventh Cavalry will move out from our cozy little Camp Forsyth and set up a forward base about a hundred miles south." Sergeant Major Kennedy paused, looking around at the sergeants of the regiment. The tent was packed. "Anybody want to guess what it all means?"

Sergeant Boye grinned and said, "No more nearby Buffalo City whores and bars?"

Kennedy put up his hands to stop the laughter. "That too, John Boye, but much more. You all have seen Lieutenant Colonel Custer is back. His court-martial sentence was cut short by General Sheridan, so's he could take us on a winter campaign against the

Cheyenne. All eleven troops is going, along with five infantry companies under Captain John Page. Now, shut up, Goddammit, and let me finish." He had to yell the last part, as chatter broke out among the assembled non-coms.

"Jaysus, Walter, you said eleven. What troop is staying behind?"

"None of us here, Sergeant Vandusky. 'L' Troop is still up at Fort Lyon, Colorado Territory. And if you'd stay sober a day or two, you'd know that." Kennedy paused for the laughter again. "Anyhow, Custer has been busy. He's got us some winter gear, fresh horses, some medicos, thousands of Spencer rounds, a vegetable ration, and over five hundred New Model Army Colts."

"You serious, Sergeant Major? Did they remember ammunition for 'em?" Boye was serious himself, now. Since the regiment's formation in 1866, most of the troopers had fought without pistols.

"About a ton of paper cartridges, John Boye, and they even remembered primers. And only took 'em, what, two years? Fifty pistols to each troop, and they go to the fighters. Don't let me catch any cooks, clerks, bandsmen, or quartermaster types with one. I think they's enough old Remingtons around to cover the rest, but the Boy General is trying to get more Colts, so's ever'body can have one. So much for the good news." Kennedy took a deep breath. "The next won't set so well, but it is something that is going to by God happen, and we're the ones as will do it. We're going to organize the troops by the color of the horses."

There was total bedlam in the tent for several minutes. Kennedy lit a cigar and stared at the others until they calmed down.

"Sweet Jesus, I don't know whether you sound more like old women or officers with all your pissing and moaning. Hell, half of you was officers in the war, on one side or the other. Well, this is the way of it. We don't get to vote. The troop commanders will get to pick their colors, based on rank, but Custer has said we'll have four troops of bays, three sorrels, a black, a brown, and a gray, and the junior commander will get the mixture of what's left. Once the choosing is done though, we have to make it happen, and fast. There won't be no exceptions. Questions?"

"Scouts?"

"We got twelve or thirteen Osage. They hates the Cheyenne, and vicey-versus. Got Ben Clark as chief scout and California

Joe Milner, and a new one who was just in the Cheyenne's camp. Name of Penn. He'll lead us, once we leave the forward base."

ON NOVEMBER 12TH 1868, the Seventh Cavalry, its supporting infantry, and hundreds of wagons left Camp Sandy Forsyth. As 'H' troop rode out, Captain Benteen saluted the Boy General, and Sergeant John Boye waved to Sergeant Major Kennedy. The band struck up, "The Girl I Left Behind Me."

* * *

"WE LEFT MY WIFE BEHIND? WHERE?" Bear's eyes showed no sign of their former alertness, as they peered from under the huge bandage on his forehead.

"In Fort Worth, Bear. Yesterday. I done told you this twice. We had to leave Shelly 'cause she was hurt so bad. Even after Doc sewed her tit back on, 'scuse me, she was in bad shape." Buck could see the confusion on Bear's face. Somewhat confused himself, Buck continued. "She's being looked after by Boss Melton's sister. Melton wanted to buy a wagon and bring her, but the regular doctor in Fort Worth said 'no way'. We'll go back and get her in the spring."

"How'd she get hurt?"

"Jesus, Bear, you're scaring me. Big bear swatted her, damn near tore off her tit."

"But I'm Bear. Listen, Cher, I'm just trying to understand. Why would I hurt her?"

"You didn't. A big damn crazy man-eating bear done it, while she was trying to scare it away. You don't remember none of this? 'Cause we been talking about it for two days."

"What happened to the bear?"

"It made off with part of our prisoner. You remember Bobby Joe Jackson? Buffalo hunter, rode with Red? You don't? Well, what a surprise. Anyhows, me and Cherokee Jim tracked it at dawn and killed it, not a half mile away, whilst Doc was sewing up you and Shelly. The bear still had Jackson's head in his mouth. God almighty, Bear, it was you and Shelly that captured

Jackson. Shelly cut him, two ways – deep and continuous."

"All right, Buck, don't get mad with me. Me, I jus' need to understand. Capturing this Jackson - is this how I got hurt?"

"No, no, no. Jesus, Bear, listen to me again. Melton's horse kicked you, when Jackson screamed, when the other bear bit his head off. Doc thinks that's why you can't remember Jack-squat for three minutes now."

"Where we going, Buck?"

Buck sighed in exasperation. "Home, Bear. Maybe one hundred more miles to the Red River, then another hundred and fifty to Canadian Fort. Least ways, it's what Cap'n Dobey tole me."

"Canadian Fort. Tres bien. Be good to see my mama again. Eh?"

Buck stared at him in horror, then yelled, "Doc, you better drop back here and ride with Bear a while. I ain't doing so good with his questions."

Doc slowed his horse and fell in beside Bear, while Buck pulled ahead alongside Cherokee Jim. Farther ahead, Dobey and Boss Melton set a strong pace through the light snow.

"Bear, do you remember me now?" "Ah, oui, Doc. For sure. Why?"

"You didn't, for a while. A horse kicked you hard, in the head. Might well have killed a lesser man. You now suffer from something which I think is called amnesia, which just means you can't remember everything. And your mind seems to flip back about every three minutes. Is anything about the last few days coming back yet?"

"It is, Doc. Buck explained a lot to me just now, so it's starting to make sense. Except for one thing."

"What's that, Bear?" "Where's Shelly?"

Chapter Twenty-One

"I've just sent General Sully back north to Fort Harker, so you now have command of this expedition." General Sheridan was hunched over a mug of coffee in the mess tent of the newly established Camp Supply. "He should have let you follow that Indian trail we crossed enroute here."

Lieutenant Colonel Custer sipped his own scalding coffee. "Yes, General. I believe we might have back-tracked it, and found an undefended camp. Though I'd prefer to chase the war party, I know your wish is to destroy their bases, rations, and horses."

"Exactly," said Sheridan. "And you can begin that process tomorrow. I'll stay here, and wait for the Nineteenth Kansas Volunteers, though God only knows where they are. Take thirty days rations, and strike out at six tomorrow morning. Perhaps you can still cut that trail, though this blizzard may have wiped out a major chance."

"Sully wiped out that chance, General, when he wouldn't cut me loose. But we'll find them. Who goes with me?" Custer stood and stretched.

"Just your regiment. I'll keep the infantry and the nigger cavalry company here, and finish building. And I'll write Billy Sherman my thoughts on Sully. Will you find the Indians in this snow?"

Custer smiled, "It's our advantage. We can move and fight in bad weather. The Indians cannot."

Sheridan, squat and feisty, hated it when the lithe Custer stood over him. "All right, General," Sheridan spat, addressing Custer by his brevet rank. "Find them, and punish them. Now, get out of here and let me write some letters. It's what real generals do, you know."

Custer grinned and gave the little general an exaggerated salute. "Yes, Sir!"

* * *

"BOSS MELTON, how come the Cap'n didn't leave Bear back there in Fort Worth, too? He don't seem no better off than Shelly was."

Melton stared at Buck for a moment, during which time Buck realized he might have asked another stupid question. He shriveled somewhat.

"Well, Buck, you and Bear being such good friends, you might have noticed he's some darker than the rest of us." Melton nodded toward Bear, to insure that Buck knew that he was referring to the only Negro within eighty miles. They had halted for Doc to give Bear a powder for pain.

"Well, yeah, Boss, I know, but..."

"You figure them good ol' boys in Fort Worth were gonna take good care of an uppity Darky? 'Specially after I braced that storekeeper over him?"

"Oh. Yeah," Buck nodded. "See, I forget..."

"Well, don't. Use your damn head for something 'sides a hat rack. And where in the hell is that Cherokee Jim? He should'a been back by now. You see anything, Cap'n?"

Dobey scrambled back down the rocky outcropping to join them. "He's on the way in. Maybe five minutes out. Coming fast, but no one trailing him." Dobey put his telescope back in the saddlebag, and mounted. "We better be ready to ride, though, no matter what his news is."

CHEROKEE JIM DISMOUNTED and began unbuttoning several layers of clothing to relieve himself, even as he reported on his ride to Dobey. "It's them Mexicans, Cap'n. Same ones we come up on before. Easy for me to spot the fat one. They got several wagons of hides. Looks like they'll get to the next river before dark. Probably camp there."

" Yeah," said Dobey. "Be a good place, this side of it. I think it's the Wichita, or a fork of it."

Buck perked up. "The Washita? We that close to home already?" He wilted as he saw Melton's expression.

" Cap'n said, 'Wichita.' We ain't nowheres near the

Washita River or home, and your wishing it won't make it no closer. Dumbass, lost-soul Eastener. It'll please me no end the day you can find your own ass with both hands." Melton gave Buck a dismissive wave, then turned back to Cherokee Jim. "Go ahead on with your report."

"That's all I seen, Boss."

Dobey asked, "Anybody trailing them?"

"No, sir, Cap'n. I rode a circle around 'em. Used Boss's scope to check their back trail, too." Cherokee Jim handed the scope back to Melton. "There is more snow coming, though."

Dobey looked at Melton, who shrugged. "No reason to skirt around 'em, Cap'n, that I can see. Whyn't we just meet 'em at the river?"

"Good plan, Jimmy. See have they seen any of our missing culprits. Be good if we could get 'em to make some resupply runs to Canadian Fort, too. You know, trade 'em skins for guns and food and such."

Melton gave Dobey a rare grin. "So, what you saying, Cap'n? You don't cherish pushing a wagon, three-four hundred mile, back and forth among the Comanche?"

Dobey took a pull off his canteen. "And Kiowa. And Dog Soldiers. And snakes, and bears, and snow and prairie dog holes."

"Murderous scoundrels," added Doc. "Ornery lawmen," said Buck.

Cherokee Jim finished relieving himself, and remounted. "Freezing rain has always been my favorite. What about you, Bear?"

Bear smiled, looking around. "Where's Shelly?"

* * *

MANUEL ROSARIO NODDED and passed his tin cup for another serving. "*Chili con carne*. That's very good, Senor Book. I better have some more, before Poco Tino finishes it. *Por favor*." Hearing his name, Tino stuck his plate out for his third helping.

Buck dished out the thick stew. "Buck," he said. "My name's Buck."

"Si, Senor. Tha's what I said, Book." He took the steaming cup. "*Gracias. Madre de Dios*, this would be good on a hot day on the Llano Estacado, but here, on this cold night, you are *los angeles*."

"Say what?"

"He is saying you're an angel," put in Doc. "I've often had the same thought."

"Si, angels. But maybe not to gringo buffalo hunters, no? You played a pretty good trick on us with that guard you left at the wagon," Rosario said.

Poco Tino laughed, and jabbed his spoon toward Melton. "Hanging around. That was a good one. You hang any more *hombres malos*?"

Melton said, "We hung one more, then cut one and fed him to a bear. Still missing two of 'em. You see any more of them two?"

Rosario put his cup down. "They called each other Red and Penn. Said they were riding to Fort Worth, but Little Rock had some men track them. They circled back to *norte*. Caught a herd of cattle, this side of the Rio Canadian."

BEAR, bored and confused by the conversation, decided to look for Shelly, and wandered away from the fire toward the river. He soon spotted her under a tree and rushed her, shouting, "Ma Chere! Where you been? Where you been?"

To his amazement, she spun and clubbed him with a carbine butt. He stumbled sideways two steps, hit a log, and went over the embankment into the freezing Lower Fork of the Wichita River.

* * *

THE STARTLED GUARD, vaquero Benito Cruz, had not anticipated an attack from behind, not with the fire only forty yards away, and certainly not from a giant. There'd been no time to turn, cock and fire his Remington. He'd done well to side step the charge and buttstroke the man. Now he ran toward the fire, shouting a warning in Spanish, praying he wasn't too late.

"Jefe! Tino! They're trying to pick us off. They're robbers, compadres, I'm coming…"

Blinded by the fire, Cruz hit some dead wood and went down. As he fell, he triggered the Remington, and the fat rimfire bullet creased Tino's leg before smashing into the cook-pot and fire logs. Sparks and chili con carne flew.

Rosario yelled, "He's one of mine," and scampered to kneel by Cruz, drawing an ivory-handled Colt as he moved.

Dobey and Melton both yelled, "Hold fire." There was no more firing, incoming or otherwise.

* * *

AS ROSARIO QUESTIONED Cruz in Spanish, Melton checked the perimeter and Dobey looked to his own men.

Cherokee Jim and Doc knelt beside Buck, sitting against a tree trunk, facing the fire. There was a smoking hole in his coat, and a dripping red stain on his shirt underneath. He looked up at Dobey, and gave him a wan smile.

"It don't hurt, none at all. I'll be all right."

Doc muttered, "Shock," then, "All right, Buck, we're just going to lay you down here, get this shirt open and have a look."

Melton came up, moving low. "Ain't nothing moving I can see, Cap'n. Mexicans is covering the river." He glanced at Buck, "Oh, Jesus."

Doc said, "Yes. Get your whiskey, Cossack, and my little bag."

Rosario yelled from the other side of the fire, "My little Benito says he was charged by a giant, and he knocked the giant into the water. My men will check the river. Stay careful."

Dobey looked around. "Anybody seen Bear?"

Melton again said, "Oh, Jesus," and started running for the riverbank.

Dobey was right behind him, shouting, "Rosario – tell your men not to shoot. The giant is one of ours."

* * *

"DO you think I am healing fast? I have always been a fast healer, even after I had my babies. The first ones did not live, but now I have a good one. A boy. I hope he is a fast healer, too. Little boys get hurt a lot. This is good coffee."

Kate smiled, "Well, Shelly, maybe if you didn't talk so much, you could finish it 'fore it ices over." The two women were sitting by the stove in the kitchen of the Gilded Lilly.

Shelly gave the big madam a sheepish grin. "Yes. My husband says I chatter like a prairie dog. Your brother says so, too. I like your brother. Others are scared of him, but he's a good father. He was a good husband, too. He's a little crazy now, because those men killed his woman."

Kate snorted, "Yeah. He ain't 'specially tolerant of men who hurt women. I guess she was a good one?"

"Oh, yes. Very much good. You know she was my mother-of-law?"

Kate stared, agape. "You mean, mother-in-law?"

"Oh, yes. She was my Bear's mother, but she was not black, like him. He is like my coffee, but she's like yours, with cream in it. Or she was. I miss her." Shelly suddenly teared up and bowed her head. "She was not as dark as me, and her daughter is more like you."

"Jaysus. Jaysus wept. So, so, let me get this straight. This makes my brother sort of your father-in-law? I must be your aunt or cousin or something. Jaysus,

Shelly, we're some kind of relatives. I don't have none others, 'cept Jimmy. And you got a son?"

Shelly nodded, "Are you mad?"

"Lord, no, Child. It's just that I didn't know I had any family left, 'til Jimmy showed up this week. I'm just having trouble taking this in. It's coming a little fast."

"There's more," Shelly said. "My Bear has a sister, Honey, and she's married to Boss Melton's partner Dobey, and they got a baby girl. Dobey's got a mother and a brother there, and the brother got a Mexican wife. Oh, and she have a sister. It is her which is keeping my little Black Dog and Boss Melton's little Mikey."

"So, Jimmy's boy is Mikey, and he plays with your puppy?" "Oh, no. We don't have no puppies. I did not tell it good. See,

Black Dog is my son." Shelly paused, her brow furrowed in thought and some pain. "We need to get some real dogs. They are special good for warnings and stew."

They heard the front door slam, and a gust of cold air billowed the doorway drape between the kitchen and the parlor. A man yelled from the other room, "Anybody up yet?"

Kate muttered, "Oh, hell," then in a louder, sweeter, less sincere voice, "In the kitchen, Deputy. I'll be right out." She whispered to Shelly, "Shh. Stay here."

The drape was brushed aside and a scar-faced man stepped in, stamping his boots to knock off the snow and mud. "Kitchen's fine, Kate. I was hunting coffee, anyways. Oh, my, what we got here? Fresh blood?" He grinned at the Indian girl.

Kate stepped between them and handed the man her coffee mug. "It ain't that way, Deputy. She's Miz Shelly Weathers, and she's getting over a bear attack. She ain't a working girl. My brother asked me to look out for her. Shelly, say hello to Deputy O.C. Pell, a small but vocal part of our police force here."

Shelly smiled and nodded, as the lawman gave her an open leer. "Yeah, right. Soon as you're feeling better, you let me know. I'll let you teach me some Indian tricks. Ain't had a squaw in a while. Matter of fact, I don't see nothing wrong with your mouth right now."

Shelly kept smiling, but placed her pistol on the table between them.

"Back up, O.C. I told you she ain't for rent." Kate moved out of the line of fire.

The front door banged open and shut again, and a shrill voice said, "God Almighty, it's cold out there. Ain't that Pell's horse outside? Pell, you here? You been summoned." The speaker, a small blond woman, pushed into the kitchen. "There you is. I just come from the sheriff's room. Said if I seen you to send you. He thought you might be here, sniffing around." She winked at Kate and Shelly, and pulled off her coat.

"Don't reckon you saved me any, did you, Saw-Tooth? Did the sheriff wear you out?" The deputy turned toward the blond but his eyes kept flicking back to Shelly's pistol.The young woman poured herself some coffee and replied over her shoulder, "I done told you, O.C. Anytime you got the money, come on by. You'd be total amazed how friendly I become."

He snorted, "Bet you didn't charge the sheriff

nothing."

She turned and gave him a sweet smile. "Well, that's his business, ain't it? But I'll tell him you asked. He did say for you to hurry on. Probably wants you to fetch him some breakfast."

"I don't fetch for him, Goddammit," he blurted, as he stormed out. "And I won't stand for no squaw to pull no gun on me, neither."

As the door slammed behind him, Kate grinned and said, "Actually, O.C., you just did. Well, weren't he touchy? Shelly, this here's Saw-Tooth Alice, my best whore and the sheriff's favorite. Alice, meet Shelly Weathers."

Alice nodded and said, "Nice pistol. Was he trying to push a free poke at you, too?"

Kate's laugh was throaty and real. "Oh, yes. And you should'a seen his eyes when she eased that .32 into sight. Well, let's see. Shelly here was with her man, who's my brother's son-in-law. Them and some others run into the man-eater ever' body's been fretting over. He 'bout tore off her teat, 'fore they chased him off and killed him. I told 'em Shelly could lay over here 'til she's better. Her man is hurt too, but since he's blacker nor the ace of spades, my brother didn't think it would be good to leave him here. What with all the local tolerance and all."

TINO SAW HIM FIRST. The giant was clinging to a dead tree in fast water, thirty yards downstream from the attack on Benito Cruz. The white head bandage, now around his neck, gave him away.

"There he is, Jefe," Tino shouted in Spanish. "You want me to shoot him loose?"

Rosario yelled, "No, no, no shooting, compadres. The gringos say he's one of theirs. Cruz, get a lariat and pull him in."

Bear was fully conscious and even able to walk once pulled ashore, but his teeth were chattering too much for him to talk. Melton took over.

"Get him to the fire. Get some more logs on the fire. Help me get him out of these wet clothes. Goddamn, do I have to do everything? Bring my brandy. Doc, look at his head. Get some damn blankets on him, will you? And hang these clothes on sticks to dry. We ain't got all night."

Even Dobey scrambled for firewood, as the Mexicans stared in amazement. Buck dropped a two-foot log on the fire, sending up a shower of sparks.

Melton glared at him. "Thought you was bad shot. I seen your innards."

"Not exactly," muttered Buck, and hurried away for more wood.

Melton turned to Doc. "Whose blood was it?"

"Nobody's. Except for a spark-hole in his coat and a greasy shirt, Mister Buck Watson's just fine, thank you."

"Lemme guess. His own damn stew?"

"Rather quick thinking, for a Cossack. Yes. Tomato sauce, mixed with pieces of prairie dog meat and peppers to help fool a poor old dentist."

"Fooled me too, Doc. How's Bear?" Melton handed

Doc the brandy, after taking a pull himself.

Doc poured brandy on the open head wound. Bear was shaking so badly it was impossible to tell whether he flinched. "The vaquero hit him just where he was kicked, and re-opened the cut, but it appears that the freezing water stopped it from bleeding much. As soon as he stops shaking so, I'll re-stitch it. Drink some of this, Bear."

Ten minutes later, Doc had finished his needlework and re-bandaged Bear's head. Across the fire, Poco Tino sat on a rock, pants around his ankles, as Rosario began to stitch the big man's leg. Doc walked over and offered Rosario the bottle.

"Gracias, Senor Doctor, but maybe I better wait til I finish this, no?" He smiled at Doc.

"Pour some on his cut and your hands now, then both of you can have some later. Perhaps his leg won't turn green and fall off."

Tino understood enough to say, "Listen to him, Jefe."

Bear suddenly stood, looked around and said, "Where's Shelly?"

Buck shook his head and said, "Oh shit, here we go again. Bear, it don't matter, 'cause you ain't gonna remember in five minutes no how."

Bear stared at him. "I know I been out, Cher. Last I remember, that hoof was coming at my head and some-body was screaming. I don't remember these Mexicans catching up with us, and me, I don't remember this river at all. The horse kicked me into it? It's just, why ain't my woman taking care of me? And where's the prisoner? Did we hang him already?"

Chapter Twenty-Two

MEOTZI GROANED AND TURNED OVER, trying to get comfortable. The child had been growing in her stomach for seven moons now, and comfort was harder to capture. She finally pushed off the buffalo robe, sat up and stirred the embers of the fire. Only then did she notice the other woman sitting across from her in the darkened tipi of her father.

Moon Calf wasn't really mean to Meotzi, but she was also not Meotzi's mother. She had died years ago. Meotzi's father, Chief Little Rock, had taken Moon Calf as his woman back then, and they were nice enough to let Meotzi live with them now since her own marriage had not worked out. Meotzi suspected that Moon Calf was a little scared of her, unsure who held the greater standing with Little Rock.

Moon Calf laid a small log on the fire. "It is not very late. You sleep a lot now. It would be better if you had your own tipi. You should not have shot your husband.

You are fifteen summers old, your baby is coming in two moons, and your father and I are too old to have a crying child here with us."

It took a lot of Cheyenne words to say all that, and by the time Moon Calf finished, Meotzi was awake and testy.

"Did my father say this? Anyhow, I didn't kill my husband. I only shot him in the leg. I am certain I will have a new husband soon."

"But your father had to give him back all those ponies. You had to leave his tipi. Why did you shoot the man?"

Meotzi shrugged. "Because I was carrying his baby, he wanted to take me from behind. It hurt. I told him to stop. He said I belonged to him, and he could do whatever he wanted. He hit me. I shot him. He stopped."

"Well, you are a spoiled young woman. And lucky your father was here to take you in, and willing. What if this were not true?"

Meotzi thought about that. "I might have done things differently. I think one does what one has to do, to live." She smiled. "I'm glad I didn't have to stand for such treatment. Or bend over for it. Where is my father, anyhow?"

Now Moon Calf stirred the fire. "Little Rock does not talk to me like he talks to you. But I overheard there were problems at the peace meeting at Fort Cobb. Black Kettle and Little Rock just came back from there, and Black Kettle asked Little Rock to go down river to the other camps and warn them, and ask if we can move closer to them, tomorrow."

"I am sorry my father must go riding at night in this snow. What is the warning? Do you know?"

"The White Chief at Fort Cobb said he couldn't promise us safety, even if we don't want to fight. Black Kettle said the White Chief was mad because the Dog Soldiers from the other camps are still raiding up north of here."

Meotzi shifted as the baby stretched. "Yes. Some boys from our camp are riding with the Cheyenne and Arapáhoe Dog Soldiers right now. Black Kettle and my father cannot control wild boys. Aieeyah, this is crazy. The Dog Soldiers won't let us camp near them, because Black Kettle and my father want peace. They have threatened to kill all our ponies if we come closer. And because we want peace with the Whites, we are in danger of being attacked by them because our few lodges are up here away from all the other camps, and the Whites think we all look alike. Don't you remember four winters ago at Sand Creek?"

Moon Calf frowned. "I think we should move down closer to the others. We are only fifty lodges, maybe one hundred fighters. And I think the Dog Soldiers are just making big talk. No one would kill eight hundred ponies. How could they? They can't even kill eight hundred buffalo."

"I hear horses now. Many of them. It must be the raiding party coming back."

The two women put small robes around their shoulders, and went outside. The snow had stopped but it was several inches deep. It was a crisp, clear night, lots of stars, a big moon, but biting cold. A few yards away,

Black Kettle and his wife stood with his sister Mahwissa in a muted discussion outside Mahwissa's lodge. As Meotzi and Moon Calf approached them, the raiding party suddenly let out a few yips and thundered away downstream toward the other camps, out of sight around a couple of bends in the river.

The few young raiders from Black Kettle's camp dismounted and began their loud reports of the raid to any and all nearby. One Kiowa boy, Follows The Enemy, detached himself and walked over to Black Kettle.

"Are you all good, Chief Black Kettle?"

"Yes, Follows The Enemy. Thank you for asking. My Cheyenne boys seem afraid or ashamed to approach me with a report. Did you lose anyone?"

"No, Chief. I was not with them. I was hunting alone. As for them, they took some horses, killed a few cows. It was a good raid. I think there will be much celebrating and dancing tonight."

"You are a respectful young man. Thank you for your report and courtesy. Have a good time tonight."

"Yes," added Mahwissa, "everyone thinks that you are a fine young man, and we are happy to have you stay with our camp. Enjoy yourself. All the girls will want to dance with you tonight."

"Thank you. Nice words, but no dancing for me. Chief, our scouts reported Bluecoats out in force, maybe coming this way. I'm going to go to my little dugout in the valley wall, sleep hard and fast, and move downstream with my horses early in the morning, closer to the other villages. You should, too."

Black Kettle nodded. "Yes. But the others won't let us come. Myself and Little Rock and a few others are going to ride out and try to find the Bluecoats tomorrow, and tell them that we don't wish to fight. That is what the White Chief at Fort Cobb said to do."

Follows The Enemy frowned. "Well, then, be careful. I think the Bluecoats do wish to fight, or they wouldn't be out in this snow."

Chapter Twenty-Three

"Don't look like we're gonna have a real daybreak today, does it, Dobey? Just sort of gone from black to gray."

"Fact is, Buck, you're right. I think maybe Boss Melton stared it down."

"The sun, you mean. I guess anybody could do it, it'd be Boss. How come he don't want it, Cap'n?"

"Ever since Bear got his mind back last night, he's been raring to go back to Fort Worth. To get Shelly, or at least stay with her 'til she can travel. Doc means to go with him. Melton doesn't think they should go, so he'd like to put it off."

"Doc? Doc's going too?" Buck perked up some.

Dobey poured himself more coffee. "Yup. Says he's got to take care of Bear, which is true, I guess. But I think he wouldn't mind passing some more time with Melton's sister, too."

Buck went on full alert. He glanced at Melton, who was still out of earshot. "That, uh, whore, Cap'n?"

"She's a madam, Buck. There's some difference. I 'spect she was one on her way up, but now she runs the place. Prob'ly doesn't help her girls with the working part."

"Why?"

"She doesn't have to, Buck. They don't do it for fun." "Then how come Doc wants to spend time with her?"

"He's going to try to get her to bring her girls to Canadian Fort. Try again, I mean. He tried it already, but she didn't seem stuck on the idea, exactly. Sort of told him to go piss up a rope." Dobey poured the dregs of the coffee on the small fire and stood up, stretching.

"You think there's more to it, Cap'n? I mean, what's the difference? It ain't been but a few days." Hope, long suppressed, was exploding in Buck's chest.

"Who knows, Buck? Maybe it's more than business. Nobody likes being turned down."

"Who don't know that?" In his mind's eye, Buck already faced a doleful Junebug. *Who'll take care of me now, Buck? Who can I trust?*

"Guess we better say our farewells," Dobey said, as Buck snapped out of his reverie. "Mexicans look like they're ready to roll."

"Yessir, Cap'n – I mean Dobey. Leastways it's good Doc and Bear can ride with Rosario and his boys. They is going on to Fort Worth, too, ain't they?"

"Yeah, Buck. Said they'd probably sell all the hides there, split up and visit their families or girlfriends a while, then load up with supplies and head up to see us after the snow. Told 'em we'd have plenty of hides by then."

Bear and Doc were mounting as Dobey and Buck walked up. Melton handed Bear the rope from the spare horse.

"We'll watch out for your boy, since you're bound and damn determined to do this," Melton said, glaring at Bear. "I ain't sure you ain't ruint your brain."

Bear grinned at him. "Me, I'm fine now, Boss. Must have scared you good while my mind was gone, but you know, was you in my place, you'd go too."

Melton shrugged. "Maybe so. Anyways, maybe it'll work out y'all can come back with these same Mex's."

"Seem like a good outfit." Dobey said. "If that doesn't work out, try to hook up with somebody else. I hate to think of just the three of you making the trip alone."

Doc smiled at him. "Well, we may be accompanied by a wagonload of working girls."

Melton snorted, but Buck said, "I surely hope so, Doc. And don't you worry none about Miss Junebug. I'll keep an eye on her for you."

Buck thought the look Doc gave him was sort of sharp, and hoped he hadn't overplayed his hand.

Doc nodded slowly, and said, "Yes, I'll bet you will." He suddenly slapped his thigh with his gloves, and added, "You take good care of her."

Buck had no idea what he meant.

AS THE WAGONS began creaking out of the camp,

Rosario rode past and touched the brim of his sombrero. "Hasta luego, compadres. A little later, no?"

Dobey nodded and saluted him. Melton turned away and yelled, "Load up, girls. We don't want to get caught in no blizzard."

Chapter Twenty-Four

HENRY WATSON WATCHED the two men ride in and tie off across the street. They had the look of Easterners, maybe lawmen. He didn't know what it was that gave him the impression, but he knew they weren't locals. Didn't much care, anyways. He was just enjoying some coffee on his front porch on a cold afternoon, relaxing after his regular noon crowd had eaten their chili and left.

A boy was sweeping in front of the hardware store. The two strangers spoke with him for a moment, then turned to stare at Henry. One of them tossed the boy a coin, who then untied their mounts and led them toward the stables. The two men crossed the street straight at Henry.

Hazel Watson brought out the coffee pot to warm Henry's mug as the men approached. "My stars, Henry, it's biting cold out here. Don't you want to come back in now? Me and Button has about cleaned up."

"Maybe too soon, Missus. I 'spect these gents is looking for hot food. Just rode in. Still got snow on 'em." Watson stood as the men clattered up the three steps. "Howdy. As I just spoke to my missus, I 'spect y'all are looking for a hot bite of food."

"What you got, old man? Anything better than beans?" Watson smiled, even though he was somewhat taken aback

by the rudeness. "Ain't got anything but beans. We do, howsomever, mix 'em with red peppers, tomatoes and wild meat. Onions too." He'd learned not to say prairie dog meat. "It's right good."

Inside, the riders pulled off slickers to reveal at least two pistols on each man. Ten minutes later, Watson brought their second serving. "It's all right then?"

The heavier man wiped his mouth and looked Watson over. "It's damned good, is what it is. Set a spell. Talk with us. Maybe your old lady can bring us some coffee."

The man's tone made Watson nervous, but he sat. Felt strange, being ordered about in his own place. Probably an officer in the war, thought Watson. Or maybe a sergeant.

"Been here long? I mean, running this place?"

Watson nodded. "Late sixty-five. Came out after the war." "We looking for some people come out then. Most people as pass through town eat here?"

"I don't know about most," Watson said. "A lot do. Maybe most. What are y'all, some kind of law?"

"We're Pinkerton detectives. Private law, but on

government work. Looking for some murderous rebels, two of 'em, maybe traveling with some darkies or breeds. You seen anything like that?"

Watson swallowed hard. Buck had warned him to watch for this, but it came on so fast he just couldn't think. "Well," he gulped again, "they's been a mess of rebels through here..."

He was interrupted by the slamming door. The gust of wind that came with it was cold, but not enough to explain the terrible chill he felt.

RED STOOD JUST inside the door of the cantina or whatever the hell it was, and slapped snow off his slicker with his gloves as he surveyed the place. Three men at a table, food in front of two of them, a nervous woman in the kitchen doorway.

"What's it take to get fed around here? Been weeks on the road from Camp Dodge, eating nothing but army beans and stringy buffalo meat, and I'm standing here starving to death, several seconds at least." Red gave them his best grin. "Maybe I could borrow somebody's horse and go somewhere hospitable?"

The man without food jumped up. "Yessir. Yessir. I'm truly sorry to hold you up like that. Just set down right here, take my place whilst I run you in some stew. Coffee, too?"

Red nodded and tossed his hat and slicker over a chair near the Franklin stove and limped over to the chair before examining the other two diners. When he did, alarm bells went off in his brain.

"Well sir, looks like I picked a safe place to set. Y'all county or town law?"

"Neither," said the burly lawman, giving Red a slow look-over.

"Well, I be go to hell. U.S. Marshals, by God? I know y'all's the law."

"Naw, not them neither." The lawman pushed his bowl away and pulled a handkerchief to wipe his mouth. "We're on U.S. business, but we're Pinkerton Agency detectives. You heard of us?"

Red nodded thanks to the storekeeper as he brought a bowl of stew and a mug of coffee, then withdrew. "Oh, yeah, y'all are right famous. That big eye that never sleeps, right? Must be serious business, they put you on it." And at least it ain't got nothing to do with me, he thought.

The skinny lawman took a toothpick from a saucer on the table and began to work it while he talked. "We looking for a small gang, maybe some ex-rebels, robbed and murdered three men, some time back. Thought to of come this way. You hear anything?"

Red's mind raced. Government wouldn't have no interest in them three men we took down. No way. "All they did was rob and kill three men, how come the government to get involved?"

The bigger man leaned forward. "Did my partner say that was all there was to it?"

Red smiled on the outside. "Well, he didn't say no more than that. What else they do?"

Skinny ran his finger through his bowl and licked it, then laid a Starr revolver on the table. "Digging into my side," he said. "See, might be they's a marshal involved in this, too. Any of this starting to ring a bell?" Skinny glanced sideways at Burly.

Bells were going off like crazy, but only Red could hear them. That damn marshal from Mason's Landing. But he was a town lawman, not a U.S. marshal. Wasn't he? Red wanted to pull the badge from his pocket and look at it again. "Naw, 'fraid not," he said, faking calm. He took a bite, then turned back toward the kitchen, looking for another door. "Mighty tasty chili, ma'am." Back door must be in the kitchen.

Red's bowl was knocked in by his lap as Burly grabbed his coat and snatched Red's hideaway pistol. "Well, well, well, Slim, lookee here. You mark as the report said one of them dead Yankees had a sawed-off .32 Smith, funny serial number, come up missing too?"

Slim cocked the Starr and pointed it at Red's chest. "I did mark it too, Johnny. How's this one look?"

Johnny smiled. "Five-fifty-five. Ain't that a bad luck number? All this time, and this dumb sumbitch walks in and sets down with us. What're the odds of that?" He drew a Colt Navy and cocked it, leaving it pointing toward the ceiling. "Now where's the money?"

Money, Red thought, what money? What the hell's going on? I didn't get the little pistol from them dead men. He up-ended the table on the two Pinkertons as he stood and drew his Colt. The table splintered as Slim's Starr went off and the shot was almost deflected.

The mangled lead ball clipped Red's temple as he

caught splinters in the face and neck. He fired two quick shots through the table, got two grunts in return, then moved right, still shooting. He hit Johnny in the chest and the head, then shot Slim in the back as he tried to crawl from under the table.

Blood streamed down his face and through his red hair, his head throbbed, his heart pounded. *Don't nothing ever go right for me,* he thought. He picked up the superstition pistol and shot each lawman in the head.

The storekeeper had retreated into the kitchen. Red holstered the .32 and his Colt just long enough to pull on his slicker and pick up his hat, then pulled his Colt again and headed for the kitchen.

The storekeeper and a boy stood by the back door, to the left. On Red's right, the old woman cringed, biting her hand. She got bad nerves, Red wondered, or did she burn herself on that simmering pot of chili? His head was simmering too. "Boy," he said waving the Colt, "you just go bring my horse around back here, and I won't hurt these folks. Big bay, right out front, red blanket on the bedroll. Get on, now. Not a word to no one."

The storekeeper said, "Go on now, Button, do 'xactly as he says."

"But, Daddy…"

"Daddy? Your daddy? This here your mama too?" Red cocked the Colt as he pointed it at the whimpering woman. He shouted, "You want me to kill 'em?"

"Yessir—I mean, nossir, don't hurt 'em. Ain't no need. I'll get your horse."

"Do it and be quick and y'all will be fine." Red's head

was splitting with pain. As the door slammed behind the boy, he pointed the pistol at the storekeeper. "You know I just lied to your boy. Y'all just seen too much…" He hesitated, put his hat on a table, then pulled the old badge from his coat pocket and held it up in front of the old storekeeper's face. "Lemme ask you something first. Anything about this would make you think I was a U.S. marshal?"

The old man peered at the badge, then whispered, "Town Marshal. Nossir, I can't say as it would."

Red yelled at him, "Then why in hell is Pinkertons after me? Shit. Now y'all really seen too much." He dropped the badge back into his pocket, swinging the pistol toward the old woman as he did. "Time's up," he grinned.

Red screamed as the chili was dumped on his head, scalding his face and eyes. His shot went into the floor, and he stumbled out and went face down into the snow. He wiped his face and eyes, lurched around the corner, and ran into the boy pulling his horse through the alley. He jerked the reins away and mounted.

"What've you done?" The boy backed against the wall, yelling at him.

"My head's on fire, damn you all." Red leaned close, put his barrel against the boy's forehead and snapped on an empty cylinder.

"Nothing," he shouted. "Don't nothing go right." He holstered the empty Colt and lashed the bay south. As he disappeared into the driving snow, he heard the boy yell, "Kill him, Daddy, kill him."

The air around him sizzled with buckshot as he

heard the twin booms. He felt several stings in his arm and back. His horse stumbled but kept going. He held on. "City people," he sobbed, "they ain't no damn good."

Chapter Twenty-Five

"So, you think these is them same Cheyenne you seen when you come through?" Sergeant Boye whispered as he stamped his feet. His arms were folded so he could keep his gloved hands under his arms.

Penn nodded and pulled off one glove to blow hot breath on his numb fingertips. "Got to be, Sergeant. I mean, we come in from more to the west and across the stream, but I seen this big knoll. It's them, all right." He changed hands.

The two men stood on a ridge less than a mile north of the Washita River. Six inches of crusted snow crunched beneath their feet as they shivered under a full moon, waiting for a dawn which approached every bit as fast as a snail. "A damned old crippled snail," muttered Sergeant Boye.

Sergeant Major Kennedy turned and said softly, "Say what?" About eight hundred men and horses of the Seventh Cavalry waited with them, strung out along the ridge. Strung out in more than one way, plus freezing and tired. Tension lay on them like a twenty-pound buffalo robe.

The previous day, Thanksgiving, the command had covered thirty miles in the snow, taken a one-hour break at 9:00 P.M., and arrived here around midnight, looking like a mile-long black

snake on the snow. No talking, no trumpets, no smoking, no jangling. They were tracking a party of maybe 150 warriors.

Boye grumbled, "Sorry, Walter. Thinking out loud, I guess. Has the Boy General decided what to do yet?"

Sergeant Major Kennedy rubbed his hands together and shrugged. "Oh, we'll attack 'em. He's down there along the river now, scouting them close and making his plan. Now that Major Elliott convinced him there's really a village there."

The scout Penn snorted. "Hell, Elliott trailed that war party here, must'a been thirty miles. Joe Milner tole me. Showed Custer the horse herd, hundreds of 'em, and he said they was buffaloes. Wouldn't believe nobody 'til he heard a baby cry and then heard them bells they puts on some horses. And all them yapping dogs."

"If we're gonna do it, I don't see why wait," Boye said. "Got a full moon, they're asleep, we ain't. Ought to just go right in amongst 'em."

Kennedy looked at his watch. "Be a good way to scatter 'em, which he don't want to do. Naw, he'll wait til closer on dawn. Wants to surround 'em, don't let none get away. He's down there right now figuring how to split us up. Still got several hours of dark."

Major Elliott scrambled up to them. "All right," he whispered, "I've briefed the officers. It's two o' clock now. I'm taking G, H, and M Companies, dropping behind this ridge and moving left. Work our way down to the river beyond the camp, cut 'em off that way. Captain Myers will go to the right with E and I Companies, come in from that side, and Captain Thompson with B and F will circle to the right all the way around to get on the far side. The General will lead A, C, D, and K right through the middle. If everybody finds their way, and we don't wake up the hostiles first, we'll hit 'em at daybreak. Signal will be the band playing 'Gary Owen,' or gunfire."

Kennedy nodded. "Any chance J Company and the main wagon train catches up afore morning?"

"No chance, Walter. Maybe the small train, those couple of wagons with Lieutenant Bell and the ammo. They're only a few miles back." Major Elliott swung into the saddle. "Let's get 'em moving. This moon is going to disappear in a couple of hours. I want to be in place before then and let the men get a couple of hours sleep."

As they started the careful descent into the valley, several baying dogs bounded into their midst. "What in God's name?" snarled Major Elliott. "Are we discovered?"

"Hell, those is Custer's foxhounds. We left 'em with the main train, back on the South Canadian. Must of broke loose and trailed us, what, twenny miles?" Boye said. The hounds swarmed around him, yapping and licking as he dismounted.

"Kill them," said Elliott. "Strangle 'em, cut their throats, before they turn us out and ruin the whole attack."

Two hours later, Custer's favorite greyhound also showed up and began responding to the dogs in the sleeping village. He was quickly garroted too.

Boye groaned. "I hate that. But I always said the damn dog talked too much."

Chapter Twenty-Six

THE GUNSHOT SOUNDED like it was fired beside her head. Before Meotzi could get to her knees, she heard yelling and some garbled bugle calls.

As her father strapped on his pistol belt, Black Kettle stuck his head in the tent. Little Rock said, "Did you shoot?"

Black Kettle shouted, "Yes. The horse herders warned me. Soldiers are upon us. Get out and run. I must warn my other wife and my sister."

Little Rock pulled his wife Moon Calf and Meotzi outside into the dawn as gunfire and screaming erupted through the camp. "Head downstream toward the other camps," he yelled and he was gone.

Chaos ruled. The morning mist was torn by dozens, then hundreds, of gun flashes, and the mist itself was soon thickened by the pungent gunsmoke. Hundreds and hundreds of Bluecoats rode among the fifty or so lodges, firing revolvers left and right.

The crescendo of gunfire, men yelling, women and wounded screaming, and a thousand horses whinnying numbed Meotzi's brain.

Black Kettle's young nephew Blue Horse rode by and yelled, "Run. Run down river," then spun to fire his pistol at a Bluecoat officer, wounding his horse. The officer fired back, shooting Blue Horse from his mount.

Moon Calf pushed Meotzi aside as Black Kettle almost ran them down. He and Medicine Woman Later were on the big gray horse he kept tethered by his tipi. His wife clung to his back as they thundered by toward the river, and Meotzi heard her say, "I told you we should have moved last night."

Seconds later, man, wife, and horse were dead in the river, caught in a barrage of Bluecoat bullets.

Moon Calf screamed in shock, then yelled, "I will tell them we don't wish to fight." She stepped toward a mounted civilian with her arms open. He rode close and fired his Colt into her face, pivoted on his horse and fired at Meotzi, missing her. As the scout cocked again, the wounded Blue Horse struggled to his feet and grabbed the man's reins. The white man kicked Blue Horse away, shot him down, then shot him again on the ground.

Mahwissa appeared from the mist and smoke, grabbed Meotzi's arms and said, "Run with me."

They ducked around a tipi, then pulled up as a buck-skinned officer on a black stallion raced by; a tall civilian scout who rode with him pointed his pistol at them. Mahwissa held up her hand and said in English, "No shoot." The scout nodded his head and rode on.

"Why didn't they shoot us?" gasped Meotzi, as they crunched through the snow.

Breathing hard, the older Mahwissa said, "I think they saw we were not warriors. That first one was a chief."

"How can you know that?" Meotzi said.

"The way he rode," said Mahwissa. "He may be their main chief. But he was surely a chief."

To their left, many Cheyenne broke through the thin ice of the Lodge Pole River and tried escape downstream in the freezing water. Soldiers fired on them from both banks.

Meotzi said, "My baby will die in my stomach in that icy water. Let's run for the deep grass instead."

As they cleared the village, Black Kettle's second wife Mosaio ran out of her tipi almost beside them, and angled left toward the river. Her toddler son was slung on her back, and she pushed her two daughters, nine and six summers old, ahead. Suddenly she tumbled, shouting, "Amithneh!" The toddler flew over her head. Mosaio had been shot in the back. The older child Amithneh ran back and tried to raise her mother, while her younger sister picked up the toddler and ran to the river, shouting, "He's not hurt."

Mosaio's eyes were already glassing over. She said, "Run with the other women. Take care of your brother and sister. And don't look back."

Amithneh looked at Meotzi and said, "The bullet must have gone between my brother's legs." Tears pouring down her face, she stood and raced after her sister into the river. Behind her, Mosaio's face slumped into the snow.

Meotzi and Mahwissa broke to the right. In the deep grass along an old road they stumbled on Moving Behind, an orphan of fourteen summers, hiding with her old aunt.

"Come with us." Meotzi paused for breath. "We're heading down the valley to the other camps."

"No," said Moving Behind. "We'll stay here and play dead. One soldier already stopped and stared at us and rode off. We were staring back at him, just waiting to die. He must have felt pity for us."

* * *

AS THEY CLEARED THE VILLAGE, Captain Benteen wheeled his horse around and halted, breathing hard from the excitement of the dawn charge. Sergeant Boye pulled up beside him. "You all right, Colonel?" Boye addressed Benteen by his brevet rank.

"By God, that was a good charge, John Boye. Yes, I'm fine. I hated to shoot that youngster, but after he shot my horse I had no choice. Easy, easy boy." Benteen patted his horse's withers, then wiped blood from the animal's shoulder. Corporal Daniel joined them.

Sergeant Boye grunted. "Orders, sir? And I think I see the General up on that little hill with the chief of scouts." He nodded to a knoll just south of the village.

Benteen squinted through the haze. "Aye, that's him and Ben Clark. Corporal Daniel, spread the word. Stop shooting the damn women and start putting them in these tents. Boye, you go up there and see do His Majesty have guidance for us from On High. And Daniel, let me know if we lost anyone." Benteen lit a cigar.

On the knoll, Sergeant Boye nodded to Ben Clark and saluted Custer. "Top of the morning to you, General. And a fine charge it was. Colonel Benteen sends his regards. I don't think we lost anyone in our battalion, and we're putting the women and wee ones in them Indian tents down there. Any special orders for us?"

Custer seemed fidgety and ecstatic. "Yes, by God, it was magnificent." He slapped his leg with his gloves. "Captain Hamilton was shot from his horse right beside me, just as we entered the camp. I want to know his status immediately." Custer nodded toward a lieutenant, who saluted and rode back down into the village.

Returning to Boye, Custer said, "Yes. Well, Colonel Benteen knows what to do. He's an old soldier and needs no help from me. I wish that were true of others. You stay here with us, Sergeant Boye. I may need you to carry orders. The real work begins now, as we dig out the warriors and finish them."

Boye looked over at Ben Clark and shrugged. Clark handed John Boye a cigar and they both lit up.

For the next several hours, Boye listened as Custer took reports, bitched, and issued a stream of orders. "Put all the women and children in tents after searching them for weapons. Round up the Cheyenne horse herd. Tear down the unoccupied tents and put them in a heap. Collect all weapons and food and get a count. Get a count of the Indian horses. And blankets. And prison-ers." As time passed the Boy General became more testy. "Put Captain Hamilton's body in a wagon for return to camp. Pick out the best tipi and roll it up and put it in a wagon for me. Well, do it when the damned wagons get here. Must I explain everything? And just where the hell is our ammunition train?"

At one point, an officer asked about wounded women and children. Custer replied that if the ammo wagons ever got there, they would be used to carry Seventh Cavalry casualties back and therefore would not be available for Indian wounded; if the wounded were unable to ride, then they'd have to be shot, just like the wounded warriors. "Lightly wounded can go with us, of course. These people heal very quickly."

Later, the Chief of Scouts said, "General, look back there. That's Captain Myers' boys. Them and their Osage scouts is running down and killing women and children. Do you want that?"

"No, by God, I do not. Custer does not kill women and children. Ride there and stop them immediately. Take Sergeant Boye with you. When you've done that, find Major Elliot and get me an update from him." Custer snorted. "I don't know why he hasn't reported to me. He must have forgotten that he no longer commands my regiment. And see if my damned sergeant major is with him."

Sergeant Boye was surprised at Custer's petulance regarding Major Elliot.

As he and Ben Clark rode toward Myers' men, Boye said, "It ain't so much that he resents young Elliot. I understands that, right enough, but he shouldn't ought to be talking to us about it. That's just wrong. Ain't nothing right about it."

Clark nodded. "Custer can't stand the thought of anybody running the Seventh Cavalry but himself. Don't know as he can ever forgive Major Elliot for doing such a good job while the Boy General was gone."

Boye said, "Yup. Most everybody likes young Elliot, too. Half the officers don't hardly care for the Boy General."

They found Captain Myers and gave him Custer's orders, then turned east to look for Major Elliott and Sergeant Major Kennedy.

Boye said, "I think that's them up ahead. But Jesus, Ben, look around. This is like a giant fornication with goats. Ain't no focus, troopers riding this way, then that. Squads chasing Indian ponies, then leaving them and going after a few women and kids, then taking on two boys shooting arrows over a log. Jesus."

Clark spat, "Yeah, but we ain't losing men. And it is like trying to pick up water with an open hand. Keeps running through your fingers. Looks like Sergeant Vandusky's got a few rounded up over here."

Chapter Twenty-Seven

ALTERNATELY RUNNING and playing dead in the tall grass, Meotzi and Mahwissa made it across an open area. As they took cover in a ravine, old Pilar joined them, carrying a young girl.

Mahwissa said, "You old fool Mexican, you've been a slave so long, you run with us. Why didn't you escape to the Whites, instead running from them?"

"You know, you are right. I'm going to surrender right now." The old Mexican stood and walked out of the ravine carrying the girl and was immediately surrounded by troopers. Mahwissa and Meotzi raised their hands and joined him.

A sergeant said, "That a little girl?" Pilar smiled and shrugged.

In English, Mahwissa said, "He don't understand you. But yes, that's a girl."

The sergeant said, "Bring her here."

Mahwissa translated, and Pilar handed the girl up to

the sergeant. Pointing with his pistol, the soldier said, "Now tell the old bastard to run back up that gully he come out of."

Mahwissa explained again, and Pilar, looking confused but anxious to please, began shuffling through the snow back into the draw.

As two more White men rode up, the sergeant shot old Pilar in the back, then shot him again when he tried to rise.

* * *

STRIKER AND WEASEL watched from a hundred yards away, uphill in heavy foliage.

"Oh. Oh, did you see that, Striker? The Bluecoat shot old Pilar. Why would he kill one of our slaves?"

Striker shook his head. "Evil, like a water moccasin. He's a sergeant. We'll circle around, try to get close enough to kill him. Easy to track, with those falling yellow tipis on his arm."

* * *

"WHAT THE DEVIL were you thinking, Vandusky? He was a Mexican. Probably a prisoner hisself. He did what you asked. Why kill him?"

"You don't tell me what to do, John Boye. See, it don't matter to me. Brown nigger, red nigger, black nigger, who cares? Now, me and the boys is gonna take these two women and this here little split-tail right in them woods there, and have us a little taste. Ben Clark, you can join us. John Boye, you can take your highfa-lutin' ways and go straight to hell."

Sergeant Boye raised his eyebrows to Ben Clark, who nodded and drew his shotgun.

Boye said, "No, you miserable drunken, back-shooting son of a bitch, you ain't gonna do no such thing. I'm gonna trade your sorry life for that little girl's." He drew and leveled his Remington at Vandusky, and Ben Clark waved the sawed-off ten-gauge at the three other troopers.

"I'm with John Boye on this, boys," Clark said.

Sergeant Vandusky looked ready to gamble whether John Boye would shoot him while he held the child. He cocked his head and squinted against the blinding snow glare. "You pull down on me whilst I'm holding this baby? You shoot and I'll drop her."

Boye shrugged. "She'll live. You won't." Vandusky fidgeted and bit his lip. "Weighing your chances, are you, Van? I'll get off one shot afore she hits the ground, and two more while your unsnapping that holster and drawing that darling new Colt again."

The tension snapped when the older Cheyenne woman spoke. "I am Mahwissa. The old Mexican Pilar was our prisoner, a slave. He tried to surrender. He was a good slave. We called him White Bear, because of his hair." She lowered her head. "I am sorry. My fear makes me talk too much." She clutched the pregnant girl's hand.

While the others stared in surprise at so much English coming from the Cheyenne woman, John Boye dismounted, putting his horse between him and the mounted Vandusky. Boye's pistol was now resting on his saddle, unwavering, pointing dead at Vandusky's face.

Clark said to Mahwissa, "Why don't you take that little girl, and you and your pregnant friend come back to the camp with us?"

It was a near thing, but Major Elliot rode up at that moment with Sergeant Major Kennedy and a mixed section of men from several companies.

Clark said, "We got us a situation here, Major. Needs some defusing."

Elliot glassed the valley to the east and said, "There's a lot of escaping Indians yonder; come on, boys, let's take 'em in."

Vandusky dropped the child into Mahwissa's arms and sneered, "They's plenty more where that came from. And I ain't forgetting this, John Boye. Nor you either, Ben Clark." He rode off after Major Elliott.

Lieutenant Hale rode up at that point with another group of prisoners, a couple of troopers and the new scout, Penn. Elliott yelled back at Hale, "Here goes for a brevet or a coffin."

Hale saluted and said, "Go get 'em, sir."

Sergeant Major Kennedy stared after Elliott as he rode away. Finally Boye said, "Well, Walter, you coming back with us?"

Kennedy shook his head. "I've come right fond of the young Yankee major. I'll go keep an eye on him, I guess."

Clark said, "Y'all could be going into a hornets' nest down river. Penn, you go with 'em and report back what all you see."

Penn gave him a sour look and said, "Yes sir, Mister Chief of Scouts, sir." Kennedy and Penn soon disappeared into the trees behind Elliott, and John Boye's group headed back toward the Cheyenne camp. It was not yet 10:00 AM.

* * *

STRIKER AND WEASEL circled the hills south of the camp to keep an eye on the twenty Bluecoats who were starting down the valley. As the Bluecoats came out of the trees, they surprised two Cheyenne men in the open and shot them down.

"Aeeyah," said Weasel, "that was the boy Crazy and some old man. Can you tell who he was?"

"Maybe old Fool Man." Striker shook his head and clucked. "We must get closer."

As they worked their way down through the trees, they came upon a Cheyenne from one of the downstream camps; he was kneeling, holding a boy whose chest was pouring blood. Two other youths looked on from horseback.

"He's just a boy," said Weasel. "Aren't you Cut Arm?"

"I am. These are my three sons. This one dying is my youngest," moaned the father.

The boy looked up and winced. He said, "Keep my horse, Father," then coughed once and died.

Cut Arm kissed his boy and stretched him out. "No, he's going with you, son." He stood and walked to the boy's pony and fired his carbine into the animal's brain. The pony staggered sideways and collapsed against a tree, showering the men with snow. The warrior remounted and with his other two sons rode back into the fight upstream, shouting blood-oaths.

Walking onto the valley floor but staying in the bushes along the edge, Striker and Weasel saw that the Bluecoats had captured several women and children. On foot, they were no match for the speed of the mounted soldiers. While the main party continued downstream, two soldiers and a civilian scout started pushing the captives back toward the camp, and away from Striker and Weasel. One of these soldiers was the sergeant whom Striker wanted to kill.

"He's bleeding," said Striker. "We have to hurry. He may die before I can kill him."

Striker took off at a slow run. A creek ran through the valley floor toward the river and gave him some cover. Weasel grunted and started after him, muttering, "Sometimes I don't know if you think about the things you say."

MAJOR ELLIOTT RUBBED his chin and said, "Damn. I didn't shave. Tell you what, Sergeant Major, you take these seven and shepherd 'em back to the camp. Sergeant Vandusky can help you. He's hit and needs treatment anyhow. Penn, you go too. You need to tell Ben Clark and Custer that there's a bunch of mounted Indians in the hills, both sides of the river. Cheyennes and Arapahos. Got to be another camp down here somewhere. We'll run down them two boys that got away, do a little scout downriver, then come on back. You got it? All right, boys, let's go."

At this point the river briefly gave up its wild undulations and flowed almost directly east for some distance. The valley floor south of the river was perhaps a half mile wide. Thick trees and brush lined the river's banks, but the floor itself was flat and covered with buffalo grass, often three feet high. And snow. Lots of new snow. Penn's eyes were killing him and his head was splitting from the glare.

Kennedy, Vandusky, and Penn pushed their reluctant group closer to the river, taking a direct route back to Black Kettle's camp. Seeing a boy prisoner fooling with something under his blanket, Penn jabbed the boy with his carbine and said, "Give it up, boy."

The boy grinned and sheepishly produced an old Navy revolver. Penn leaned down and grabbed it away. Vandusky said, "Shoot the bugger."

Sergeant Major Kennedy said, "No need. Just keep 'em moving,"

Minutes later a female prisoner pointed to the bare feet of one of the children, and made signs of binding it. Kennedy said, "Oh, hell, go ahead," and they paused again while the child's feet were wrapped.

As they fretted, Vandusky said, "Hey, Sergeant Major, I think I seen a squaw over by the river. I'll go pick her up." The river was only two hundred yards to their right.

Kennedy said, "Hurry back." He began to circle around his prisoners.

As he rode away, Vandusky winked at Penn and

whispered, "What I'm gonna do is get me some squaw tail in them bushes."

Penn thought about going with him, but what he wanted more than sex was to get back inside that circle of seven hundred cavalrymen around the camp. He heard gunfire behind them and looked back to see Elliott's group run down and kill the two boys they'd been pursuing, a half-mile downstream in the open.

He also saw another group of women and children, maybe twenty of them, come up from the riverbank beyond Elliott's command and head downstream. Elliott's men let out a whoop and started after them, moving farther away. While that bothered him, something else bothered him more. As he stared down the valley, two warriors ran down the creek they'd just crossed, racing toward Vandusky, who was searching the bushes along the riverbank. There were Indians between him and Elliott's men. Sweet Jesus.

And as he spurred toward Vandusky shouting a warning, he saw the worst thing, the thing which chilled him to the bone. Four Arapaho warriors had crossed the river between them and the camp, and were riding hell for leather straight toward the Sergeant Major and his prisoners. The Indian ponies kicked up a chunky mist of snow. Penn wasn't sure where all the screaming came from; was it the Arapahos, or their horses? Or maybe him?

* * *

STRIKER HEARD the yell just after he and Weasel ran

behind the prisoners with the big sergeant and the scout. He didn't care. He couldn't believe his good fortune. The man he wanted had ridden off by himself and was now alone, looking for something or someone along the riverbank, not more than one hundred yards away. He heard Arapaho war whoops behind him and to his left, and glanced over to see four warriors on horseback bearing down on the prisoners, and the scout riding hard after him and Weasel.

Weasel spun and fired at the scout, and Striker saw blood and dust fly from the man's saddle. The scout immediately veered left and raced for the camp, cutting between the river and the Arapahos.

The creek bed curved away to run parallel to the river at this point, and Striker and Weasel ran up out of it. Their target, the sergeant who had gunned down old Pilar, was broadside to them, staring dumbstruck at the Arapahos charging the other sergeant, and at the scout fleeing upstream. If he'd noticed the two men charging him, it didn't show.

Weasel went down on his hands and knees and said, "Use me. Shoot him."

Striker dropped beside Weasel and braced his Sharps over the older man's back. The gun roared, and Striker stood upright to look over his smoke. He saw horse and rider tumble over the

embankment. He yelled, "Got him. Come on, old man!" He reloaded and sprinted forward again. Weasel reloaded too and crunched through the snow to catch up, heaving and blowing tired white breath into the frigid morning air.

PENN WAS TOO scared to look behind him, but he could see what happened to Sergeant Major Kennedy off to his left. His prisoners had broken and run toward the river, crossing somewhere behind Penn. Kennedy got off one shot toward the Arapahos and tried to chamber another round, but his horse bolted away from the screaming Indians. In seconds, they ran him down, counting coup on him with clubs, then dragged him down and swarmed over him.

Penn's heart was beating so loud that he could barely hear the shouting and screaming. He never even thought about going to help Kennedy. He glanced to his right to see if Vandusky was riding to escape with him, but he was nowhere to be seen. Those two Cheyennes must have hit him and me, he thought. All he knew was, there was blood on his leg and there were bad people behind him. Again.

* * *

AS THEY RAN up to the river bank, Striker yelled back at Weasel, lumbering along behind him. "Careful here, old man. I think I hit his horse, not him. He may want to fight."

Weasel grunted acknowledgment, but there was a flurry of female chatter from below the embankment. Cheyenne female chatter.

Without exposing himself, Striker yelled, "I am

Striker, from Black Kettle's camp. Did I kill the Blue-coat? Can you see him?"

"You killed his horse, but it landed on him," a woman yelled back. "It's on his leg. Hurry. He's trying to reach his gun."

Striker and Weasel cocked their carbines and scrambled over the embankment to find the sergeant pinned by one leg. He was wide-eyed in fear, trying to get to his Spencer, just out of his reach. A woman and a girl cowered against the embankment, shivering wet.

Striker counted first coup by whacking the soldier with the barrel of his carbine. Weasel hit the man too and said, "Second coup." He yanked the Spencer from its scabbard, then pulled off the soldier's carbine sling and slipped it on himself. As he clipped it to the Spencer, he said, "He should have used this. He is both mean and foolish." He pointed his Sharps at the man, who moaned and held his hands up. Striker turned to the females. "You are White Elk and Little Elk. Am I right? Little Rock's people, from our camp. Are you hurt?"

The woman nodded. "My leg is hurt. My daughter is helping me. We were running with Little Rock and some others, but I had to rest here. This Bluecoat had a pistol, too. He dropped it when they fell over the bank. It's there." White Elk pointed toward blackberry brambles near Striker.

Striker retrieved the Colt from the snow and checked it. "Pull him out, Weasel. Get his knife first."

When the sergeant was upright, Striker signaled him to drop his pistol belt and run away upstream, back toward his own people. The man looked confused and stupid first, then almost melted in gratitude. He turned and started limping upstream.

Striker shot the man in the back. The heavy Sharps bullet knocked the sergeant face down on the sandbar. Weasel walked over and spat on the gasping, writhing Bluecoat and said, "See how that feels?" He tossed the man's knife to White Elk. "Take his clothing. It's dry. When you're through with him, put him in the river. It's full of dead people and blood already, and we will have to move away from this place anyhow."

Striker offered her the man's pistol but she said, "No. You keep it, and take his ammunition too. Go help Little Rock, but leave your hatchet. We need it to finish him. Little Elk will bring it back to you when this fight is over."

Weasel was already jogging downstream carrying two carbines and a shot tube for the Spencer. Striker strapped on the sergeant's holster and belt, then grabbed paper pistol cartridges from the sergeant's saddle bag and ran too. Behind him, the dying sergeant began first to cry and plead. Then to scream.

Chapter Twenty-Eight

AFTER MAJOR ELLIOTT rode away downstream, Sergeant Boye and Ben Clark helped herd the several captives back toward the Cheyenne tent area. Clark constantly scanned the hills around them, grunting and pointing out different assemblies of warriors. On horseback.

"Them are fresh, and mounted," he said. "Some Arapahos and Kiowas amongst 'em. The ones we ran over, we got their horses right here." Clark gestured at the hundreds of Cheyenne ponies milling in several groups. "Means more villages downstream. I best go tell the Boy General."

Sergeant Boye nodded. "What about these horses, by the way? Ain't no way we can herd 'em all back, and if they's more hostiles coming, we needs to be easing away from here."

Clark pulled up. "Here's the thing, John Boye. Custer needs to kill these horses, but there's yet no sign of the ammo wagons, and these boys is burning bullets like pinestraw. I don't know as we got enough Spencer cartridges to hold off these hostiles, let alone kill seven or eight hundred ponies." He wheeled and rode off, shouting over his shoulder, "What the hell do I know? I just work here."

Boye grinned and yelled after him, "If you see Captain Benteen, tell him I'll hook back up soon's we deliver these prisoners."

Downstream behind him, Boye heard a flurry of gunfire. He looked over at Lieutenant Hale and jerked a thumb over his shoulder. "There's Major Elliott, carrying the battle to the enemy. You reckon he'll save any for us?"

* * *

SHORTLY BEFORE NOON, Ben Clark rode up to the knoll from which Custer was directing the battle, issuing rapid-fire orders, exulting in his quick and total victory. Repeating himself.

"No looting. If you have everything assembled and tallied, then burn it. Tents, robes, weapons, food, clothing, powder, tools. Bullet molds, axes, you name it, I want it destroyed. Except that one, that tipi right there, put it aside for the wagons, if they ever get here. And start killing their horses. Kill them all. Without their horses, they're ruined. Can't hunt, can't raid, can't fight, can't run. Can't move their camp. Did you see me shoot that one boy?"

Clark touched his hat brim. "I did, General, and he

were no boy. See now, though, on them horses, we might want to put these prisoners on mounts for the trip home, so's they don't slow us down or die in this snow. And we ain't got enough carbine ammo to shoot 'em all, nohow."

Custer slapped his leg with his gloves. "Cut their throats then. Hamstring them. We can't leave the horses unharmed. Where the hell is the ammo train anyhow? Somebody find Major Elliott and tell him I want him to put together a squadron to find those ammo wagons and bring them in."

Clark said, "Have to be somebody else, General. Elliott's gone down river with a section, chasing hostiles. And he'll find 'em or they'll find him."

Custer peered at him and shushed the officers around them. "What do you mean, Chief Scout? Are you trying to tell me something?"

Clark spat. "Yessir. They's fresh Cheyenne, mounted, mixed with Arapahos and Kiowas in them hills all around us. More coming from downstream steady like. Got to be several more villages downstream. We just stumbled on an outlier here." Clark pointed across the river to the hills from which the cavalry attack had been launched. "Lookee there. See 'em? Damn Indians just found them overcoats we left."

In preparation for the attack, the regiment had stashed their bulky coats on a hill a half-mile north of the river. The command group stared and cursed and shivered as the Indians shouted and waved the captured coats. The curses changed to cheers as the Indians suddenly scattered. The missing mule-driven ammo wagons raced through them and bounced down the snow-covered hill to the river, through it and into the camp. Cheers changed to panicked shouts as one of the wagons burst into flames. Troopers quickly unhitched it and turned it on its side, using snow to put out the fire.

Clark grinned. "That driver was riding that brake all the way down that slope, and the axle tar caught fire. I bet you couldn't drive a ten-penny nail up his ass with a sledge hammer right now."

Custer clapped him on the shoulder. "You see? Custer's luck still holds. I knew we needn't worry. Get that ammo out, get skirmishers out in all directions, and send a company to try to retrieve those coats. Have four companies start shooting those horses. As soon as the prisoners have mounts, of course, and spare personal horses for the officers. And make sure each prisoner has blankets, one for their horse and one for themself."

Clark noticed Sergeant Boye shepherding his group of prisoners by the foot of the knoll and trotted down to rejoin them. As he did, the new scout, Penn, galloped in from downstream.

"Where's Elliott?" Clark shouted.

Penn gulped air and dismounted. "I think I'm hit. Got blood all down my leg. Am I hit, Sergeant Boye?"

Boye said, "I think your horse is hit. Now where the devil is Walter Kennedy and the Major?"

"He, uh, he sent me to tell you they's Indians both sides of the river, and he'll come in directly he finishes his scout." Penn's head bobbed as he blurted out his report. "Said to tell Custer these was new ones, coming from downstream. He was fine. Going after some more of 'em, he was. Yessir."

"This was Elliott, right? And what of my boy Walter Kennedy?" Sergeant Boye leaned down and thumped Penn in the chest.

Penn frowned. "I ain't responsible for no Sergeant Major Kennedy. I just did what Major Elliott told me. And don't be thumping me. I don't have to take that. I ain't no soldier."

"No, for a fact you ain't." John Boye swung out of his saddle and handed his reins to Penn, saying, "Here. Hold these." Left-handed, he drew his revolver and clipped Penn's temple, dropping him. Boye turned to Clark and said, "Ben, you got a problem with that, seeing as he works for you?"

"Nope. Looked to me like he snatched your reins away from you."

Boye turned back to the dazed Penn, now sitting up. Boye cocked his revolver and placed the muzzle to Penn's other temple. "I ast you once, boyo. You're evading me. I think you run out on'em. Where's Kennedy? And gimme back my reins."

Penn said, "Jesus, Sergeant, last I seen him, Elliott had sent him to squire some women and kids back this way. He'll, uh, he should be here any time now. They was pretty squirrelly, you know? Jesus. I'm seeing sparks."

Clark spat out the piece of grass he'd been chewing. "Listen up, Penn. You go find Romero, help with the prisoners, and get you another horse afore the General kills 'em all. Take these prisoners with you, 'cept the one speaks English." Clark nodded to Mahwissa. "You come with me. You're gonna meet our chief."

Mahwissa said, "I saw you with him when you rode through our village at dawn. You almost shot me." She turned and spoke to the pregnant Cheyenne girl, who burst into protests. Turning back to Clark, Mahwissa pleaded, "Can she come too? She's family, and scared. I am teaching her your talk. She's a chief's daughter. Name of Meotzi."

"Bring her then. More the merrier, I always say. Get your head looked at, Penn. Tell 'em you was wounded in battle. Just don't mention who the battle was with. C'mon, John Boye, ladies, let's go meet the General." Clark nodded toward the command group. As they rode slowly up the knoll, Clark winked at Sergeant Boye. "Mister Remington makes a fine club, don't he?" He patted his own.

John Boye grinned. "It's why I kept mine, when everyone got new Colts. You whack a hard-headed sumbitch like that with a Colt, you'll knock your barrel loose for sure."

"Choose your tools careful, I always say. Here comes your boy Jim Daniel."

Corporal Daniel rode up and nodded to the chief scout. "Howdy, Ben. John Boye, Captain Benteen says see if Custer will let you re-join us. He's got the company running faints against the hostiles."

"Feints, James."

"It's what I said. Faints. Only they ain't fainting. We charge a little, they pull back, like they want us to follow. They've 'bout quit even shooting at us, 'lessen we's close."

"Scared of hitting our prisoners," said Clark. "Might be why they ain't rode over us yet."

Daniel drew up and looked at Clark askance. "Ride over us? With what?"

"I think they's more of them here than us."

Daniel's eyes widened as he considered that. Ben Clark was known for being more right than wrong. "Well, don't matter. Three times as many as us, still ain't no way they ride over the Seventh By-God Cavalry."

At the top, Clark made introductions. "This here's Mahwissa, General, Black Kettle's sister. Speaks passable English. Young'un's Meotzi, Little Rock's daughter. Black Kettle and Little Rock is the two chiefs of this village."

Custer stared at Meotzi. "Comely. Very comely, eh, gentlemen? Keep her separate, so they don't compare answers. I may want to interview her more, later." He grinned, then turned to Mahwissa. "Are there more villages downstream? Do you understand me?"

She nodded, and held up four fingers. "One big camp, three smaller, but bigger than us. Maybe this many chiefs," she held up ten fingers, "and only two here."

"So," said Custer, "eight more chiefs to deal with."

Mahwissa shook her head slowly, still holding up ten fingers. "No. This many. And almost all the Dog Soldiers are in those other camps."

Custer shrugged. "Well, at least we have all the horses."

She shook her head again. "No. These are all ours. They have many more, like the trees in the forest."

As that sank in, someone in the little crowd muttered, "Jesus. Jesus H. Christ."

* * *

AS THEY RODE to join Captain Benteen in the valley, Daniel said, "Don't sound too promising, does it? Tell you though, this morning Benteen had to send me to tell the boys no killing of women and children. You believe that?"

"Fearful, James. Where's the honor in it, killing defenseless ones?" Boye shook his head.

"That's what I'm saying, John Boye. I'd done rode right by a pair hiding in the bushes, first thing this morning. Looked up at me like they's sure I'd shoot 'em. Girl and a ol' woman."

"You take 'em in, did you, James?"

"Naw, John Boye. Hell, they looked so pitiful, I just left 'em."

Boye grunted. "They might not have been so sweet to you, was things turned 'round."

Chapter Twenty-Nine

STRIKER QUICKLY PASSED OLD WEASEL, and as he jogged down the edge of the river he heard shooting ahead. He ran into shorter grass and saw the band of mounted Bluecoats, only two hundred paces ahead, charging the slow group of women and children led by Little Rock. Little Rock turned and fired at the Bluecoats, and a young Kiowa warrior with him let fly four arrows. An even younger boy, a Cheyenne, was handing arrows to the Kiowa. The bluecoats faltered and swerved away, and Striker, still unseen by either party, stopped to wait for Weasel.

Weasel ran up, gasping. "I'm too old for this," he wheezed. "Five Arapaho crossed the river behind me back there, and they're coming up behind the Bluecoats. A little closer and we can attack from this side."

They ran again, gaining another fifty paces before the Bluecoats rallied for another charge. Little Rock stood to face them, pointing his revolver when a bullet hit him in the head, throwing a spray of blood. The Kiowa tossed his bow to the third man, ran forward, picked up the pistol and fired two shots.

"I know that Kiowa. His name is Trailing The Enemy," shouted Striker, and he fired too. As he reloaded, Weasel lumbered up, leaned against a small tree and loosed three quick shots from the captured Spencer. The gunsmoke hung thick on the cold valley floor, but Striker saw the troopers pull away, surprised by the flank attack, only to be hit by the mounted Arapahos that Weasel had seen. As the Bluecoats turned to face the new threat, another group of Indians charged them from the far side.

More warriors crossed the river behind Trailing The Enemy, and he sent the group of women and children on downstream . He jogged over to join Striker and Weasel and said, "I may have one round left in Little Rock's pistol. Can you help me?"

Weasel said, "Take my Sharps and this ammo bag. I'm about to die, carrying two guns and all these bullets, trying to keep up with young Striker. Let's move up on them. They've dismounted."

Striker nodded grimly. "We have them now."

As they fired and closed in, several Cheyenne and Arapaho warriors raced their mounts through the circle of white men, counting coups and scattering the Blue-coats' horses. The hot breath of men and horses added steam to the acrid layer of gunsmoke, as men grunted and cursed, groaned and yelled, cheered and died, sweating in the freezing cold.

* * *

DOC THOUGHT he was making some headway. The sun was almost down as Doc, Big Kate, and Shelly sat around the table in the kitchen of the Gilded Lilly, drinking coffee. Except for Kate.

The madam took another sip of whiskey and honey, and said, "No way."

Shelly said, "Please, Kate, come with us. We are family, and your brother needs family, what with his wife murdered."

Doc said, "To hell with that cossack, I need you to run my brothel. Be my partner. Think of the opportunity. How many brothels are there in Fort Worth?"

Kate shrugged. "Only one. This one. But there are a bunch of cheap-assed lowlife whorehouses, for a fact."

"Hah! My very point," said Doc. "We'll have the only one for a hundred miles at Canadian Fort. Soldiers, buffalo hunters, Mexican traders, Cheyenne if you want 'em. We'll have a lock on the market. And food."

Kate shook her head. "No. Y'all are sweet, but it ain't gonna happen. And if I was interested, I wouldn't think about making that trip in this weather. Y'all oughta wait too. Go home in the spring."

Shelly said, "We cannot. I miss my baby, and my man wants us back there before the weather gets worse. He worries about his sister. She was hurt bad. Worries 'bout me living here in this place."

A door slammed, and Bear pushed through the curtain from the mud room. "Found one, I did," he said, shucking his coat.

"One what?" asked Kate.

"He was looking for a wagon for Shelly," said Doc. Turning to Bear, he said, "What kind?"

Bear took a mug of coffee and sat. "Big one, she is. Covered. Family came from Georgia in it, don't need it no more, and needs money. Livery, they been trying to sell it for months. Six mules, too."

"One of them big old wagons, for one little Indian girl? A smaller one would move faster. Buckboard. You could get a cover on it," Kate said.

Bear looked around. "Doc, he tole me to get a big one. Said maybe you and some of your girls would join us. I got extra buffalo robes too."

Kate frowned. "Just how you paying for all this? You rob a bank or something?"

Bear made a strange face and looked at Doc. "Not exactly."

Doc coughed. "He means we have dollars from my practice and from our trade at Balliett's Post."

They were interrupted by a commotion upstairs. Furniture crashed, shouts, a scream, then the sound of feet on the stairs. They all crowded into the parlor at the foot of the stairs.

Saw-Tooth Alice was helping a fat girl to a bench. "It's that bastard Pell, Kate. He's drunk and he cut Lula Bell here. Lie down, hon, we'll get you bandaged."

"It ain't bad, Kate, but my dress is ruint along with my pantaloons. He cut my arm, then Alice cold-cocked him with her sap. Oh, shit, it's starting to hurt." The young whore showed them a three-inch slash on her left forearm.

Doc pushed in to take over. "Get my bag, Shelly. It's up in my room."

"Why'd he cut you, Lula Bell?" Kate handed Doc a towel and a water pitcher.

Lula Bell jerked as Doc wiped off the wound. "Ouch. He's just mean drunk again, Kate. He couldn't do much, needed special handling, then didn't want to pay. I tole him I'd tell everybody what a pitiful little worthless prick he had if he didn't pay, and that sent him off."

There was another flurry of noise from the landing above them, and Shelly scuttled down the stairs shouting, "You stay away from me."

Deputy Pell appeared at the top step, shirtless, bootless, bleeding from the forehead, but wearing a gun belt. He stumbled down two steps and said, "I'ma kill the whore 'at whacked me, then I'ma have that squaw." Noticing the men finally, he slurred, "What you staring at, nigger? I'ma blow your kinky head off." He pulled his pistol.

Two shots rang out, almost together, deafening in the closed space. Doc's bullet snapped Pell's head back, and Bear's 300 grain Remington slug bounced the man off the wall, then through the railing to crush an armchair below. The deputy's pistol clattered down the stairs.

"Now he's ruint my bannister and a good chair too. Sorry, no-account..." Kate surveyed the wreckage through the gunsmoke.

Lula Bell cried out, "He's still flinching."

Big Kate stepped over Pell's feet, a stiletto suddenly

in her hand, and jabbed it in his ear. "Now he ain't," she said, wiping the thin blade on his pants.

Doc thought out loud, "I've simply got to have this woman."

* * *

THE SHERIFF WAS irritable and raw when Saw-Tooth Alice finally got him his breakfast.

"What took so damn long? Me freezing here, no coffee. You forgetting you're a whore?"

"Easy now, Sheriff. I ain't just a whore no more. Big Kate sold out to me last night, headed out to find her brother. Took half the girls, but she cut me a deal."

"Well, I will be damned." He sipped the coffee, choked, then sputtered, "Shee-it, that's scalding. I suppose my deputy's hanging around the Gilded Lilly, seeing as he just got paid. You go back, tell him I said get over here."

"Nossir. Matter of fact, Pell left last night, too. Cut Lula Bell, then departed. Went south."

"You don't say. His family's back east, over Houston ways." "Naw. He definitely went south."

* * *

"IT IS NOT TOO long until the sun is down," said Moving Behind. "The soldiers have all gone back to our village. I know you are tired and hungry, Corn Stalk Woman. Let's try to get to that next village before dark."

Her aunt, a woman of over fifty summers, just

270

grunted and started shuffling east down the valley. After a little time, she said, "If you were a good child, you would have thought to grab us some pemmican before we ran."

"You are my mother's sister, and I respect you, but you must remember that I have kept us alive since before dawn, with killers all around us, and I have only fourteen summers behind me." She helped her aunt over a creek and pulled her up the far embankment. "Maybe you should stop complaining, save your breath, and try to move faster…"Moving Behind's voice trailed off as she saw the look of dismay and fear on the face of her aunt, who pointed downstream behind her. The girl turned to see the most horrible, inexplicable sight she'd ever witnessed.

Corn Stalk Woman whispered, "I do not understand this…" Moving Behind said, "To the woods. Run."

Chapter Thirty

CORPORAL JIM DANIEL caught up to Sergeant Boye as Benteen's company started back across the Washita at sundown. Daniel wore his usual worried frown.

"You seem afret, James. Can't you just enjoy the music? They're playing our song," Sergeant Boye smiled.

The lanky corporal cocked an ear, as if he hadn't noticed the band's efforts. "Our song, is it? Ahh. Yiss, 'tis indeed. 'Ain't I Glad To Get Out Of The Wilderness.' And I will be, John Boye. But have you noticed we ain't out yet?"

Boye spurred his horse up the far bank, then pulled up to watch the last of the company cross. "And what news for me, James?"

Daniel reined in beside him. "I brung the last of the scragglers, as you told me."

"Stragglers, James."

Daniel's frown deepened. "Faith, John Boye, what

did I just say? Yiss, I did, and some news too. They ain't found Major Elliott nor none of the boys was with him."

"Whoa," said Boye, "Walter Kennedy went with him."

"Nor him," said Daniel. "Nor that asshole Sergeant Vandusky. A section rode down this side of the river around noon, heard heavy firing downstream, but couldn't see nothing through the trees, and then they's driven back. Custer sent another patrol down the south side couple of hours ago. Said they went two miles, didn't see nor hear nothing. That what we're doing now, going looking for Elliott?"

Boye shook his head. "No, James. Captain Benteen says we're faking an attack on the other villages. Soon as the hostiles pull back and dark sets in, we'll wheel about and head home. I fear for Walter Kennedy and them others. Maybe they fought their way across the river and is waiting for us up north."

"You believe that, John Boye?"

"No, James, I don't. And I don't like leaving 'em, neither." "Other than them, how'd we fare?" Daniel clucked his horse

to fall in with Boye behind H Company.

"Captain Hamilton was killed right off, and one trooper. Three officers wounded, one of 'em bad, and twelve troopers. One of them is our boy McCasey, arrow in his lung. He's alive but he ain't good. Four of our H Company boys was part of the eighteen what rode off with Elliott and Kennedy. Let's head up front." Boye spurred his mount to pass the company column.

Corporal Daniel caught up and slowed. "And the hostiles, John Boye, how'd we do there?"

274

Boye cast him a funny look. "We got over fifty prisoners, all women and wee ones. The Boy General says we killed over one hundred, but I only seen maybe ten dead warriors and maybe that many again in women and children. 'Course, Elliott must've killed some downstream."

"So we come out ahead, huh?" Said Daniel.

"Tell that to Walter Kennedy and Elliott, when you see 'em." "Jaysus, you're touchy, Sergeant. I knows you's worried

about Kennedy and them others. Faith, John Boye, and I'll pray for them."

"Aye, James, and it might be a good time for that." "Well, I will then, John Boye. Soon as I take a leak."

* * *

AT SEVEN MONTHS PREGNANT, Meotzi could not find a comfortable way to ride the pony Mahwissa had chosen for her. Whatever her discomfort, it was better than trying to keep up on foot. In the snow.

The Bluecoats had formed up and jabbed at the other villages to scare them, then turned and hurried away from the battlefield after dark.

Mahwissa looked at her and knew she was suffering. "Meotzi, I think their chief likes you," she started.

"Likes me?" Meotzi spat. "He doesn't know me."

Mahwissa said, "All right, all right, then – he wants you. That better? Whatever, if you want to live and have this baby, you must do whatever he wants. Do you hear me? He can't be worse than that husband you shot."

"I don't want to think about it."

"Well, think on this. Maybe he wants you enough to let you ride in a wagon. I'll go ask him. Or maybe that scout. You pray, little girl."

As Mahwissa trotted away, Meotzi noticed the goosebumps on her arms, and realized they were not just from the cold. She raised her free hand, palm up, and started: "Hear me, Ma'heo'o, creator of all life. I have one of your creations in my stomach, over six moons now. It is my first, and it's already part of me. Help me to do what I need to do to finish bringing this one in, and if I must submit to these soldiers, let them not be too rough on us. I hope you have protected my father, Little Rock, and if you let him come save me, please watch over him and guide his steps. And look out for old Mahwissa. She is ancient, over forty summers, and she's been kind to me, and she can help all of us captives because she knows the tongue of these devils. I hope you're awake now, Ma'heo'o. You weren't much help this morning. Maybe you were sleeping. Right now, though, this baby is pushing my stomach again. I've got to get down and make water."

As Meotzi turned her horse out of the column, Mahwissa trotted up, crunching snow under the bright glow of the moon. Mahwissa glanced up and, "Dog Soldier moon. Maybe the Dog Soldiers will come after us, but I don't expect it. They're probably riding circles around the other camps, looking for another attack by these people."

Meotzi said, "Tell these Bluecoats that I must go in

the bushes, so they don't think I'm trying to escape. And what did you learn?"

Mahwissa gave her a funny smile. "Well, little one, I have good news and bad news."

Chapter Thirty-One

"WE SAW some some dead white men down there in the valley, before we found you. Lots of them, in a circle. Maybe this many." Moving Behind flashed all her fingers twice. "There was a lot of smoke and fire, and they had no clothes. We ran." She and her aunt were crouched in a cramped dugout in the valley wall. It had been Follow The Enemy's place, but now the two women shared it with Striker and Weasel.

Weasel grunted. "So you saw the fight."

"No," said Moving Behind. "There was no one else around. The smoke and fire came from the dead men. They were very jumbled. One's face looked at me, but his body was turned away."

Striker said, "You must have hurt your head," and groaned as she put more mud on his wound.

Weasel shook his head. "No. I know what she saw. The smoke was steam coming from the warm insides of those Bluecoats, cut open there in the cold. The fire was all their blood, still red, not even frozen and black yet, all bright against the snow."

Moving Behind nodded. "Blood-red. Like our river. And we thought they were burning. We ran away."

Weasel crawled to the entrance of the dugout and pushed back the blanket serving as a door. "It's not so bad out there now. We need to leave here."

"But why, Weasel?" Moving Behind looked up from Striker's wound. "We are warm here. There is certainly enough horseflesh to feed us all winter, the cold keeps it fresh, and the creek water is clean even if the river is not. And Striker is hurt."

Weasel grinned. "He's not hurt that bad. He just likes your attention. No, we'll move. The Bluecoats will come back to find these dead men they left behind. They almost always do. It's been five nights since they left, and with the weather better, they'll come soon. We'll head north and west, go by Balliett's Post and warn our friends what happened."

"Good idea, Old Man. Maybe get their medicine man to look at my arm and get something to eat besides horse and dog meat. And get away from these wolves and vultures," Striker said, picking up his meager belongings.

From outside, Weasel said, "Bring our carbines and get out here, Striker." His voice was low but urgent.

Striker scrambled out and handed Weasel his new Spencer, then covered his eyes to peer upstream toward the destroyed village, just past the slaughtered pony herd. The dugout was high in the south wall of the valley, above the trees. They had a clear view of the big covered wagon and two riders that had ridden down into the shallow valley from the south.

"They've seen our smoke. Take the women and run," said Weasel. "Wagon is probably full of Bluecoats. I'll delay them and join you later."

"Fight them if you want to, old fool, but I'll not help you." Striker grinned.

Weasel spun to stare at him, dumbfounded. "What?"

"Big one near us is Bear, from Balliett's Post. You remember their tracker, the black man? I think the little one is Doc. And that wagon is full of women. They are clucking like birds."

"Sacred Spirits," said Weasel. "This is not funny. They almost scared the yellow water out of me."

BEST ANYONE COULD FIGURE, it was near Christmas, end of this year of 1868. While there were individual bright spots, like Doc, Bear, Shelly and those whores with Boss's sister getting here all right, Junebug didn't see it as much of a joyous season.

Sure, little Black Dog was tickled to be with his parents again, and Shelly's healing was amazing, and durn if Boss Melton weren't about speechless to see his sister here. And Shelly did bring a bunch of dogs from that burned-down Cheyenne camp, not so good in stew, but pretty tasty fried. Still...

Junebug slipped out onto the eating porch. Wrapped in a fifteen pound buffalo robe, the cold still took her breath. "Got to do this quick," she thought; "Either

Buck'll come looking or I'll freeze afore I finish, lessen I'm fast." She bowed her head and started: "Dear Lord, we both know I ain't nothing but a common whore, but who else can I go to? Listen. I can't help worrying about them Cheyenne women and children that the soldiers took. I know soldiers. Them women, specially the fresh ones, they's getting passed around right now. I know, I know – from what Doc and Bear seen in that valley, Cheyenne women ain't no wilting flowers them own selves.

"Still...you know what I'm saying, soldiers and all. Nailed you bang-on to a durn cross, didn't they? Good thing the Indians ain't learned that one. I'll try to get Boss or the Cap'n to take me up to Camp Dodge to check on them prisoners. You help me, all right? Once the weather's some better?

"And I need help here, too, Lord. I owe Doc. He was my way out of that Mason's Landing whorehouse, and he's the first to let me feel I had value other than some-body's toy. He don't need me much, though, and the boy Buck do, but I fear Doc'll shoot him. Just let Doc settle in with Boss's sister, all right? Doc don't need us both.

"I remember what that circuit riding preacher said, the one you sent us when I's young. You don't make deals with the Lord, he said. You take what he gives you and be grateful. I don't know about that, but here's something for you to think on. You didn't do me no favors with that son of a...that man you made my daddy. You want to play catch-up, Boss Melton really needs help now.

"He's just an old soldier who never did have no

particular woman before Marie-Louise, then for three years he had her. Had a baby with her, and that woman was feisty, smart, good-looking and the bestest momma you ever seen. Then she's taken in such a awful way, and Boss ain't even caught her killer. He's eat slam up with it, and he needs you, and he don't know it. Manuela is mighty young for him, but she could help him, and you know I'm right.

"Worse though, is Honey and Dobey. See, he loves her but he knows this ain't his baby coming. Already hardened his heart against it, and you know Honey's gonna love it, even if it is Red's. Try and show him he's wrong, and help him and Boss find Red and Penn and clear them accounts. I do appreciate you keeping that Marshal Butch Fetterman away from us. Just don't help him none, all right? Wheresomever he is?

"If you could, let things come back around to more like they was here. Or better. God knows they ain't no good like they is.

"Thanks for letting me unload, Lord. I hope I ain't been too hard on you. I got to go now. I'm 'bout to freeze out here, and I got to pee."

1869

_____

Chapter Thirty-Two

"WELL, Doc, sure and I hate to take you away from your business but it's surely good you was here to take care of Corporal Daniel's abcessed tooth." Sergeant Boye paused and grinned. "Though I don't know as he's ready to thank you for your loving care just yet."

Jim Bob Daniel groaned and held his swollen jaw. "Didn't give me near enough likker," he mumbled. "Hurts like hell its ownself."

Doc raised an eyebrow. "I gave you exactly what you paid for, Corporal. You are welcome to buy more."

The three men were in Doc's office in the Northern Lilly, as the newly finished restaurant, bar, dentistry, and whorehouse was known. On the north bank of the South Canadian River, in the tiny new community called Hogtown. Across the river from Canadian Fort, the Northern Lilly was a joint project of Doctor Charles John Thomason, Kathryn Melton Jackson, and the ex-slave, William Black. Known as Doc, Big Kate, and Big

William, they were the dentist, the madame, and the cook of the establishment as well as the owners. They were also the enforcer, the manager, and the bouncer respectively.

As Doc finished up the wiping of his instruments, Sergeant Boye stood and said, "I'll be fording the river to say my farewells to Dobey and the others, James, m'boy. You git them other troopers to have their pants back on and ready to ride in half an hour."

Corporal Daniel muttered, "And if they're too drunk to ride?" "Then you have them tied face down on their bleeding horses,

James, and you pull them back to Camp Supply, don't you now?" It wasn't a question.

Doc re-corked the whiskey he'd just used to clean his tools and said, "Give me two minutes, and I'll cross over with you."

Daniel moaned again. "You put more likker on them pliers than you poured in me."

* * *

HONEY BROUGHT coffee in to the small group gathered in the main room of the trading post. Doc and Sergeant Boye had just joined Dobey, Bear, and Shelly in front of the fire.

After handshakes all around, Dobey said, "So y'all overran Black Kettle's camp. I tried to tell Custer he was a peace chief."

Boye shrugged. "Dobey, we trailed a war party there in the night, in the snow, and at dawn, we hit 'em. We didn't know it were Black Kettle's village. Don't know as it woulda mattered if we'd known. I mean, some of them bucks in that war party had to come from that village, even did most of 'em go on downstream. And a lot of 'em from that camp got away."

"The hell you say, John Boye," Dobey said. "There weren't but about one hundred fifty in the camp. Y'all killed over thirty, took over fifty prisoners, and wounded a bunch of the rest."

Sergeant Boye frowned. "Killed thirty, d'ye say? Custer's claiming we killed over one hundred warriors."

Doc gave him a shrewd look. "And what do you say, Sergeant? You were there."

Boye shook his head. "Aye, and I was there, during the whole thing and again, two weeks later. All I seen was maybe thirty dead Injins, including women and wee ones. Only maybe half was warriors."

Doc nodded. "Bear and Shelly and I were there perhaps a week after the fight. We counted thirty-two Indians including non-combatants, mostly Cheyenne. More dead horses than I could count, but over five hundred. There were also sixteen dead white men in a circle, and one more by himself, mid-valley. All naked, all frozen, all horribly mutilated. Are they why you came back?"

Boye lowered his head. "Just so. The shame of the Seventh Cavalry, or at least the shame of Custer. That was Major Elliott and his little band of adventurers. The lone one were my good friend Sergeant Major Walter

Kennedy, whom you well knew, Dobey. And had you but seen what they did to these boyos, Dobey, y'might not feel so sad for the heathens."

Boye choked up for a second, then pushed on. "They was only two mile or so from us, and they fought a long time, surrounded as they were. Could have saved them. Should have. We never even found Sergeant Vandusky's body. Sorry bastard that he was, he still shoulda been buried like we did the others."

Doc hesitated a moment, thinking about his response. He really didn't want to tell this tough old sergeant that he had brought Striker back to Canadian Fort briefly to nurse his wounds. "A couple of Cheyenne warriors from that camp passed through here after the battle. They confirmed the number of Cheyenne, Arapaho, and Kiowa dead. They said they tracked and killed one sergeant in the river, and four Arapahos killed another lone sergeant near a creek. All the others were killed in the circle, after a long fight."

Boye said, "We missed the one in the river. Had to be Vandusky. This sorry ass of a scout said he seen Van ride off from Kennedy to chase down some Injins along the river. I think the scout left 'em and ran. Custer wanted to keep him, but me and Ben Clark finally run him off."

Dobey said, "Why'd Custer want to keep him on if you and the chief of scouts didn't cotton to him?"

"He's the one as led us to the camp," Boye said. "He'd been there not long before. And he's also the one as steered that fine little chief's daughter to Custer, the one he's so taken up with now."

Shelly perked up. "Chief's daughter? Was she carrying a baby?"

Honey stood and left the room.

Boye gave Honey a long look as she hurried out. "Sure and she was," said Boye. "Had herself a little girl, end of January. And the way the Custer brothers is going at her, I don't doubt but she'll soon be having another."

Shelly said, "That must be Meotzi. Little Rock's daughter." Boye said, "That ain't what the Boy General calls her, but she

is Little Rock's daughter. Cheyenne translator woman, 'nuther captive, tole me so."

Shelly shook her head and looked away for a moment. "When you go back, you must tell her that her father was killed. Striker and Weasel are Cheyenne fighters and they saw it. He was shooting a pistol at some bluecoats down the valley, trying to protect some women and children. After all them bluecoats went into a circle and was killed, Weasel went and looked at Little Rock. A bullet had went through his head. Tell Meotzi he didn't have no time to suffer."

Dobey stopped pacing and cut in at that point. "Back up now. You said some scout had been there before. Was he red-headed?"

John Boye gave Dobey a funny look. "No, he wasn't. But he did come into our camp with a blow-hard name of Red. Said they was on a cattle drive, up from Texas. Got in a scrape, Red was shot up some so's he couldn't come back with us, so's it was Penn as led us to the Injins."

Dobey said, "You got any idea where these two are right now?"

"Red headed for Santa Fe with a wagon train of pilgrims. I heard Penn went toward Fort Hays after Clark fired him, but I ain't sure. Dobey, I can see you're about to bust wide open. Why you so interested?"

Doc thought it might be easier for someone else to deal with that, and started to answer. "Well, Sergeant..."

Dobey cut him off, pushing a silencing palm toward the dentist. "They owe us something. Nothing we can't settle on, once we find 'em. I'd thank you not to let on that we're looking, but get word to us if you hear of their whereabouts. It's kind of private."

Boye shrugged. "Well, I owe you too, so I'll keep it under my hat but ask around. Guess I'd better get back to Hogtown and get my boys moving back towards Camp Supply."

On the porch, Dobey shook Boye's hand again and said, "Good to see you, John Boye. Glad you weren't hurt. Wish I could tell you more, but it might be best you don't know."

Boye grinned. "You're a man of many secrets. And another you ain't tole me about is your bride, who seems to be pooching a little. Easy to notice, her being so tiny and all. So you two are expecting another wee one?"

Doc winced, and it was Dobey's turn to give John Boye a funny look.

"Yes," Dobey said slowly. "She is."

Chapter Thirty-Three

"No REMINGTONS LEFT, least ways no conversions. I do have a couple of Lefaucheux metal cartridge pistols. They's old, but still solid."

"What kind, you say?" Dobey was in a store in the 'town' of Fort Hays, Kansas. A store which sold guns. A store that wasn't a bar, whorehouse, funeral parlor, barber shop, hotel or café. Maybe the only one that wasn't.

"Lee-fow-sho. Lefaucheux. French, they said. Called 'em 'twelve millimeters', which I thought was .48 caliber, but they measures as about .44." The proprietor laid two heavy six shooters on the counter, then produced several boxes of ammunition. "They's pinfires, see? Which I have seen before but mainly in fancy shotguns. The hammer drives the pin, which hits the cap, which is inside the cartridge. Pin slides right into them slots in the back of the cylinder. Ejector rod to push out the empties."

"Where'd you get 'em?" Dobey was dubious.

"Some Frenchy trappers, flush you know, wanted to trade up for Remingtons. Got my last two conversion models."

A well-dressed tall man, apparently a gambler, had been nursing his coffee and watching with an amused expression. He hefted one of the pistols.

"Lot of Union officers had 'em. They ain't for fast shooting, I'd say." He nodded toward Dobey's belt. "Not like that cut-down cross-draw Navy. You a sporting man?"

Dobey stepped away from the counter and faced the dandy. "No. And the men who might use these will either be family or maybe buffalo hunters. Just looking for waterproof cartridges and faster loading. Why?"

The dandy grinned. "Feisty, ain't you?" He put down his mug without taking his eyes off Dobey, and squared off. He pushed back his coat to show two ivory handled Navy Colts in crossdraw holsters. And a badge.

The proprietor backed away, but said, "Sheriff, he's a regular. Runs a trading post, over to the Canadian River. You start shooting my customers, you can get your damn coffee somewheres else."

"I don't know who'd shoot who, no how." Big William was standing just inside the door, his Colt revolving shotgun pointing loosely at the lawman. "I seen the Cap'n shoot two men, real fast, and they started it. Down in Arkansas."

"Were they armed?" It wasn't quite a sneer. The dandy's eyes flicked between Dobey and Big William.

"Oh, yassuh, Mr. Sheriff. One went to pull his pistol, and the other was holding a shotgun."

"He kill 'em?"

"Nossuh. He knocked 'em down. Wasn't in my hands, but this old Avenging Angel, she finished 'em." The old black man patted the barrel left-handed, but now held it steady at the sheriff. "Boss Melton, he was holding it back then."

"Well, it don't matter nohow," spluttered the proprietor. "They ain't done nothing wrong, Sheriff. Get yourself some more coffee and let me make this sale."

The sheriff stared at the cavernous mouth of the ten gauge for a moment, nodded, then picked up his mug and backed carefully toward the stove. "Go ahead on then."

Dobey picked up one of the revolvers. "Looks fine, but I won't buy no old pig in a poke. Where can I shoot it?"

"Out back. Better yet, Bill, you ain't been shooting yet. Whyn't you take him with you?" The proprietor turned back to Dobey. "Sheriff likes to freshen up his pistols 'bout every afternoon. Shoots the old charges for practice, then loads 'em up new. Don't you, Bill? Don't want no damp powder, just like this gentleman."

The lawman shrugged. "We could do that. Let me pick up some powder, caps, and balls."

Twenty minutes later they were out on the plain, which was already turning cool for late September. There was maybe an hour of daylight left. As they dismounted, the sheriff said, "Don't want no one to sneak up on me. Hard to do that out here. Now what I do is, I empty one Colt at one of them rocks there. Then I clean it, re-load, then do the other."

"Don't want to be caught with two empty pistols, do you," said Dobey.

"Exactly."

The plain was soon covered with gunsmoke and dancing rocks. Ears ringing, they emptied then re-loaded two pistols each. Dobey finished first by several minutes.

"Old thumb-busters shoot and load just fine, but they are clunky. Can't beat a Navy Colt for handling. And you're a hell of a shot with 'em, either hand." Dobey snapped shut the loading gate on the second Lefaucheux pistol.

"I need to be," the sheriff grinned. "It's why I do this, most days. I'll tell you though, best shot I ever made was with a damn old four pounder Dragoon. Fellow named Tutt did me wrong over a watch, back in '65, Springfield, Missoura. He opened up, and I laid that old horse pistol on my left arm and dropped him, first shot. It was about seventy-five paces. Killed him, deader 'n a doornail."

"Head shot?" Dobey was skeptical. "Hell of a shot at a hundred feet, let alone seventy-five paces."

"Heart. Or maybe lungs. Slug went through him, side to side. Now, you know I was lucky. I had a eight inch barrel on that Dragoon, and I'd put a rear sight on it, too, and I am pretty good. Still, he was sideways and shooting, and my front sight covered half his body. I was just looking to hit him in the body, you know, just to stop him. I was pretty durn happy to see him stagger around and go down." The lawman flicked his mustache with his trigger finger. "He had a few friends nearby. Odd how fast they calmed down."

Dobey smiled. "I can see how. My sawed-off Colt, I'm happy to hit somebody at fifteen yards. Don't matter what you say, that was still a hell of a shot."

"Not half so good as I tell people. Somebody started the story that it was one hundred paces. With my legs that's a hundred yards. You're a shooter. You know how hard that would be. They also say I can put six rounds from a Navy in a playing card at fifty yards, either hand." He grinned. "I like for folks to believe that. Nice to have an edge, you know?"

Dobey laughed. "I guess."

"Guess, hell. Think on it. You really drop those two men, like your man said?"

"He ain't my man, Sheriff. I did shoot 'em. They were pretty slow and stupid. Maybe drunk. I wasn't, and they weren't even ten yards away."

"Shoot-fire. I think I's half drunk every time I shot someone." He shrugged. "Anyhows, you need your man to say it was six of 'em, and you took 'em with six shots. Left handed. 'Less of course, you just like killing."

"Why?" Dobey mounted as he waited for the answer.

"Well, if you boost up folks' expectations about what you can do, you might avoid a gunfight every now and then. Generally when somebody wants to get crossways with me, somebody else will say, 'Hold on, there. That's James Butler Hickok, old Wild Bill hisself. He's killed over a hundred men, not counting Indians and Rebels.'

You'll see 'em pop a sweat on a cold day, and start apologizing."

Dobey chuckled. "Who starts these stories?" "Me, mostly. I do like an edge."

As Hickok swung into the saddle he said, "You meet me in Paddy Welch's bar in an hour, I'll buy you a drink. Bring your man."

"That won't be a problem?"

"Oh, hell no. Not for me, anyways. On top of the Seventh Cavalry, I've scouted for the Tenth Cavalry too. They's all colored. Pretty good troopers, too."

They parted ways at the railroad tracks and Dobey rode back to the store to complete his purchases. Inside, the proprietor poured him a coffee and said, "Hell of a shot, ain't he?"

Dobey grinned. "You might have warned me he was Wild Bill Hickok. I mean, I guess he is, right? He admitted he ain't always truthful when it comes to getting a jump on some other shooter. Told me about a remarkable long shot back in Missouri. You know is there anything to that story, or was he just working on one of his 'edges' with me?"

The proprietor handed Dobey his change and ammo, then leaned on the counter and said, "Davis Tutt and Bill was friends, sort of. Drank and played cards a lot together, but this one night they was drunk and Tutt had a bad patch at cards and tole Bill to pay him the thirty-five dollars he owed him. Bill said naw, it weren't thirty-five, it had been, but Bill had give him ten of it at Oak Hall already, he had it all writ down in his room.

Tutt says, 'Maybe it was forty-five,' and grabbed Bill's watch off the table, said Bill could get it back once he paid up the forty-five. Bill said, 'I'd ruther fuss with any man on earth other'n you, as you've accommodated me time and agin, but I won't pay you more than the twenny-five unless my book says I remember it wrong. But don't you go on the square with my watch till I check my figures.' Well, Tutt he promptly heads out into the square and Bill yelled at him, 'Don't do this,' but Tutt drew and fired and Bill fired back. Tutt dropped his pistol, said, 'Boys, he's kilt me,' or some such, staggered around a pillar in the courthouse door, back into the square and went down dead. Bullet went in under a rib on his right side, come out under the same rib on t'other side. It was seventy-five yards, measured. I was there."

He took a sip of coffee. "See, he ain't a bad man. And don't take no guff off him on these pinfires. He carries one hisself when it rains. A thirty-six caliber. Bought it from me."

JOHN WALSH'S saloon was known as Paddy Welch's and, like most frontier drinking establishments, was long and thin. Its long side paralleled Fort Street. Dobey entered its main door in the narrow end fronting on Main Street and the tracks of the Kansas and Pacific Railroad. The bar itself ran most of the length of the wall on his left, and at the far end stood Sheriff Hickok, surveying the small crowd and nursing a whiskey.

Noticing Dobey, he nodded, then signaled the bartender to bring another glass.

"Where's your man?" he said, pushing the bottle to Dobey. "Big William? He decided he'd do better to stay by the

wagon. Ain't much of a drinker, anyhow."

Dobey took a sip. "I been wondering, since you said you scouted for the Seventh Cavalry some, you ever run across a scout name of Penn?"

"Fact of the matter is, I did. Didn't much care for him. Don't seem to be sort of person you'd hold in very high esteem, neither."

The lawman downed his drink and poured another. "I'd guess he's an in-law you're wanting to stay clear of. Or you're hunting him."

"I'm hunting him."

"Well, you've missed him. He was with them at the Washita fight last year, but Custer's wife and some others didn't care none for him so he got run off."

When Dobey just stared at him, Hickok grinned and continued. "Yup. Seems your boy Penn was who intro-duced some fine young Cheyenne maiden to the Custer brothers on the way home from the Washita, last November. Pregnant girl, some chief's daughter they captured down there, maybe fourteen, fifteen year old. The Boy General took a real liking to her, and soon as she had that baby, damn if him or Brother Tom didn't get her pregnant again. I say that 'cause some say the General is firing blanks after a bad case of the pox years back. I don't think he knowed his brother was partaking too, but I seen your boy Penn dragging her to Tom's tent a time or two. Hell, Custer and his wife Libby ain't been able to come up with no baby neither, all these years. I mean he took the girl on patrols, had a Sioux squaw with 'em as a nanny, and called this girl his translator, though I don't know as she spoke a word of English. Monahsetah. Yeah. That's what he called her, but it weren't really her name. Anyways, he kept one more prisoner, this girl's aunt, who could translate, kept her and the girl and her baby and the nanny over to Camp Supply, and sent all the other prisoners to here, maybe fifty squaws and kids."

They both took a sip. Dobey said, "And how long did Custer's wife put up with this?"

Hickok laughed. "Oh, Miss Libby weren't here then. She was back East. It become common knowledge, and she got here pretty damn quick. Mid summer, it were. He knew she were coming, of course, so the girl and her baby and the others was in the stockade here when Mrs. Libby Custer arrived. No more special treatment for them, I tell you. And right off, Miss Libby wanted to see the prisoners and That Girl."

"You serious?"

'Oh, yes. Elizabeth Custer is a piece of work. Some kind of a woman, I'm here to tell you. She don't think badly of me none, neither, and I'd take her off the Boy General's hands in a minute, 'cept she knows she's hitched to a star. Anyhow, I guess the girl Monahsetah figgered out that her and the others was about to be cut loose with no more'n the clothes on their backs and her near 'bout six months pregnant, so she walks right up to Custer and the missus and offers them her little girl.

Baby girl was only born in January, so she's, what, seven months? Guess she figgered the girl had a better chance with them than with her. Translator even said the girl figgered she was sort of Miss Libby's sister, Cheyenne style, as they was both married to the General. They declined to take the baby of course, and she were sent on her merry way with all the others. Hell, she'll be having that second baby inside a month now."

Dobey shook his head. "Jesus. Tough kid, huh?"

"Yeah. Now why you looking for that asshole Penn?"

Dobey really didn't want to answer that.

Before he could think of a dodge, they were interrupted by Hickok's deputy. "Could be trouble, Sheriff. Over to Bitter's Saloon. Old man Bitters ast for some help. Says Strawhun's got a bunch of his boys in there, looking for blood and payback."

Hickok said, "Strawhun. That popinjay. I did ask him to leave Hays."

As the three men walked south in the dark across Main Street and the tracks, Dobey said, "So. You killed a lot of men, like folks say?"

Hickok stopped for a moment, staring at Dobey, and let his deputy walk on ahead. "Not so many, outside of war. Prob'ly like you. Couple back in Nebraska in '61. Dave Tutt in '65. Rounder name of Mulvey here, just last month. It ain't like I just go around shooting folks."

Bitter's place laid out parallel to the railroad tracks, with the front door on Fort Street. As they walked in, John Bitters yelled from the bar on their left, "Sheriff, these boys is taking my beer glasses out the back door and ain't bringing 'em back. They's trying to break me up, 'cause I'm on the Vigilance Committee."

Sam Strawhun turned his bleary eyes on Hickok and waved at the eight men with him. "We's wolfing tonight and chooses to drink from fresh glasses, by God. And don't nobody better bring none o' them dirty ones back in or they face me and my wolves."

Hickok strolled through them to the far end of the bar, making soothing gestures with his hands. "Boys, this ain't no way to treat an old man. Can't drink without glasses. Let's go out in the side lot and everybody bring a few back in now."

"They do and I'll throw 'em right back out there," slurred Strawhun.

"Do, and they'll carry you out," said the sheriff. He pushed through the rowdies and retrieved four glasses from the lot next door. As Hickok set them on the bar, Strawhun grabbed one and started to swing it to bash Hickok's face. There was a flash and a blast, Strawhun's head snapped back, and he collapsed like an empty sack. Hickok stood, back to the bar, a Colt in each hand, both cocked, one smoking. "Anyone else want to dance?"

The nervous drunks backed away, staring at the pool of blood spreading from Sam Strawhun's head.

Jesus, Dobey thought, *I never even saw him draw.*

"He's done now," Hickok said. "Y'all go ahead and carry him out."

* * *

DOBEY AND BIG William had just finished hitching the

team to their wagon when Sheriff Hickok strolled up, carrying his coffee. It was not yet 10:00 A.M.

"Kinda early for you, ain't it, Sheriff?"

Hickok yawned and stretched. "Yup. Had a hearing on Strawhun's death 'bout an hour ago. Ruled justified. Guess you're heading for Fort Dodge with the army resupply wagons?"

"Yep. Then Camp Supply, then home. Ought to beat the snow."

"Home. Nice sound to that. You got family there?" Hickok helped Big William load the last box of canned goods into the wagon.

Dobey frowned. "I do. Little girl, wife, and she's got a boy from another man."

"Never had no kids myself. How old?"

Dobey's frown deepened. "My girl's four. The boy was just born this summer."

As the significance of that set in, Hickok frowned too. "I'm right sorry to hear that."

"Not as much as me." Dobey swung into the saddle, and touched his hat brim to the lawman. "Thanks for the drink and shooting lesson, Sheriff. See you. Big William, I'll meet you at the water point. Let's roll."

As Dobey trotted away, Big William shook his head and sighed. "It ain't like he let on, Sheriff. She was took by force. Beat and shot, too. He's lucky she lived, but he don't feel too lucky. It's why he's looking for that man, Penn. There was another one too, name of Red, but he run South. You see how it is, now?"

Hickok tossed the dregs from his mug. "I do. Thankee, Mister Big William. You take care of Dobey, and tell him I'll keep an eye out for Penn. He scouted for Custer once, he's likely to again."

Big William nodded, and clucked the team into motion to start that long, sad trip back to Canadian Fort. It could be neither longer nor sadder than Big William's face.

Chapter Thirty-Four

RED KICKED a sleeping dog out of the doorway and entered the adobe cantina. Inside, a fire crackled in one corner while old Paco wiped glasses behind the bar. It was still too early for either hungry prospectors or thirsty soldiers from Fort Bayard.

Red shook off his coat, nodded to Paco, and tried to stamp some of the cold out of his feet.

The old bartender mumbled, "Si, Boss," and poured some mescal. Red took it and pushed past a drape into the cooking area in the back of the building. Frank Barney, his partner, leaned against a table, mescal in one bloody hand, a thin cigar in the other. The smell of blood and innards was almost overpowering.

"It's near sundown," Red said. "They'll start coming in soon. We ready?"

Barney nodded. "Nearly 'bout. This is working pretty good. I skin 'em, gut 'em, cut 'em small here," he nodded to the gory table behind him. A machete lay on the table, and a bucket of guts beside it. "Girl takes the pieces out to the cookshed. Got two pots going out there. First one boils the meat off the bone, second one's got her beans and chilis simmering in it. Once she moves the meat to the chili pot, we keep the first pot as thin soup for the cheap trade. Maybe put in a onion. Chili pot comes back in here, we add tomato sauce and onions, we ready to go."

Red nodded approval. "What'd you get for meat today?" Barney scratched his scrawny butt. "Shot about ten prairie dogs and one fox last night."

Red gave him a hard look. "That's pretty damn thin, Frank." "I know, I know, Red. Got started late. I got Paco to kill us a dog this afternoon, and I bought a good sized armadillo off a Mex boy, too. It'll be thick enough."

"Was he dead?" Red finished his mescal.

"The armadillo?" Barney wiped his hands on his pants nervously.

Red exploded. "No, goddamit, the boy you bought him from. Yes, the goddam armadillo. I'm wondering, if he was dead, how damn long was he dead. Did you smell him?"

"Well, no, Red. I mean, yes he were dead, but you can't smell nothing in here…"

Red gritted his teeth and took a deep breath. "Listen to me, Frank. This is looking to be a good thing here. Timing is good. They finding some silver here, pretty soon they'll bring in some nigger cavalry to go with the nigger foot soldiers over to the fort. Silver will really bring folks, miners, whores, all that. Name'll change from San Vicente to Silver Creek, Silver City, something like that. We need to keep this going, build up some cash, maybe get some whores. What we don't need is to kill nobody with bad meat. Was you to bathe every now and then, and get rid of them innards, it would help too. Jesus."

"I unnerstand, Red. I do." Barney ground out his cigar and grabbed the gut bucket. "You want me to bathe right now too?"

Paco's chubby daughter Consuela probably saved Barney from a beating by kicking open the door back at that moment. She backed in, lugging a steaming pot, a rag wrapped around the handle. Dropping it on the floor, she groaned, knuckled her back, shoved the door closed, and turned to face the men.

"Ready for the mixing, Senor Frank. Ah! Senor Red! Buenos tardes, Jefe!" She smiled boldly at Red, shaking a finger. "And you never tole me, why is you called Red? You are not as red-haired as me."

"I used to be. Anyhow, mind your own business. Get this stuff ready. People are starting to come in."

THE CROWD WAS NOT BAD, he thought.

Five prospectors, four Mex's, eight nigger soldiers, and two white officers. And a lot of 'em going for seconds. As he watched, a scruffy prospector broke in the refill line in front of two soldiers.

Red started over. Never believed I'd be taking up for no niggers, he thought. But they is a lot more of them than prospectors. And that boss at the fort did say he'd put me 'off-limits' if I didn't serve 'em. I can't stand line-jumpers nohow.

He tapped the prospector on the shoulder, and the man turned, his face hostile, ready for a fight. The hostility disappeared before Red could speak, the man's eyes bulged, and he threw up on Red's boots. Red shoved the man against the wall and shouted, "What the hell?"

Behind him, one of the white officers stood, grabbed his stomach, and lunged toward the door. He almost made it, but spewed on the overcoat of the fort's commander, who had just stepped inside. The sick lieutenant went to his knees and crawled outside, still vomiting. The senior officer wiped his coat with his hands, stared at his hands with disgust, then wiped them back on his coat.

"Brand new!" he shouted, then, "That's it. Shut this filthy pig sty down. I want it closed today, you hear me, Sergeant Major? And who's the owner? Any of my men die from eating this swill, I'll hang him."

Red said, "He's out hunting, Colonel. Be back tonight." As he turned away, he hung his head and muttered, "Well, good-bye, City of Silver Dreams. Look out, El Paso, here I come."

Chapter Thirty-Five

MELTON HAD TWO ROOMS, one of them pretty large, in his part of the adobe fort which now comprised Balliett's Post. He was nursing a brandy on a cold night, trying to convince himself that he really wished he was on the road with Dobey, somewhere between Hays City and Canadian Fort right now. He wasn't having much luck. It was damned cold out, gusting snow, and it was damned comfortable inside.

Manuela eased out of the smaller room, closing the door carefully behind her. "He's sleeping good now, Boss. Can I fix you something else to eat?"

Melton shook his head and smiled at her. "Naw, I'm all right. You go on and get some sleep. That boy sure likes you. Don't know what we'd have done this last year, wasn't for you."

She walked close behind him and rubbed his shoulders. She'd never touched him before. It startled him.

He groaned. "Durn, that feels good. My wife used to

do that." Manuela bore down on his knotted neck muscles.

"I like taking care of little Mikey, and I could do more for you too. Why do you make me walk back to my room on such a cold night? I'm not ready to sleep. I'm too young to be sleeping at this hour, and there are no men for me to dance with."

Melton grabbed her wrist and pulled around to face her. "That's the problem, Manuelita. I'm way too old for you. I'm near forty, and you ain't twenty yet. Not even near."

She grinned and touched his face. "Don't worry, Boss. I won't hurt you." She walked to the door, bolted it, and began unbuttoning her shirt.

* * *

DOC CAME into the kitchen and brushed off the snow.

"Ah, coffee. Nectar of the gods. Plenty cold out there this fine morning, children. Rejoice that we're not on the road with Masters Dobey and Big William."

The other early risers mumbled greetings over their own steaming mugs. Honey looked up from nursing Baby Robert, and nodded, bleary-eyed. Crying? Lack of sleep? Both, maybe.

Bear stood to get more coffee himself and grumbled, "Me, I don't remember you being so cheerful of a morning before you quit drinking. Or so loud."

Doc smiled. "You're as cranky as that damned cossack Melton. Had some drinks with him last night, didn't you? You seem to be bleeding to death from the eyes. Speaking of the cossack, where is he? We were to hunt today."

Buck said, "Ain't seen him yet. Him nor Manuela. Maybe you missed him."

Carmela giggled. "No, I don't think so. Little Manuelita didn't come to her bed last night. Boss Melton may be too tired to hunt today. Or too happy."

Bear's belly laugh mixed with Shelly's happy squeals and the bedlam seemed to infect everyone. Except maybe Honey. And Buck.

Doc could tell the boy was uncomfortable, and was pretty sure he knew why. He fixed Buck with a squinty stare.

"You see no humor in this, Master Buck? The talk of sexual matters puts you in a state of unease? We're mainly adults here. Baby Robert understands less than I about such things, and the other brats are still abed. Surely we can talk of such things."

Buck stood, and the laughter died behind him. "I don't know about all that, Doc, but I do want to talk with you. I know it's cold, but could we go outside?"

Doc continued staring, letting Buck stew for another moment, then shifted his gaze to Junebug. "Why, certainly. That would certainly be better. Let's do it."

Junebug surged upright. "Doc, don't you..." Her voice failed under his glare.

"Refreshing, out there. That's all. Not to worry your pretty young head. Buck, why don't you bring us two fresh mugs of coffee into our courtyard?"

Outside, the light snow gusted and swirled inside the large mud fort, but it was still far better than being outside the walls where the biting wind raged down across the Canadian River from the north. Nothing to slow it down for hundreds of miles, thought Doc. Unstoppable, almost, rather like what's about to happen here.

Buck eased out into the open area and handed Doc a mug of scalding coffee. Doc took it left-handed without looking away from Buck's eyes.

"Your hand's shaking a little there," Doc smiled. "Really cold, isn't it?"

Buck said, "I ain't shaking because it's cold, Doc. You know I'm scared of you. Just can't stand by and let you treat her so."

Doc's right hand rested on the ivory handle of his little Colt. He said softly, "How's that?"

Buck coughed. "You know what I mean. You and Big Kate. You don't need both of 'em. I need Junebug, and she likes me. She's just afraid you'll kill me if she switches over."

Doc said, "Oh, I've seen that she likes you. Noticed you both 'missing in action' at the same time, a few times. Do you think me blind?"

"No, sir." "Stupid, then?"

"Nossir. But we ain't flaunted it."

Doc snorted. "But you're ready to die for her. You know I can kill you before you can drop that coffee."

Buck spilled some coffee and said, "I don't want to die, Doc. I just can't stand by no more, and can't run. I'm hoping you'll just let us leave and not come after us. She don't deserve this."

Doc tossed aside his coffee and mug and grabbed

Buck's right wrist with his left hand. The move caught Buck by surprise. "You're right, son. She deserves better than me. I've just been waiting for you to prove you were the man for the job." Doc grinned. "Took you long enough. Regardless of that, I see absolutely no reason for you to leave. You're both well-loved here."

Behind Doc, in the shadows of the blacksmith shop, Junebug quietly lowered the hammers of the shotgun.

Chapter Thirty-Six

JUNEBUG FINISHED CLEANING the dishes from the midday meal and thew the soapy water out the side door. She took off her apron, and with a second thought, snugged it back on again. Annette and Big Kate were still at the table, while Honey sat in the rocker with the baby.

"Miss Honey, I'm gonna take that baby now. He's fed. I can clean him and make him belch. You just go get some rest." Junebug squeezed Honey's shoulder as she spoke.

"But, but I…" Honey sputtered.

"But, nothing," said Big Kate. "Jimmy, Doc, and Cherokee Jim have taken the wagon out for firewood. Buck and Tad are on watch. We got nothing to do. Go sleep. Dobey's liable to come home any day."

Honey handed up Baby Robert to Junebug and struggled up from Annette's rocking chair. "Guess I ought to let my mother-in-law have her chair ever' now and then. But I don't see as how Dobey's in any hurry to come home. He hates me." She burst into tears. Again. "Hates the baby too."

Annette hurried to put her arm around the girl. "Shh. Hush, now. No such thing. He don't hate neither of you. He's messed up, I grant you, but if he hates anybody it's himself for not being here to stop what happened."

Honey snuffled, wiping her nose on her sleeve. "Acts like he hates us, then. Won't hold the baby, won't touch me. Mama Balliett, he don't even look at me."

Annette eased her toward her room. "Men get all screwed up in the head when they can't fix things, you know? Especially for their women and family. He can't fix this. He knows it ain't your fault. Hell, child, you shot the man that done it. But tough as they is, and my Dobey is some kind of tough, they's as fragile as glass about things below the belt."

"I don't know what you mean, Mama Balliett."

"I ain't sure neither, but he might wonder did you like it some, despite how it ended."

"Oh my God, Mama Bee, how can you say that?"

"I'm just telling you, Honey, he's messed up. He's wondering did that evil son of a b..., that monster, was he built better'n Dobey? Did he know things a woman might like, that Dobey never knew to do with you? See, I ain't saying that's so, I'm saying that's the kind of crazy horse droppings that's in Dobey's head now. Like, did you do something to make him think you was interested?"

Honey sat on her bed and stared at Annette, horrified.

"Why do you even say these things? You can't believe that. Neither can he. Oh my God!"

"Honey, I don't believe a bit of it. Matter of fact, I know it ain't so. Could he just clear his head, he'd know too. You got to help him get by this."

"Help him? I'm the one was raped. And shot!"

"I know, I know, Honey, but men, they just ain't as strong as us. You got to be even stronger. You find a way to tell him that monster's pecker was no bigger'n your finger. I don't care if he was built like a horse, you tell Dobey he was tiny. And say he didn't know what he was doing neither, which is partly why he beat you so, 'cause you laughed at him. And you wished you'd killed him, 'cause it's all been so hard on Dobey."

"On Dobey. Not on me." Honey stiffened, and stopped crying.

"Trust me, Honey. Dobey ain't a mean man. He's just a man. Get past this, and he can't help but love you and the boy." Annette turned away as if embarrassed and said, "Ask that girl Junebug about getting him back in your bed. I 'spect she's got some ideas. This ain't no time to hold back."

"And you think, with me doing these things, it will somehow be all right?" Honey fixed her mother-in-law with a granite-hard stare.

Annette shrugged. "Prob'ly not. Spent my whole life out here, and I ain't never seen something like this work out, short of a miracle. But life goes on."

Annette was interrupted by Tad, who pushed into the room followed close by Buck.

"Momma, they's two big wagons crossing the river

right now. I seen 'em from the north tower. Had some Nigra horse soldiers with 'em, but they ain't army wagons and they ain't ours. The soldiers stayed across the river at Doc's place."

Annette perked up. "Must of come from Camp Supply. We'd best get busy, get ready for some business. I s'pose Big William's across the river too?"

Tad nodded. "Yes'm, but Mary Belle is here."

"Tell her and Carmela and Manuela to fire up the kitchen. Buck, whyn't you ride out and meet 'em, come back and give us a heads up on what to expect?" It sounded like a request but everyone knew better. Buck took off like a bullet.

Twenty minutes later Buck rode to where Annette stood by the gate. A young boy rode in front of him, holding the pommel with both hands and sporting a huge grin. He looked vaguely familiar.

Annette shielded her eyes from the sun and said, "My, my, what a handsome, sweet-looking young man! Can you tell me what's your name, and how old you are? And where you're from?"

The boy nodded. " I'm Tommy Christmas and I'm this many." He stared at his hand for a second and held up four fingers. "From 'Bama."

Buck said, "He wanted to know was I his daddy when I come up to 'em. Then he wanted to ride back up here with me, when I told him his daddy won't here."

"And just who's his daddy?" Annette's brow furrowed in confusion.

"Woman on the wagon said his momma's dead, and his daddy was a Texas horse soldier name of Thomas

Walls." Buck grinned. "Might be known as 'Dobey' or 'Captain'. Looks like you got another grandchild, Miz Annette."

* * *

MARY BELLE WHITE brought the pot of chili and beans onto the eating porch and served Janey Green another portion. Janey thanked her, and continued her story.

"Your boy and Jimmy Melton stayed over with us one night in April '65 at my farm, with me and Bobby Sue, that is. Bobby Sue Peterson was my sister-in-law. Both our husbands was kilt and we was living hand to mouth. Your boys helped us with food and a little money, we had a pretty good time that night, and Tommy was the upshot of it. Born on Christmas Day, 1865. Bobby Sue said she couldn't give the boy her dead husband's name, just wouldn't have been right, nor Dobey's neither as they won't married. He's been Tommy Christmas ever since. The birthing was hard on her, her being nigh on forty-year-old, and the rest was worse. Her growed children cut her dead, wouldn't have aught more to do with her, and o' course people talked."

"O' course they did," said Annette. "It's a lot easier than helping out."

Janey eyed her, then decided Annette wasn't being sarcastic. "Ain't that the gospel truth. My kids, they was fine, pitched right in but it was still a struggle. When the carpetbagging buggers running the state took all our land for taxes, we headed thisaway, but Bobby Sue was heartbroke. Weak. Got some bad water in Arkansas. It shouldn't have killed her, but it did."

Annette said, "So I guess Dobey had told you where he and Jimmy were heading, and y'all decided to join us?"

Janey laughed, deep and rich. "Lord, no. We was heading for Santa Fe, maybe California later. But when Bobby Sue was dying, she made me promise to try and find Tommy's daddy. Said he ought to be allowed to pass on the boy if his plate was full, seeing as the child was her fault, but he ought to have a choice."

Annette snorted, "Her fault, my old tired butt! Ain't that the way a man would see it?" She stood and walked to the edge of the porch to look at Tommy playing with Mikey, Millie, Black Dog, and Shelly. "No, ma'am," she said. "That darling boy is my grandson and a godsend. And when my boy Dobey shows up here, that child is gonna pull him back into the real world in a heartbeat. And Honey, don't you go too easy on Dobey when he starts explaining all this. No, ma'am. Tommy Christmas is our little miracle, the one as we been waiting for and didn't even know it. He's home."

A Look At Higher Ground

BY MCKENDREE LONG

Raw, unvarnished, and authentic, Mike Long doesn't pull any punches when he writes anything western. The detail about the historical events in this book are spot on, including his riveting depiction of what it must have been like to be fighting the Battle of the Big Horn, also known as Custer's Last Stand.

Long's command of the language, his use of imagery and his knowledge of weaponry make this a book for any western, adventure, or historical reader.

COMING FEBRUARY 2019 FROM MCKENDREE LONG AND WOLFPACK PUBLISHING

About the Author

McKendree R. (Mike) Long III is a former paratrooper with tours as an advisor to Vietnamese Army artillery and infantry battalions, in 1966 and 1970. His awards and decorations include the Parachutist Badge, the Combat Infantryman's Badge, the Silver Star, and the Vietnamese Cross of Gallantry (Gold and Silver Stars). He is a graduate of Coker College with a Bachelor of Science degree in Business Administration.

After retiring from the US Army in 1980, he was a Financial Advisor with a major investment firm for 29 years, retiring as a First Vice President (Investments) at the end of 2009. Since then he has completed and has published four historical novels and eight short stories.

He and Mary were married in 1960; they have two married daughters, four grandchildren, and four great-grandchildren (plus one on the way).

Mike is an avid collector and shooter of guns of the Old West; readers of his works may learn much about them, whether they set out to or not.

McKendree Long now devotes his time to his family, research, writing, and travel. He is often found on Seabrook Island, SC.

www.ingramcontent.com/pod-product-compliance
Lightning Source LLC
Chambersburg PA
CBHW030638020726
47493CB00006B/1770